Straight off the Sea

Susannah Pearson

Michael Terence
Publishing

First published in paperback by
Michael Terence Publishing in 2018
www.mtp.agency

ISBN 9781912639168

All names have been changed

This book is dedicated to my dear mother and father, who moved heaven and earth to make sure I had a life full of opportunity; to my friend, Rachel, who has encouraged my writing efforts over the last twelve years; to Paul Blaney, whose great evening classes at City University inspired me to try to write a novel.

Straight off the Sea

Susannah Pearson

Chapter One

"For heaven's sake," she told herself, "it's only a house."

But earlier this morning she had felt life would never be worth living again – and now here was this glistening white stranger smiling at her and beckoning her from across the road. Already, in her bones, she knew it was more than a house. She stared back, entranced, and then she saw the sign on the gatepost.

For Sale.

Two Bedroomed Top Floor Flat.

She fumbled in her pocket for her mobile.

"Certainly," replied a voice at the end of the line, "I can take you round now if you want. I've got keys. Stay put. I'll only be five minutes."

She stood there, waiting for the agent, in a ridiculous fit of excitement, turning first one way, then the other, unable to decide which was the better view. It was a brilliant Indian summer of a day and the terrace of white houses gleamed blindingly beneath an intensely blue sky. Behind her was the sea, an even deeper blue, rippling like a lake stroked by the gentlest of breezes. The sun cast a blinding silver streak from the horizon, across the pier, and right down to the shingled shore.

The houses were built on the top of a cliff, and Felicity was standing looking at them from the very wide pavement on the shore side. It had to be wide to accommodate the vast amount of people traffic – joggers, cyclists, rollerbladers, lovers, lone thinkers, lurching toddlers, and babes in arms with their proud parents There were all sorts and conditions of dogs – to say nothing of an amazing cat on a lead, lolling superciliously on a human shoulder – all safely contained by a long, long railing in Art Deco blue as they processed along Kingscove seafront.

"Ms Green?" came a voice to her left, "I'm from the Estate Agency. I believe you want to view the penthouse in Augustus House?"

*

A couple of days later Felicity and her friend and colleague, Ann, were relaxing on Ann's balcony.

It was one of those mellow autumn afternoons when it was really pleasant sitting watching the Thames slide by. There was a tourist boat crammed with passengers on the river, but the wind was blowing the noise of the commentary towards the other shore so it was all very peaceful. Now that they had finished their weekly business meeting, making decisions about what to recommend clients to do with their money, they were enjoying just relaxing as friends.

"You mean you've actually put in an offer?" It took a great deal to surprise Ann, but, for once, she looked quite incredulous.

"Yes," was Felicity's triumphant reply, "And it's been accepted. I'm going to buy a flat in a really old house right on the seafront."

"But why Kingscove?" Ann wanted to know, "I didn't think you'd ever been there."

"That's right, my first visit ever. Dominic had just told me about Cheryl. You can imagine how I felt. I'd not had the faintest idea there was anything between them. I just couldn't stand there listening to him telling me how he'd always be fond of me and how he hoped we could stay friends. I wanted to hit him.

I rushed out of the house and caught a bus to London Bridge. Then I got on the first train that was due. It was going to Gatwick, then Kingscove. I nearly got off at Gatwick, but I realised just in time I'd probably need my passport there, so I stayed on till Kingscove.

I can see you think it's completely out of character but I couldn't help myself."

"So if the train times had been different you might have ended up putting in an offer for a flat in Dartford?" suggested Ann, with that straight face she did so well. She could not believe this. She'd worked with Felicity for quite a while now in financial services, and she knew she was really good at her job, but making sudden decisions was just not something she did.

Felicity shook her head amusedly. "That's a thought, but I don't think so. I'm sure Dartford's very nice, but I can't see it casting quite the same spell on me. I really felt as if something was drawing me there - as if it was meant to be. I've never seen such an amazing place. I reckon you could do anything there - even I could."

"Did you go *intending* to look for somewhere to live?" Ann was becoming more and more intrigued. She sipped on her gin and tonic, trying hard not to show how curious she was.

Flat hunting had been the last thing on Felicity's mind that morning. When she'd got off the train she'd been swept along out of the station by crowds of high spirited trippers. They were all making for the distant sea at the bottom of the hill. Their exuberance had been in total contrast to her own mood and she'd found herself almost wishing she'd gone somewhere else. Then she'd stumbled on a left turn down a very steep road and managed to shake off most of the crowds.

As she'd descended, the area had begun to take on a personality of its own. It was a hotch potch of little streets with a hotch potch of little shops – all completely different. Very classy little dress shops stood next to whimsical, eccentric boutiques. The wares of most of the vendors spilled out on to the pavements. Rickety stands of knitted woolly hats jostled for space with crockery and cooking utensils. There wasn't a chain shop or a multiple in sight – no cloned shop fronts here. That applied to the humans as well, she'd realized. Everyone, including the toddlers, and even the babies, seemed to be their own distinctive people, comfortable inside themselves.

On she walked, intrigued. There were pots of flowers on shop doorsteps, boards on lamp posts advertising who was performing in which Kingscove nightspot, boards propped on the pavements extolling "All day veggie breakfasts" and "We sell sheepskins for babies and washable nappies", windows full of ethnic artworks, carved wooden statues, green glass iguanas, brightly, brashly coloured sputnik ceiling lamps alongside elegant refined table lamps – a veritable treasure house of eclecticism all packed into a few narrow little, mostly pedestrianised, streets. Where traffic was allowed there seemed more cyclists than motorists. Cyclists of all ages, the younger ones mostly in helmets, the older ones, whom Felicity thought probably more in need, almost universally without. An old man, carrier bags swinging on his handle bars, toiled up the hill. He had the solid look of someone cemented to his cycle seat.

There were large quantities of young women – all looking as if they'd just tossed their outfits together, yet ending up looking so stylish. She noticed one intriguing older woman as well, moving slowly but confidently, a white stick probing the space in front of her. She was very effectively dressed too, in an almost theatrical way, with a jaunty white cap and red scarf. One could imagine her spending her working life in repertory, doing panto at Christmas, and progressing from role to role as the years passed - Dick Whittington and Ophelia, followed all too quickly by the Fairy Godmother, and finally the wicked witch and Miss Marple. Now here she was, retired, doing her daily shop through the Kingscove Market.

What a fantastic place, Felicity thought. She had a bite to eat at one of the little pavement cafes before continuing her walk, ending up somehow by the pier.

She'd been standing by the pier railings looking east when she'd suddenly seen the vision - a long row of wonderful old houses climbing up the hilly road to the top of the cliff. They were beautiful, white, stuccoed houses, five and six storeys high, stretching out into the distance, smiling out to sea, stunning in the sunshine. They'd looked as if they'd been waiting for her, she told Ann.

"Yes," I expect they had," was the reply, "Just been standing around waiting for 150 years or so for a sucker like you. I suppose you found an estate agent who looked about twelve years old to take you round a few and tell you what a hotspot the place was in the property market, and how you'd better make your mind up quickly before someone else snaffled it?"

"Stop it, Ann. You're making out I'm a complete idiot."

"W e… e… ll…, "Ann admitted, "I do sometimes wonder about you - perhaps you lead a double life - financial genius at work, complete idiot at home. Anyway, tell me a bit more about this wonderful flat." She poured them a couple more drinks and sat back waiting.

It would be difficult to find two women less alike. Felicity was tall, almost gangling, with a short fairish bob of hair and a shy hesitant smile. She'd just taken off her spectacles and suddenly looked much younger. They made her seem over-earnest and did not do her justice.

Ann was a lot shorter and probably ten or so years older, with sharpish, livewire features and long hair, pulled back today in a 'workmode' bun. She always seemed brimming with self confidence.

Such opposites often seem to work well together, and these two definitely did - both professionally and socially.

"You're right," Felicity admitted grudgingly, "He did say the area was on the up. I took a bit of convincing - the down and outs were starting to congregate, in the shelter on the seafront opposite, for their evening bread and soup, and there were lots of burst black sacks in the forecourt with rotting rubbish spilling out everywhere. He explained that it was rubbish collection day, and that the seagulls pecked the bags open to see what they could forage. Later on I saw some doing it, so he wasn't fibbing.

My flat has a glorious position. It's up four flights, right on the top floor. The agent called it a penthouse. The view is impossible to describe."

"Yeah, well… I bet I could describe it for you on a wet, windy day."

"I'm not going to tell you anything else," declared Felicity, "if you're just going to be sarky."

Ann managed to look penitent, so Felicity went on to tell

her about the blue front door, which did, she admitted, have a slight touch of damp, and how it stuck when you tried to shut it, showering bits of flaking plaster on your nose, and how, yes, she supposed the bathroom was dire, with mouldy walls looking like cave paintings. She told her too about the very dubious balding green shag pile carpet which covered the bathroom floor and continued right up the wall behind the toilet and washbasin.

Ann shuddered. "Do you think they've slaughtered and skinned an elderly muppet and stuck him up there?"

Felicity looked at her warningly. "The view makes up for everything," she assured her. I'm going to be miserable wherever I live, but when I walked in and saw that view I just knew I'd be so much happier being miserable there - if you see what I mean. There were boats zig-zagging around like little white swans, and the sea just lolled about like a lazy old sailor in a lovely new navy blue suit."

Ann raised an irritating eyebrow. "Really!" she said, "Are you gearing up to be the next Poet Laureate?"

"Go on. Laugh!" was the reply, "You never take me seriously. You can keep your trendy loft. I'm going to live somewhere seriously romantic - somewhere where *real* people have lived for a very long time."

"You'll be telling me next," Ann leaned towards her conspiratorially, "that there's a ghost."

Felicity hesitated. Something had certainly been drawing her towards Augustus House. When the Estate Agent had opened the front door the main hall had seemed very familiar, but she decided that perhaps Ann thought she was mad enough already.

Her friend grinned affectionately at her. "You're better

than a novel, you are. I'm only teasing. You should know me by now. I'm delighted you've found somewhere you like so much, though I'm a bit worried about this quick decision. It's so out of character. Are you really sure you want to move there? You've only been there once. Shouldn't you hang on a bit and then see how you feel?"

Felicity's reply was verging on tearful. She *couldn't* go on in that house if he was living just next door with that awful Cheryl. Couldn't Ann see how impossible that would be? She didn't think she could stay there another week, even. She was going to find a bedsit until she'd completed on the flat. Ann was quite taken aback. This was so different from how she would have reacted. She would have gone on living there just to see how difficult and embarrassing she could make things for him.

But no way was she going to have Felicity miserable in a poky little bedsit. "I'll put you up. Don't argue. I've bags of space. And I really do think you've done the right thing - I'm so glad you're getting rid of that awful Dominic."

"You mean he's getting rid of me," Felicity interrupted gloomily.

The main thing, Ann assured her, was that he was through the exit. She'd never told Felicity how much she'd always disliked his pomposity, always suspected him. He'd certainly lived up to her expectations. Now that she realised that Felicity was so determined about this flat she would put all her energies into safeguarding her friend's interests.

"Are you sure you've made a sensible offer? You didn't get carried away?"

Felicity assured her that she'd offered way under the

asking price. She'd really only intended it as a figure to open negotiations and had been shocked in the best sense when they'd accepted. He'd got a new job in York and was obviously pretty fed up with weekly commuting.

Ann had a bit of a reputation as a man eater, so Felicity was quite surprised that she hadn't asked her whether there seemed to be any nice available men in the house. She got in first, and told her about the somewhat tasty man she'd almost fallen over on one of the landings where a light bulb had gone. Long legs up to his neck, she informed Ann, and a brilliant smile that had almost done away with the need for a bulb.

"There you go again," tutted Ann, "what an incorrigible romantic! Just try to be practical for a minute. How easy is it to get up to town? After all, you won't be able to skulk on the coast all the time, will you?"

Felicity told her about the fast trains, and about 'the lovely little bus' she'd caught which had swept round onto the seafront - just like a little Toytown bus.

"It was dusk when I finally left," she went on, "I could see the pier all lit up and twinkling like Christmas - and I could hear the people screaming on the rides. It was like trundling up to Trumpton Station, not Kingscove."

"Idyllic," grunted Ann, "That's just you hankering after your lost childhood."

It *had* been idyllic, thought Felicity. It was what had finally clinched the matter. Two old ladies had been sitting in front of her, both wearing hearing aids. They must have forgotten to turn them on, because they'd shouted their way up to the city centre, generously sharing their conversation with the rest of the bus.

"Thank you very much for the lovely letter," said the

first.

“Well, it was the least I could do,” the second one assured her, “I was going to ring, but it was a bit late. The others go to bed early. And the phone isn’t working properly. They’re having to bring a new one. It’s lost its memory, the man said. The storm affected it.”

“I dressed for cold weather,” continued the first one, “I went out into the garden to pay Godfrey and I noticed then how cold it was. We’re like you - we get the wind straight off the sea.”

She remembered how strangely comforting she’d found their conversation. It had somehow reassured her that life went on, in spite of Dominic and Cheryl. Perhaps one day life might even let her slot back in. Old ladies doing ordinary old ladyish things, tootling out for the evening with their friends, all wrapped up, sending each other letters, paying their gardeners, feeling the wind straight off the sea. They gave her hope.

Maybe, she thought, in that flat high above the sea, Time might eventually help her to heal.

The train had been waiting for her. She’d just had time to grab a coffee from the stall on the station forecourt. After she’d drunk it she’d half dozed most of the way back to London Bridge, but in one of her more lucid moments she’d realised that her mind was definitely made up. As soon as she got back she’d left a message on the estate agency phone offering for the flat which was to change her life at least twice over.

Chapter 2

"What's she like then, Andrew, this new buyer? Hubert says you met her."

Abigail and Andrew were sitting drinking tea half way up the wide steps leading up from her semi basement flat in Augustus House. There was just room where the steps curled round to reach the forecourt for a couple of chairs, together with enough space to grow a few hardy flowers. It was one of her favourite places on a sunny day. You couldn't see the sea from that level, but somehow you could always feel it. You could often hear it as well, even above the noise of the traffic that was always rolling by. Sometimes, if it was blowing a gale, you would hear nothing else but the sea - roaring, boiling and churning under the Cove Cliff upon which Augustus House perched.

The house had stood there a long time, through countless storms and crises, first proudly, then sadly crumbling and unloved. Latterly people were beginning to appreciate such beautiful old houses again, snapping them up, doing them up… and sometimes regretting it, thought Abigail ruefully, looking at the flaking, yellowing white paint. They'd definitely have to do the front again next spring, to say nothing of the roof. She'd have to work on prising the money out of them all. With some of them it would be harder than getting blood out of a Kingscove beach pebble. She sometimes reckoned they thought the fairies took care of the maintenance. Being Company Secretary for the caring, sharing freeholders of Augustus House Limited was not an enviable job.

She ran her fingers through her greying hair as she

waited for Andrew to come up with the lowdown on their probable new neighbour.

"She seemed ok," he told her, "The light on my landing had gone kaput and she nearly knocked me over by my front door. Something's bothering her, I reckon. She was trying to hide it, but her face had that pinched, tense look. Wedding ring, specs, not much make-up - didn't need it actually - nice face. Tall. Reads The Times - unless she picked it up on the bus, of course. Early thirties? Not bad for ten seconds in the dark, eh?"

"Hubert's been talking to Diana," Abigail told him, " Apparently Felicity promised them she wanted a quick sale. That's the only reason they accepted her offer. I gather it was pretty low. I would have thought they could have held out for a bit more."

Andrew disagreed. He thought they'd been very wise to accept, he told her, pointing out how long it had been hanging around and what an almighty mess it was in with its leaking roof and its ghastly bathroom.

Typical Andrew, thought Abigail, smiling inwardly. He liked things to be so totally clean and ordered - in his home and in his life. He really was too houseproud for his own good. She'd once told him that she wouldn't be all that surprised to find that he re-ironed his sheets half way through the night - a real Mr Meticulous. She was sure he must frighten off anyone who fancied him, in spite of his gorgeous long legs and lovely smile. Imagine trying to keep up with those standards!

From what Andrew had said it sounded as if the prospective buyer might fit in. Hopefully she might be a bit better than the previous two owners had been at paying up for house maintenance.

She wouldn't be getting that bad a deal, after all - a flat in a lovely old house, with nice neighbours, in a vibrant city by the sea, and a view to end all views. She'd thought of buying it herself but had reluctantly decided not. Four flights of stairs were best left to the young.

"I'm surprised you've seen Hubert," she went on aloud, "One practically has to make an appointment these days because he's so busy."

"I only bumped into him shopping in St. Peter's St. ," Andrew replied, "He said he was about to go away, but he seemed to be buying some specially nice food. He'd got a couple of carrier bags from that posh new deli. What's he up to?"

Hubert was off to the States, Abigail told him. She supposed the food was for the dinner he was cooking for her tonight as a farewell. She bit her lip and hesitated before deciding *not* to confide in Andrew that Hubert had asked her to marry him. She and Andrew were pretty good friends - surprisingly, perhaps, given that there were more than thirty years between them. He'd bought his flat only a month or two after her own arrival at Augustus House about ten years ago. His much loved grandmother had left him some money in her will, with strict instructions to spend it usefully, and he had used it as a deposit for his flat. He and Abigail confided in each other frequently. She knew she could have done so now, but at the last minute she worried that it might be disloyal to Hubert.

So what Andrew said next took her aback.

"He really likes you, doesn't he? I'm surprised he hasn't ever asked you to marry him."

Abigail shuddered. She'd long since decided that she would never marry again and she had made that clear to

Hubert more than once.

"Life becomes one long compromise when one marries," she told Andrew, " That's my verdict, anyway. Always half measures. Neither of you ever does what you really want to do - and Hubert can be a bit narrow minded, you know - it's all tied up with his wretched Victorian poetry. I worry that he takes it to such extremes. I'm all for behaving morally, but Hubert's moral standards are so very tight. They're like those constrained little houses in North St. Do you remember? You and I viewed one once and we had to go down the stairs sideways like crabs because the treads were too narrow for our feet. And another thing – his compulsive quoting would drive me to distraction if I had to live with it all the time. He's like a walking literary dictionary. I like his company in smallish doses... What are you laughing at ?" she ended sharply.

"I was just thinking what an epitaph that would make - 'We liked his company in smallish doses.' Deep down you are a very cruel woman."

Abigail looked at him defiantly, though once Andrew started to laugh it was always difficult not to join in.

"Well it's true," she insisted, "anyway, he's off to San Francisco on Monday. Some university or other's having a conference on Francis Thompson. He's reading a paper. I don't know what made us think that he'd ease off when he retired."

"Would Hubert say poetry was the new sex?" Andrew asked her, trying to look very intellectual.

"I know you're joking, but I actually think he might," agreed Abigail, " He was practising reading his paper with me as a guinea pig last night, and there was a bit about *'feel the primal sex of heaven and poetry'.*

"I really do hope it goes down well. It would make him so happy."

"Did you say you were working today?" she went on.

Apparently Andrew was off to Hong Kong and was a bit nervous about it. There'd been a sudden scourge of food poisoning amongst the First Class Cabin Crew and he was having to act as stand-in First Class Purser. "I'm back on Tuesday very early," he told her, "probably dead to the world till late lunchtime. I'll put the flag out when I surface."

Some previous eccentric owner of Andrew's flat had fixed up a flagpole, and had left behind a load of different flags. Andrew raised the Union Flag when he got up after recovering from a long flight. It was one of their silly means of communication. It meant it was safe to ring without waking him up.

The rear of Augustus House was a hotch potch of late nineteenth century add-ons built around the basement courtyard which belonged to Abigail. Andrew's unusual flat rambled round three sides of the courtyard, but three floors above it, so Abigail could see the flag from her basement bedroom window.

Little things please little minds, had been Hubert's private reaction.

She started slightly, "Can you hear that music?"

"What music? Probably from a car at the traffic lights."

"Just listen," she insisted, "Can you hear it now? What does it sound like to you?"

Andrew concentrated, "Could be the Teddy Bears' Picnic?" he volunteered.

"That's what I thought. I've heard it a few times. Who on earth in this house would want to keep playing The Teddy Bears' Picnic?"

"Perhaps it's musical burglars. Burgling Teddies. They break in, have a picnic with porridge, honey and stuff, borrow a bed and play themselves to sleep with their signature tune. Then they wake up and break out. A kind of revenge on Goldilocks. Or perhaps it's just that Tracie has her little nephew staying again and he likes to keep playing it. Sometimes I think you get far too worried about what goes on in the house. Let it run itself . It's not good for you. You just end up stressing yourself out."

She didn't say anything, but she was thinking what a mess it would get into if it ran itself – the roof would fall in in a year or two, for starters. Their wonderful builder, James, kept patching it up, but he kept warning them that one really bad storm could have disastrous consequences. She'd have to get them all organized to pay up.

Anyway, she *liked* being nosy. It wasn't malicious, she told herself – just an ultra interest in life. For Abigail, probably the best thing about finding out other people's secrets, although she may not have realized, was that it stopped her dwelling too much on a terrible secret of her own, which she had carried with her for the greater part of her life.

She'd jolly well find out about those teddy bears, whatever Andrew said!

Anyway, she needed to go to the shops, so she walked with him up the steps from her semi-basement to the forecourt just as the main front door opened. Out came the Reverend Cedric Wright, the relatively new tenant of the first floor balcony flat. He was in mufti this morning. He often was.

"Good morning, Mrs Harvey, Mr Eliot," he greeted them, and turned right towards the bus stop.

Another one to find out about, she thought. He's *definitely* not what he seems!

Chapter 3

Felicity stood at the window watching the last of her depleted possessions coming out of the removal van far below. It was mid November, and a very different sort of day than when she had first viewed Augustus House. Everything seemed so murky. She turned, and looked ruefully at her sparsely furnished sitting room. Perhaps it hadn't been such a good idea to stay with Ann till the sale went through because Dominic seemed to have taken the opportunity to pillage just about all of their joint possessions. Pots and pans, bedding, even the sofa had all gone awol. Cheryl must have lived off fish and chips on a deckchair previously.

Still, Felicity thought, she *was* trying to make a new start. Did she *really* want the plates he'd eaten off, and the sofa he'd always hogged with his lazy behind? She certainly didn't want the bed they'd shared and a new one was being delivered that afternoon.

"Cheer up," said Ann, who'd come down from London to offer moral support, "You know you're well rid. Let's put the kettle on. These poor men must be gasping."

The removal men were a bit of an unusual couple. One was about six foot six and the other scarcely five. They moved surprisingly well together and they'd got her stuff into the flat really quickly. It was just a bit of luck that she'd found their advert in the Kingscove Recorder.

"Will you miss London?" asked the little one as he drank his tea.

"No. I've had enough of living there," Felicity told him.

"Don't blame you. I hate it. Wouldn't live in London again if you paid me, "He shuddered. "Spent three months there once. Only good thing that came out of it was I met Barry."

He gestured towards the big one.

"That was five years ago. We've been together in Kingscove ever since."

They supped up and handed over a card in case she ever needed anything else moving.

'Larry and Barry – Moving up' it read 'High Rises our Speciality. Together we can do anything.'

"No job too small," said Barry, the big one.

"And no job too big," said Larry the little one, "the more stairs the better - keeps us fit."

"Weren't they good? Wasn't I lucky to find them?" said Felicity after they'd gone.

"They were splendid," agreed Ann, "I've not met any gay removal men before."

Felicity was really surprised. "How could you tell?"

"Well, the odds in Kingscove are pretty good. I think they reckon 1 in 5 in East Town is gay. You'll get the hang of it. Gay men are well on the way to being our most splendid national treasure. After the Queen, of course. Every woman should know several."

Half an hour later the new bed - Felicity's one extravagance - arrived. The bed bearers weren't nearly as pleasant as Larry and Barry. They huffed and puffed and moaned and groaned their way up the four flights of stairs, thumping the bed expertly against any corners that looked a bit too nicely painted. Proudly they displayed their beer guts to perfection over the tops of their drooping trousers and they shamelessly revealed the wonderful cleavage of their buttocks even without bending over. Worst of all, they departed sharpish before anyone could suggest they actually helped put the bed up.

It was a kingsize, and pretty heavy. After Felicity and Ann had struggled with it for a while they had to admit they needed a third pair of hands - they just didn't have the wingspan to cope. Ann put the kettle on for another cup of tea while they decided on a plan of action. Fortunately the situation solved itself as she was filling the pot.

There was a knock on the open door. It was the man with legs up to his neck, who introduced himself as Andrew Eliot. His arms turned out to be nearly as long as his legs, so the bed was up in no time.

"We've just this minute made some tea. Would you like a cup?" asked Felicity.

"It's six o'clock, Felicity," interrupted Ann, "he might like something stronger."

She fished a bottle of gin and a bottle of tonic from her large briefcase.

"I thought this might come in handy for house warming purposes. I suppose I'll have to use the tea mugs?

Two hours later they were still talking and the gin bottle had gone down quite a bit.

"I've got to go," sighed Ann, "lots to get organised for tomorrow. Have you got a cab number, Andrew?"

"Yes, but the bus is pretty good, you know - stops just round the corner. Goes straight to the station."

She pulled a face. "I think it's starting to rain. I'll have a cab. Don't let me break the party up, though."

And off she clattered.

"How long have you known Ann?" asked Andrew, as they waved her off from the sitting room window, high above the forecourt.

"About ten years. I work for her, although I suppose we're partners now. I've just bought into her business."

"She seems quite an intimidating character."

"Oh, it's mainly show. She's been wonderful to me these last two or three months."

"Yes. They say death, marriage breakup and moving are the three most stressful life events, don't they?"

"That might explain why I feel so grim, "Felicity blurted. "My marriage has failed as well. My husband's gone off with someone else..." she broke off, biting her lip in embarrassment. She hadn't meant to say anything about that.

"I'm sorry." Andrew really looked as if he meant it. "And it's no good my coming out with that junk about time healing. My experience is that it's a very long hard haul. Is it getting any better?"

"I suppose so. But it feels bad tonight. Starting again is quite frightening. You think you know where you're going, think your future's all mapped out, then suddenly everything changes and you're by yourself again, quite back at the very beginning, in fact before the very beginning. And even though part of you thinks it might be exciting, the other part thinks it's terrifying. You feel a bit as if half of you has got lost, gone missing. Would you like another gin?"

Why on earth are you confiding in this total stranger, she asked herself?

"No thanks, I'm working tomorrow afternoon. I work on the planes – have to be really careful. And you definitely shouldn't have any more either if you feel like that! Have you any coffee?"

"Yes. Somewhere in all these packing cases."

"Well let's keep unpacking till we find it…"

"This woman he's gone off with. What's she like?"

She told him about Cheryl, and how Dominic had gone round to be "neighbourly" when her partner had left her, and how that must have been the beginning of the end. And how they'd made off with most of the furniture and all her self- confidence.

"I thought you didn't have much stuff. Rotten sod. Sounds like a real life soap opera of a road, though."

"Oh it is. I hadn't realised what a sheltered life I'd led till I moved there."

"Well, a couple of years in Kingscove will complete that process, believe me."

Felicity smiled. "Yes, that's what Ann keeps telling me."

"It's impossible to be lonely in this house, Felicity, - except from choice. There's such a collection of people here."

"What are they all like?" Felicity had curled herself up on a large floor cushion. Dominic, of course, had made off with the sofa. They'd given up hope of finding the coffee and were drinking water.

"Well – it's a bit complicated," he told her, "because there are six flats. I'll start right at the bottom.

There we have Mrs Abigail Harvey – our very competent Company Secretary." He went on to tell her how much he admired Abigail but hinted that there was an air of mystery around her.

"Why is that?" Felicity probed.

So Andrew found himself trying to explain how every so often you would meet Abigail and you would find that the clouds had come down around her face. Goodness knows what it was, but it certainly could upset her greatly.

I'd better move on, he thought. There's been far too much gin and tonic swilling around here. Bottles of spirit should carry warnings proclaiming 'Even a small amount of this liquid may loosen tongues'.

But instead he went on to tell her about Hubert Jeffries, the compulsive quoter – Emeritus Professor of Poetry at one of the local universities.

"He's got a very soft spot for Abigail," Andrew confided, "but I reckon he's no chance there."

Felicity wanted to know who lived in the balcony flat which overlooked the sea.

"That's the Reverend Cedric Wright," she was told. "He rents it from someone who teaches abroad. I think he's another university type – not sure if he's a chaplain or a theology lecturer – maybe both. Seems ok, Keeps himself to himself. That always makes me wonder what people are getting up to – and Abigail is even worse that way than I am."

Felicity could see what he meant about it being complicated. "Hang on a minute," she asked him. "Let me get my head round this. You're the next one? You're above the Reverend Wright?

Andrew beamed at her.

"That's right. I'm next, on the Second Floor. I'm a purser with Excelsior Air."

"Do you live by yourself?" she asked him.

"Oh no! I'd get lonely. I live with Blackie, my goldfish.

I'm doing up my spare room and then I shall get a human lodger as well. Just under you we have Martin and Tracie Taylor. They both work for Kingscove Council. And that's it!" he ended triumphantly.

Then he raised his hands in mock horror. "How could I? I've forgotten the ghost!"

Felicity stared at him. "The ghost?"

"Yes. We have a resident ghost. Not everybody's come across it. Abigail has, and Hubert too. That really makes you wonder, because Hubert's usually so 'no nonsense'. If Hubert's seen the ghost you start to think it must exist."

Andrew was enjoying himself hugely.

"Who is the ghost then? Is it a man or a woman?" Felicity wasn't sure whether to take him seriously or not.

"A man apparently. I've not come across him myself. According to Hubert it's the ghost of Augustus Booth, a young late Victorian poet who got hooked on opium during a depressive illness. He lived here with his parents. Committed suicide after his fiancee died of consumption. Walked into the sea, I believe. His parents were devastated. Renamed the house in his memory. Hubert and Abigail both swear his ghost is still here. Abigail says she's sensed his presence more than once, especially in Hubert's Tower."

"Hubert's Tower?"

He told her all about the wonderful room at the back of Hubert's flat. The Booths, Augustus' parents, had wanted more space so that Mrs Booth could cut a dash on the Kingscove social scene. They both loved their Regent's Parade house too much to move, so they kept buying up gardens belonging to people in neighbouring houses and extending. The last extension was a large towered room, sadly almost derelict now. It had been their concert room and their ballroom. Mrs Booth used to hold soirees and Augustus would read his poetry. Sometimes they'd hire a string quartet and sometimes a small orchestra for dancing.

"How do you know all this, Andrew?" Felicity was really intrigued.

"Hubert's researched it all. The late Victorian poets are his speciality. I think he bought the flat because of the associations. The Tower's a real tip now – needs a complete restoration, but Hubert's an old skinflint."

"Anyway, what about the ghost?"

"Abigail swears that Augustus is often around. She has smelt his cologne - Eucris. Apparently it was first for sale in Victorian times but can still be bought today – a mix of spiciness and lily of the valley, I gather. We know Augustus used it because in his diary he mentions being given it as a birthday present. Abigail says she has felt him passing her in the Tower and sometimes on the stairs as well, and she's heard him weeping. What's the matter, Felicity? You really look as if *you're* the one who's seen a ghost."

"Andrew, that first day when I came to view the flat I felt someone brush past me on the stairs and I got a whiff of a perfume I didn't recognize. I thought it must be imagination, because there was no one there except me and the estate agent. I know we met you on the stairs later, but you were certainly flesh and blood. Oh it's too silly."

"Yes, of course it is really. I agree. But it makes the house seem more romantic, doesn't it? Perhaps puts a thousand or so on the price? Can't do any harm. Anyway, let's get back into the present. Have you got to go to work tomorrow?"

She was taking the day off to get unpacked, she told him, so when he offered to treat her to breakfast the next morning at the greasy spoon up the road she didn't need to be asked twice.

When Andrew had gone she had another glass of water and looked out across the sea. She could just make it out because of the lights on the pier reflecting in the water.

Suddenly she felt very alone.

Chapter 4

The Reverend Cedric Wright yawned, stretched and groaned. Writing sermons had become anathema to him. That was one of the reasons he'd left parish work. Grinding them out week after week, coming out with truism after truism, platitude after platitude, had driven him to screaming point. Combined of course with visiting the sick, tending to the bereaved, christening the babies, marrying the lovers, burying the dead, keeping an eye on everyone in the parish- and, worst of all, everyone in the parish keeping an eye on him! Yes, keeping an eye on him, but not looking after him. He had felt so alone. And still did. How had he ever persuaded himself that he had a vocation?

He'd been so relieved to get the job at the university. Most of the time there he only needed to pay lip service to being a priest. No one pried too closely into his private life- just as well because -Oh God!- what a mess that was! But you could never completely escape. There was always the old friend still stuck in some parish desperately needing a weekend off. He tried to make excuses most of the time, but every now and then he had to give in. This particular sermon was for a bloke who'd been a very good friend- Cedric was really indebted to him. Pity he'd waited till Cedric had agreed to fill in for him before mentioning that he was just reaching the end of a series of sermons from 1 Corinthians xiv. How on earth could he have got landed with this text? - 'Let all things be done decently and in order.' What's more, the friend had told his congregation that Cedric had been the best preacher of their year at Divinity College. They were probably getting excited already. So he was going to let them down with a very big bump, wasn't he?

Let all things be done decently and in order- indeed! His own life wasn't exactly indecent, but it certainly wasn't ordered by accepted churchman standards. There were things which he wouldn't want to be common knowledge. Half of him hated himself, wanted to reform, yet the other half couldn't care less, enjoying the lack of discipline which was possible when faith walked out.

What a useless way to spend a sunny Saturday. Much better to have a walk. Sod sermons. He threw his notes down on to an already incredibly littered floor. Cedric couldn't have tidied for a long time. Cleanliness was certainly not next to godliness here.

Perhaps he should chuck it all in? Move? Emigrate? Australia? That might just be far enough to be himself, with no need to worry about anyone knowing he used to be a clergyman. Then no one would expect him to lead a blameless life. Be himself? Part of the trouble was he didn't know himself. It had got lost somewhere in his sadness, and although he could sometimes hear it calling to him he could not find it.

As well as which, whenever he got just to the edge of possible escape like this a strange something inside him would hold him back. Hang on, hang in, it would say. He supposed it was his conscience. He hated it, but it would not go away.

He looked down again at the floor - a truly disgusting mess, strewn with biscuit wrappings, cigarette packets, a grubby old clerical collar, a large selection of pizza flyers, a few books, even an apple core, all luxuriating in a mulch of crumpled up pieces of rejected sermon notes. He had not the will nor the energy to clear it up. In fact, he rather liked it.

Definitely time for that walk - perhaps a stroll down to the pier, returning via St. Peter's Street to see if there was anyone he knew in The Dog House.

If only all his problems were as easy to shrug off as his messy floor, he lamented, as he strolled down Regent's Parade.

His attitude to his sermons was specially troubling him. There had been a time when writing a sermon was one of the most pleasurable things in his life - his weekly opportunity to lift the spirits of his parishioners and share so much with them, suggest new ideas to them, calm their worries, help them clarify their thoughts. Now that his powers to do this had shrivelled to dust, along with his faith, he felt very alone. Who was there to lift his spirits, to clarify his thoughts?

Loss of faith, he had often read, was akin to bereavement. He could not agree. Loss of faith was far far worse. One could be open about bereavement. There was no shame about it. People understood. They would support you at the funeral. They would help you, gradually, to move on. But loss of faith - particularly for a priest... One couldn't announce it in The Times. There could be no funeral. Not one of the normal methods of coping with a grievous loss could be utilised. It was difficult to trust even one's closest friends with the shameful secret. It had to stay hidden - and keeping grief to oneself intensifies the anguish and the anger and the terrible loneliness, giving it full rein to wrack one's soul. He felt that the light at the centre of his being had been snuffed out.

He knew he was drinking too much, and smoking too, but drink seemed the only way to camouflage the pain-apart from humour, albeit a somewhat black variety these days.

*

Things weren't going a lot better two floors up, where the same terrible feeling of loss was saddening the air.

Martin had long since left for the Planning Department, but Tracie, his wife, was still in bed in their flat, drinking yet more coffee. She and Martin had had another row last night. She felt it would soon be one row too many. Once again she felt the huge wave of sadness which always rushed in when she thought of how it used to be when they were first together- the jumping pleasure as she'd heard his key in the lock, the lingering meals together, the moonlight walks along the shore. She'd thought they'd known each other so well. How wrong one can be. Now she heaved sighs of relief when she heard the door close every morning behind him.

When they'd first met that summer seven years ago at Whitedean University she'd fallen head over heels for this gentle, thoughtful, rugby playing giant. In those moonlit walks they'd told each other absolutely everything about their hopes, their fears, their tragedies, their happiness - everything, as new lovers always do. Or so she thought. Now she could only look back ruefully to those early days and realise how little she had really known about Martin Taylor. Nevertheless, they had married, had both been lucky enough to land jobs in Kingscove when they'd graduated, and had sweated and saved for four years. They'd lived in a bedsit so small that whenever Martin sat down she had to climb over his feet if she needed to cross the room, but they'd managed to save enough for a tired little flat, almost at the top of Augustus House.

Bit by bit they'd done it up, lugging most of the necessaries back from the DIY Superstore on the bus. They had been so happy. Every Tuesday and Thursday Martin would be off to train with his rugby team, and she would curl up at home and catch up on all the things she never could fit in during the rest of the week. The only thing she had found wrong in her life was her job. They were both employed by the City Council. Martin rather liked his work and could see prospects of interesting advancement. She hated hers. The days dragged, but worse was that it held no future - neither would it look specially enticing on a cv. She needed something new, more exciting. She'd very recently had an idea for starting up in business for herself - something quite unusual, and a bit controversial, so she hadn't mentioned it as yet to anyone.

She and Martin were still pretty hard up after their flat purchase, but they always tried to go out at the weekend. One Saturday they'd had an invitation to a housewarming from one of Tracie's contemporaries at Whitedean. She was moving in to a new place with her boyfriend, whom they'd not yet met. It had been a truly foul Kingscove night and they'd seriously discussed whether it wouldn't be nicer just to stay at home. Later, she fervently wished they'd done so.

The boyfriend turned out to be an old rugby-playing chum of Martin's.

"How are you?" he'd boomed across the room, "we've really missed you in the team. Is the injury improving? Any chance you might be back this season?"

Martin had looked very uncomfortable, "Er... perhaps,"

he'd muttered, "yes. It is improving." And he'd got into conversation with someone else as quickly as he could.

Tracie just did not know what to think. She got them out of there pretty quickly, feigning a sudden migraine.

"What have you been doing for the last few months," she'd demanded when they were in the taxi, "every Tuesday and Thursday night?"

He'd come up with some fudged excuse or other, but she'd not believed him. All she could think was that her big beautiful husband was having an affair. A few weeks later when she came across a pair of lacy knickers hidden in his brief case, beautifully wrapped in the paper used by the most expensive lingerie shop in town, she was sure she was right - he must be having an affair.

A huge row broke out.

Martin had ducked and wheeled about with the truth like the master footballer he was, but in the end he had come clean. He was a transvestite.. He'd hoped he might have been able to give it up when he married, and he'd managed for a while. In the end it had turned out to be impossible. So every Tuesday and Thursday he went to a flat in East Town, freed Roberta from her suitcase under a bed, and let her spend the evening there with a few other closet trannies.

"Why didn't you tell me before we got married?" Tracie had screeched.

"Because I didn't think you'd marry me if you knew, and I so much wanted to marry you," he'd told her wretchedly, "and I'm right, aren't I? You wouldn't have."

"I don't know. I might have. But you should have given me the option. It was cowardly not to."

He'd made an effort to explain. It made him feel good,

relaxed, comfortable. But by now he was in tears and looked so wretched that she found that impossible to believe.

She'd tried to come to terms with it, she really had, but she didn't see how things could ever be the same again. Martin was a bit more optimistic. He was really relieved it was out in the open between them and he hoped they might be able to work out a way through, but Tracie couldn't bear him near her, even though she felt angry with herself. It was a cruel way to discover that her liberal principles were so fragile.

So much for romance. So much for a marriage. Both gone. Lost without trace in a Kingscove storm.

Tracie wiped her eyes. Crying wasn't going to do much good. Action, that's what was needed. She eased herself out from under the duvet and padded out in her nightie down the stairs to check the post, bumping into Andrew coming up the stairs carrying a load of little paint pots and a packet of biscuits. That Felicity had certainly got him jumping to attention already. Wonder if she realises she's flogging a dead horse there, she thought, with bitter amusement.

Someone had already picked up all the letters off the mat and sorted them carefully into the appropriate piles. Probably Hubert- that man was anally tidy. There were a couple of bills for them, a letter from Martin's aunt, and one for her. Back up in bed she opened it.. It was from the Estate Agency in West Kingscove about the place she'd investigated the other day for renting so that she could start up her new business. The letter was confirming that her offer was acceptable to the landlord. Her plans could go ahead. Time for a celebration, she decided. Just one little vodka, perhaps, before she went off to give in her notice?

Chapter 5

Right at the top of the house Felicity also had junk all over the floor- lots of back numbers of interior decoration magazines, lots of shade cards. Andrew was busy painting largish blobs of colour on her sitting room walls from some half used Matchpots he'd brought up from his own place.

"How's it going then?" he asked her. "Do you feel you belong yet? After all, you've been here two weeks now."

Felicity gave the matter a moment's thought."Yes,-" she decided, "and no. I'm coming to terms much better with the Dominic business. Getting out of London has worked wonders for that. It's not much fun living next door to your ex."

"Why 'no' then?"

To Andrew's amazement she started to tell him about the noises, the creakings, the whisperings in her ear.

"That's just old houses," he tried to console her, "they creak with the central heating. My place does. And sometimes in the night it's so still high up at the back of the house that you can hear your own inside rumbling- it sounds just like anxious mutterings."

But Felicity was sure it was more than that – Augustus, the ghost, came upstairs. She kept smelling that cologne.

"I feel he must want something, be looking for something." She insisted.

"Felicity, you're just letting your imagination run away with you.I should never have told you about Augustus. It was just a joke. You probably smell Martin's aftershave on the stairs. If your flat mutters, it's pleading with you to get a move on and peel the muppet off the wall. It wants bringing into this century, not reminding about previous ones. I think we should change the subject- what do you think of these colours?"

"I love the yellow, but is it a bit too light for here? Did you say you'd got a slightly darker shade?" Felicity didn't really want to change the subject, but perhaps it made sense.

Idiot, he told himself, as he'd gone down the two flights of stairs to his own flat to have a hunt, why did you have to tell her about the ghost? He'd have to talk to Abigail- see what suggestions she could make. Felicity had enough on her plate getting rid of her errant husband's ghost without having to cope with Augustus as well.

*

"I'd *never* have told her about him if I'd realised how impressionable she is. I was only messing about. Now she's imagining all sorts of stuff."

"She thinks Augustus goes upstairs looking for something. Did you ever hear anything so unlikely?"

"Where is Felicity now?" asked Abigail.

"She's getting ready to go up to London for a business meeting with Ann. Staying up there a couple of nights. Going to a concert I think she said. What should we do? It was all just silly talk."

Abigail looked uneasy.

"Well," she confessed, "I'm not sure if it is silly... I often feel Augustus is down here. Looking for something. Sometimes I talk to him. I've heard him weeping. I've told you this before, Andrew."

She was looking at his amazed face.

“I know you have, but I thought you were just kidding. It was that night Hubert had us all to dinner in the Tower by candlelight and he started quoting about ghosts and telling us about Augustus. We’d all had rather a lot to drink. I thought you were just going along with him.”

“No. I’d actually had the experiences I talked about. But since then there’ve been more. It’s almost as if that evening partially unlocked a way through for Augustus, like a chink of light for him to begin to edge out of his darkness. Hubert hadn’t drunk much that night, you know. He never does if he’s the host, he takes entertaining very seriously. He was *pretty* sober, but he still maintained that he’d had experiences with Augustus. And how often does Hubert legpull?”

“OK.” Andrew shrugged, “Let’s say for argument that these experiences *are* real. Why would Augustus want to come down to your place? That must have been the servants’ quarters. The young master wouldn’t spend time down there.”

“He might have done when he was a little boy. James, our builder, has shown me where there must have been a set of stairs down from the main hall to the servants’ quarters. If Augustus was a nice little boy they probably spoiled him rotten- sat him at the kitchen table with nice things to eat, played with him. It could be that he’s got very happy memories of time spent in my place. If he’s unhappy now he’s possibly trying to regain that happiness.”

“But what should we do? I feel quite guilty about it. I don’t want Felicity spooked out of her mind by herself up there on the top floor.”

“Hubert’s cooking me lunch,” Abigail told him, “I’ll see

what suggestions he's got. I'll talk to Felicity as well when she gets back."

*

Abigail knew if she got dressed up for lunch with Hubert it would give him the wrong ideas, but vanity won. Anyway, she convinced herself, his food was worth the compliment. There was no doubt about that.

Hubert was resplendent in the green apron she had bought him for his birthday in October.

"Abigail, my dear," he greeted her, gravely kissing her hand, "you are so sweet.

Sweet, when the morn is grey;

Sweet, when they've cleared away

Lunch; and at close of day

Possibly sweetest.

How's that for an Ode to Abigail?"

"It would be lovely, Hubert, but I happen to know it's Calverley's Ode to Tobacco!"

He smiled a rare smile - "Ah well I can but try. Come and have a drink. Everything's under control."

Such a poseur, she thought as she followed him into his elegant dining room overlooking the sea.

Fortunately the concentration needed for the final touches to cooking the lunch, and then the very satisfying business of eating it, put a stop to the quotations for a while.

When they were drinking coffee afterwards in the sunlounge at the back of the flat Abigail broached the subject of the ghost.

"Augustus is trying to contact Felicity."

"Really?" Hubert looked surprised. "How do you know?"

"Andrew told her about him. He feels quite bad now. If you remember, he didn't take it very seriously last time we discussed it. He only told her because he thought it would amuse her. But it's backfired. It's troubling her."

"How does Augustus try to contact her?" Hubert asked.

Abigail explained to him about the cologne, and the creakings and whisperings. She found it very puzzling, she told him, because Augustus had never gone up there when Diana and Rick owned the flat. She was sure they would have said something if they'd sensed his presence.

"You can't be sure they'd realise," Hubert's face was creased in thought. "You have to be quite sensitive to notice. He may have been there and they didn't realise. I wonder what he's looking for? It's a pity he can't tell us."

Abigail took a deep breath. She wondered, she suggested, if they might hold a séance. She fully expected to be shot down in flames. But Hubert only looked surprised.

"We could try, Abigail, but they can be a bit risky, you know. You never know quite what you might uncover."

Abigail looked at him sharply. He seemed very knowledgable all of a sudden.

"Have you done this before?" she asked.

"My mother was a medium. Haven't I told you? After my father died she used to hold regular séances as a means of income. I never decided whether she really did believe in it or just used it as a convenient way to pay the bills. Either way I suppose you could say that ghosts helped pay my way through university."

"I expect it was Shelley, and Wordsworth and Francis Thompson, then. They've got a lot to answer for, haven't they?" she teased. "Shall we give it a try? See if we can help poor Augustus?"

"I suppose we could," he replied, "I used to go to my mother's séances when I was a child. She used to dress me up as a little manservant for a bit of effect. If I'm honest, I used to quite enjoy it. Shall we try this afternoon?"

Abigail looked at him in astonishment. This was a completely new side of Hubert - getting quite animated and even splitting infinitives. Perhaps he'd had a bit more to drink than usual.

They decided to hold the séance in the Tower Room. Abigail rang Andrew who jumped at the idea.

"Good." said Hubert, "That makes our numbers right. A séance needs numbers of people divisible by three."

"How long do these things usually go on?" asked Andrew as he arrived. "I've got to leave by six. The Bangkok flight goes at nine."

"Well, if we're still here at six I should think we'll be in a pretty bad way," Hubert told him.

Abigail remembered something she'd seen about séances on the internet- something along much the same lines as what Hubert had said about risks of contacting something nasty, and that one should take suitable precautions. Unfortunately it had given no clues at all about what precautions might be suitable. She always found that was the trouble with the internet – you never got the full tale. Like that time she'd found an account of a séance with Elvis on his birthday. Apart from finding out that there was TV in heaven, and that he still liked peanut butter and banana sandwiches, she learnt nothing. She began to have second thoughts about the whole thing, but it was too late. Hubert had the bit beween his teeth.

The air of excitement grew as they rushed around getting the things Hubert said they needed. Hubert's round glass table had to be moved from the sun room into the Tower Room and Andrew brought down three of his large church candles - according to Hubert, the spirits of the past are drawn endlessly to the light. The lit candles began to cast strange shadows round the large and darkening room on the wet November afternoon.

Round the candles Hubert insisted on placing the wood of three different trees. They had to settle for shrubs as there are very few trees on Regent's Parade. They can't survive the gales. One poor thing had made a very brave effort outside the Taunton Arms just a few blocks east of Augustus House, but it had been battered almost horizontal by the westerly winds and most of the time its leaves were black with windburn. It always looked as if the elements had left it there as a terrifying example to any other tree that might dare to consider growing. Andrew found what he hoped would be the next best thing - branches from his mahonia, Abigail's camellia, and Hubert's little potted bay tree. Next Hubert demanded a circle of stones, preferably from the bed of a stream. Andrew had some lovely stones in the bottom of Blackie's tank. Abigail had given him them. He loved their pure white moonlike smoothness. She hadn't had the heart to tell him they were from the Pound Shop. They rinsed the stones in Abigail's pond water, trying to make them a bit more authentic. Hopefully Augustus would appreciate all this ingenuity.

When all the preparations were complete the three of them joined hands and Hubert spoke- although intoned might have been a better word.

"Spirits of the past, move among us. Be guided by the light of this world and visit upon us." His words echoed around the empty Tower. The plastic cover high on the roof flapped gently in a light breeze.

Nothing happened. The three of them sat bolt upright round the table, the candlelight showing up their faces in an unearthly way. Abigail could feel Andrew's fingers twitching in her left hand. She wasn't sure whether it was mirth or apprehension of imminent spirits but, knowing Andrew, she had her suspicions. In her right hand Hubert's grasp was firm and his face was steadfastly expressionless.

Again he intoned, "Spirits of the past, move among us. Be guided by the light of this world and visit upon us."

Still nothing happened, although the room got darker and darker and it began suddenly to rain. It rained more and more. It rained torrentially. In all fairness it had been threatening to do that all day. Hubert's Tower began to leak. Drip, drip, drip came the ever faster invading rain. Andrew's fingers twitched and twitched. Abigail kicked him under the table.

Again Hubert spoke, "Spirits of the past, move among us. Be guided by the light of this world. This is no séance of the idly curious. We need, we beseech your help. Visit upon us."

He was in his element. What a show off!

The light breeze had become a great squally gust of wind. The blue plastic cover over Hubert's Tower lifted with a tearing sound before settling back into place.Three spiralling columns of smoke spluttered up towards the roof and the candles almost went out.

"Spirits of the past, are you in the room? Can you help us? Give us a sign."

The blue plastic cover lifted again, then plummetted down into place.

"We wish to speak to Augustus Booth. Augustus Booth, come forth. Make yourself known to us."

Nothing happened, The torrential rain continued and the sound of the drops of water falling into the Tower buckets got louder and louder. But Andrew had stopped his silent giggling.

"Augustus. Augustus. Come forth. We offer you our help."

There was a terrible wailing sound. Just the wind surely, yet it sounded like a noise that could only come from someone in the depths of total despair.

"Augustus. Augustus. Are you there? Come forth. We offer you our help."

Abigail stiffened. She could smell the cologne. He was moving around the outside of the table. She knew he was. She could feel him. She tried to tell herself she was being an idiot, but it didn't stop her shaking. She dared not look around. She dared not look up, but she could smell him, feel him, walking around. And somehow she knew he was weeping. Desolately crying. Poor Augustus. He was weeping and Abigail began to weep too - for herself and for Augustus. Tears streamed down her cheeks, down and down, and on and on. Suddenly there was a voice. It was a moment before she realised that the words were coming from her own mouth.

"This room. Such disarray. My mother will be so dismayed. She holds a party here tomorrow, and the roof is leaking. The windows are cracked and broken. What is wrong? What has happened?"

"Augustus," replied Hubert gently, "There is no party tomorrow. It has been and gone. We have met with you from another century. We live now in this house. But we know you are here also, and you are troubled. We want to help you."

There was a great shudder from Abigail.

"Emily! Emily! My love." The voice within her wailed, "I am looking for you. I need you."

"Where is Emily, Augustus? If you could tell us then perhaps we could help you," encouraged Hubert.

"She is here. I know she is here. She has returned. She is in this house."

"How will we recognise her, Augustus?"

There was a silence. The smell of the cologne had receded to the back of the Tower, hovering round a large cupboard, rather a splendid cupboard of which Hubert was very proud. He had bought it with the flat - an original feature.

"Look in the cupboard."

Andrew gingerly moved in that direction, finding his way almost like a blind man.

"Look inside." Augustus urged.

"I c... c... can't find anything to open." The voice certainly wasn't Andrew's usual jaunty tone.

"There's a torch on top of the cupboard, Andrew. See if some light helps." said Hubert urgently.

And when Andrew pushed the two knobs that the light

helped him find at the back of the cupboard simultaneously, the back swung open. There was indeed something inside. He pulled it out. It was a picture in an ornate Victorian frame – a picture of a demure young woman. And attached to the frame a small plate on which was engraved – Miss Emily Stanton, 1859 – 1882.

Andrew brought the picture to the table and he and Hubert peered at it in the candlelight. Neither realised yet that Augustus was gone.

"I need some fresh air, please, Hubert. I feel strange." murmured Abigail, "Can you come with me ?" They both turned guiltily, having temporarily forgotten all about her.

*

Still feeling a bit weak at the knees, Abigail took Hubert's arm along Regent's Parade.

"Well, you're a surprise," he said, "did you know you had these powers?"

"I used to get premonitions when I was younger- it's tailed off in recent years. But I've never done anything like this before. I felt such a bond of sympathy with the poor boy and then suddenly he seemed to be inside, using me."

"Was it frightening?"

"No. I didn't fully realise what was happening at the time." She was improving considerably now. The rain had stopped, and a watery sun had just gone down.

"What an afternoon," sighed Abigail as Hubert deposited her back at her front door. "Thank you for a lovely lunch.

I'm going to go and put my feet up with a cup of coffee. What are you doing later?"

"Nothing of much importance." He replied.

"Well why don't you come down about eight for a glass of wine and some cheese and we can hold a council of war about all this."

"I'll do that," said Hubert, kissing her cheek and seeing her safely inside.

Abigail was so glad to be home. She fed herself paracetamol and coffee, but she couldn't rest until she'd checked out the idea that had come to her during the walk along Regent's Parade. She got out the box in which she kept all the Augustus House Ltd. documents. Putting on her Company Secretary hat she searched through for the file relating to the transfer of the top flat share in the freehold to Felicity Green. She whistled through her teeth. Yes! Her memory had served her right - Felicity Emily Stanton Green. What a turn up for the books! Wait till she told Hubert! But even a revelation like that would have to wait.

She put up her feet and closed her eyes.

Chapter 6

Abigail was dreaming. She could probably have dreamt for England, certainly for Kingscove. This time she was dreaming her father had disappeared at sea, lost inside a bottle. She kept waking up, then going back to sleep, back kept coming the dream. Non-existent, but terribly anxious members of the family waited around at the pier head - the way they used to wait for news in mining accidents in the old black and white films. The bottle bobbed around, on the sea of life she supposed, empty. Eventually she could stand it no longer and got up.

She was still at that strange stage when a dream seems real.

"Abigail Harvey," she told herself sternly, gratefully cradling the first cup of coffee of the day, "your father is *not* lost in a bottle. He has been dead for 40 years and those relatives waiting anxiously around for news of him are *not* real - they have *never* existed. Snap out of it! Go for a walk or something."

It was this Emily Stanton business, she knew. Augustus had been hovering all night, reminding her about the urgent matter in hand. She decided to speak seriously to him now.

"Augustus," she called, "we know how anxious you feel about this, and we really won't let you down. But you've got to give us some time. Please go away. I promise I'll call you back when I've worked out how to deal with this."

There was a loud creak. She knew it had to be the early morning central heating, but it was nice to pretend that it might have been Augustus and that he was off out.

She made another coffee and thumbed through the ridiculous book on dreams that she'd picked up in a charity shop. It was possibly the most useless book ever produced but she always looked in it to see if it threw any light on anything.

It did have a section on bottles and made the obvious point that it depended on what was in the bottle. If it was empty it foretold an approaching period of uncertainty. It did not hazard a guess as to what it meant if the bottle was empty of one's father. Abigail sighed. Useless as usual, she thought, putting it back on the shelf. She threw on some clothes and went out onto Regent's Parade.

*

Hubert swept open his dining room curtains. Still dark, but then it always was at this time of year when he awoke. He looked across the road to where a woman's figure was disappearing in the direction of the Pagoda, the small oriental looking building housing the lift which went down the cliff. It was Abigail. He looked at the clock- 5.45. That was pretty early, even for him. This Augustus thing had obviously got to them both. He left her a phone message inviting her to breakfast on her return. They'd got nowhere talking it out last night. Perhaps in the cold light of day…

*

"I really shouldn't have drunk so much at lunch yesterday. Then I wouldn't have been so silly and come out with such ridiculous things," Abigail declared ruefully when she'd come upstairs.

"Abigail, You scarcely drank at all. You never do." Hubert replied in great surprise.

"Perhaps I should stop drinking altogether, then -Really! Pretending I'm a medium! Hearing voices! Speaking for the dead! Ridiculous!"

"Abigail. Stop it. Stop it. We must have been convinced by it all at the time, when we promised to help Augustus. We need to help Felicity too.

You'd better speak to her, Abigail, - see if she can cast any light on Emily Stanton."

They parted company- Hubert to his poets, Abigail to the Augustus House accounts. They weren't due in to Companies House until January but she liked to get them out of the way long before that. The previous Company Secretary had never sent them in on time and so they had kept being fined. As if they were all made of money.

About 8 o'clock that evening she started to keep a lookout for Felicity, who would be due back after her meeting with Ann. There was a large streetlamp on the Regent's Parade just by Augustus House so everyone crossing the forecourt was clearly silhouetted at this time of night. From the lower ground floor Abigail got a wonderful view of everyone's legs. She knew all their legs by heart. She could recognise their footsteps, too, as they passed through the shared ground floor hall, which ran above her own hall. She rather missed Diana, now residing in York. She had always rushed in and out at breakneck speed - as if her knickers were on fire. That had been Andrew's delicate assessment of the situation anyway.

Felicity was much quieter. Abigail had already been worrying about her before this latest problem. She seemed so pale and thin – almost like a ghost herself. Hubert spent much of his time taking Abigail to task for treating everyone in the house like her children but she couldn't help it.

There went Felicity's legs across the forecourt. Abigail gave her a few minutes and then picked up the phone. Felicity still felt very lonely whenever she arrived back in her new home, so she was only too glad of the invitation. She turned down the offer of wine - saying she was gasping for a cup of tea - and chatted nonstop about Ann and the business while Abigail made it.

"How long have you known Ann?" asked Abigail.

"Since I left university. I went into a city bank as soon as I graduated and Ann was my immediate boss. She frightened the life out of me at first, but most of it is show, although she is certainly very clever and very efficient. She left the bank to start her own business and after a while I joined her."

She bit her bottom lip nervously, then went on to explain that she'd bought in as a partner just before she and Dominic had split. It had made finances a bit tight at the moment.

Abigail probed a bit further. Apparently the business involved financial advice to City women.

"We advise women on financial matters - pensions, mortgages, investments." Felicity told her, "there are lots of women working all hours God sends in the City, some making a great deal of money, without the time either to spend it or to decide how to invest it. It's no good just piling it up under the mattress, is it?"

Abigail wasn't sure. Frequently she wished she'd stashed away a bit more and she'd have been quite happy if it was only under the mattress! .

"How long were you married?" Abigail wanted to know.

"Six years. Just long enough to get a nice life together and then suddenly it's all smashed up and you're back not even in square one. Thank goodness I've had Ann around, but I moved to Kingscove to try to build a new life. I don't want to keep relying on Ann."

She wasn't sure if it was going to work, she confided. She couldn't completely relax up there.

"I keep wondering if it's just because of the split up, or if there's something else."

Abigail hoped she wasn't seeming too nosy, but she needn't have worried, as Felicity was very keen to talk. Out it all came about the smell of cologne on the stairs, the creakings and whisperings.

"Andrew told me about Augustus." Felicity continued. "First of all I thought it was great - living in a house with a ghost, something to dine out on - tell people how he'd passed me on the stairs and all the rest. But it's got to me. I feel he really *does* pass me on the stairs, and he comes into my flat. I can feel him there and he's never happy. My flat is full of sadness- my sadness and his sadness, and put together they make more than double. Perhaps I should see a doctor. Perhaps I'm going mad. Augustus cannot possibly be upstairs… can he?"

Abigail struggled to find the best words.

"My sensible side," she declared, "says Augustus is long dead, so he can't possibly be upstairs, downstairs or anywhere else. But in spite of that I have this feeling that I have met him too. In fact I feel sure I have. Only yesterday I felt he was down here."

She decided to come clean and admit that Andrew had already spoken to her, and that they had held the séance. She looked anxiously at Felicity, feeling she would have every right to be angry, but Felicity just stared, wide eyed.

"What happened?" she eventually asked.

Abigail tried to explain in as matter of fact way as possible. Then she went over to her desk and took Emily's picture from a drawer. She gave it to Felicity, who studied it intently.

"You're right. It does look a bit like a younger version of me, and those are my two middle names. I'd no idea we had any family connections with Kingscove, but I certainly did fall in love with this place the minute I saw it from across the road. Somehow, it felt as if I'd been before. What are we going to do, Abigail? Do you think he thinks I'm Emily?"

Hubert seemed to know quite a bit about things like this, Abigail told her, so Felicity agreed that Abigail should talk to him again.

Felicity looked around. "Do you think Augustus is here now, Abigail?"

"I do," nodded Abigail. "Augustus," she called, "Trust me. We *will* sort it out. Just give us some time."

There was the familiar creak which Abigail now took as a sign that Augustus had gone. She turned to Felicity.

"You're very welcome to sleep down here till this business is resolved, if you want."

"I'll be alright. I'm getting the feeling now that he trusts you and he's gone away."

She does look more relaxed, thought Abigail thankfully.

*

Hubert and Abigail were talking on the phone till quite late on Tuesday night after Abigail's evening with Felicity. One of the bonuses of such close and concentrated living was that you had no problems deciding whether it was too late to ring someone. Abigail just had to look out of her second bedroom window to see if Hubert was still up.

"So that's settled," Hubert declared, when they'd agreed on another séance. "We could have it on Friday night. I get the feeling you're nodding off already, so you'd better come up for coffee in the morning and we'll get it all organized then."

"Hubert," Abigail replied, "I find this all such a puzzle. It seems so out of character for you to get excited about something like a séance."

"I can't see why. My grandmother used to say if a thing's worth doing it's worth doing well. As well as which, seances are very poetical, and, by their nature, spiritual. One is communicating with souls. You must think me very mundane and unimaginative, Abigail, to speak like that." He sounded quite hurt and she thought she'd better get off the line asap.

"Mundane, Hubert, is the last thing I would ever think you. But you *are* right. I am practically nodding off. Sleep well. I'll see you tomorrow."

Is there something wrong with me, she thought. She would only have to say the word with Hubert, but he was so straitlaced, so puritanical. She had decided long since that three marriages were quite enough for one woman. Hubert knew she'd been married, but he didn't know she'd had three goes and still not got it right. There was a lot Hubert didn't know.

Not long after she'd put the phone down, Hubert's light went out. There'd be no more from him now other than the odd intermittent snore and a small hours perambulation to the loo. One could certainly have worse upstairs neighbours.

Even though she was tired, Abigail couldn't get to sleep. The gremlins of the past were out in force that night. As if I didn't have enough ghosts of my own, she thought, without taking on Augustus. Eventually she realized that sleep was out of the question and picked up her book. She was halfway through Brighton Rock for the third time. There was a helicopter nearby. Abigail could tell it must be hovering over the sea, level with Regent's Parade. That was always a bad sign. Someone must be in difficulty in the water. She shuddered, and buried herself in her book.

Chapter 7

Abigail was on the bus enjoying one of her favourite pastimes..Two elderly women in the seat in front were discussing their attendance at an imminent wedding and Abigail's ears were flapping as usual. The noisier of the two was obviously practising hard to be death's head at the wedding feast, although she didn't seem to need much practise.

"I've told them we shall definitely expect to have a taxi laid on. It's outrageous for them not to have thought of it. I'm not going unless they send a taxi," she declared.

Good enough reason not to send one, thought Abigail, - can't imagine having the old trout at my wedding.

"And I've told them I'm definitely not going clubbing afterwards."

"Oh, horrors!" thought Abigail, "the bride and groom must have been devastated when she told them."

Reluctantly she got to her feet. Here was yet another riveting tale whose ending she would never know. The medium demonstration was starting in quarter of an hour. There'd been a leaflet about it in the library. Erika, apparently the area's foremost medium, if you believe everything you read in leaflets from the library, was to give a demonstration . Abigail had felt she was meant to attend – see what tips she could pick up for the next séance.

The Another Way Centre was based in a pretty little gold and green building in West Kingscove. It had obviously once been a corner shop – probably gone under years back to the big superstores. Abigail's parents had owned just such a shop in the town where she had been brought up. There had been a huge frightening machine for slicing bacon, enormous slabs of butter and cheese – pieces just hacked off and wrapped in greaseproof paper as needed – pudding rice and dried prunes weighed out to order. And there was a machine for making fizzy drinks at a penny a throw – an old penny, at that. A Vantas machine , she recalled. Her Saturday job had been to make the drinks and sell them. If she sold twenty she got one free. She probably drank all the profit, and there hadn't ever been much of that. In those days there was a Grocery and General Dealer on just about every corner. And no General Dealer was ever finished for the night. Even after the shop was closed there would be fairly constant knockings on the door. And if you played awkward and refused to serve people then they'd take their custom over to the other corner of the street. It had been a funny life, she supposed. There was never any spare cash , so in that sense they were quite poor, but there was no shortage of food ever – they just ate out of the shop, and all her friends were treated to pretty good meals as well. But money for a school uniform, or money for a Sunday School trip for herself or her brother had been very hard to find. .

Her mother had been the neighbourhood wisewoman cum witch, with possibly a larger dollop of witch. One of Abigail's most abiding memories of her was when she got called out to deliver a baby because the midwife had gone down with flu. She was out delivering it all night and arrived home so proud of herself. She hadn't really had a clue what she was doing, but she'd just got on and done it, and fortunately what she did was right. She was regaling the family with the less gory details over bacon and eggs when suddenly she broke down into tears. They were tears of tiredness, pride, joy and relief. Abigail could see that now, but at the time it had scared and unnerved her. She had never seen her normally tight lipped mother cry before.

I wonder if she'll come tonight to try to get through to me, she thought. She would certainly feel at home in this old grocers' shop. Even if she didn't make it, some of the ghosts of long gone shopkeepers who'd worked in the building might attend. What would they think of the changes?

All the would be communicators with the other world were having to wait, because the designated room was still being used by another group. The queue, mainly women, but with two men, snaked around an inside corridor,waiting patiently as queues normally do, and Abigail tacked herself on to the end.

The two women next to her obviously knew each other and were deep in conversation.

"I think he forgets completely that I've got a full time job, three children and that I'm doing a PhD part- time, said the small freckled one. "When I get home at night there he is, sitting in the kitchen just like one of those baby birds in the nest with its beak wide open. He doesn't really pull his weight at all."

"Doesn't he do anything?" asked the bigger, placid looking one. Placid wasn't quite the right word – she had the long suffering look of someone who expected the worst, and was never disappointed. Goodness knows how many baby birds were parked in her kitchen.

"He actually started to cook the evening meal when I was in the last panic stages of revising for my degree finals. The night I finished my exams I took us out to celebrate. The night after that there he was back in the kitchen with his beak open again. And he doesn't pay his way."

"Why do you put up with him?"

Yes, I was just going to ask that, thought Abigail.

"I'd be lonely if he wasn't there. He's fun. And the children love him."

"I know what you mean," replied the lugubrious one. She looked as if she'd never had any fun in her entire life.

At last the queue started to wend its way upstairs into a first floor room – a large deep purple first floor room, full of deep, deep purple cushions. As she sank down, and even further down, Abigail fervently hoped that someone would be willing and able to heave her up out of all these cushions at the end of the session.. The last people in the queue found themselves standing until some folding chairs were produced. The younger of the two men decided to stay standing, leaning awkwardly against the window behind Abigail. The air was heavy with the perfume of incense sticks and New Age music tinkled on in the background. One entire wall had a startling mural painted in all kinds of psychedelic shades of orange, electric blue and fizzing green. There seemed no definite form to it, and yet Abigail found herself drawn further and further into its depths. In fact it was a very intricate composition – an absolute maze of paths, all hung with various symbols which she didn't recognise. The paths converged on a gate.

The lights in the room were dimmed. Suddenly the gate opened. It caught a lot of people off guard and there was a unified hiss of surprised shock. In the middle of the picture there now stood an extremely tall character in a flowing black kaftan, and with masses of Afro style white hair, which was topped by an exotic feathered bird head dress which masked the features.. But it was the sudden unexpected materialisation that gave people the shock. Although Kingscove is full to overflowing with people of eccentric demeanour, you don't expect one of them to jump out of a mural at you.

"Let us give up our minds and beings to those who are calling us from the spirit world!" demanded the exotic apparition.

"Friends! Friends!" the voice boomed out again. "You are not concentrating. I can feel them. I can feel them – longing, thronging behind me. Thronging to come through this gate. Longing to speak to you. I have someone for each of you. News for each of you. Cleanse your minds of unnecessary thoughts. Have faith in me. I can feel the sceptics. Their disbelief shackles me. Have faith in me. Faith in yourselves. Faith in the departed. Faith in all the armies of spirits who have passed over. Look at me! Look at me! Concentrate! Concentrate!"

"I've a gentleman here very anxious to speak to his daughter. Margaret? Have I a Margaret here? I think it's Margaret. Definitely an M. Mary? Margot? Martha?

A frightened whimper came from near the back - "Yes, I'm Margot."

Erika turned her searing eyes and quivering feathers in the direction of the hapless Margot.

"He says it is time to change, Margot. He says it has gone on long enough.

Does that mean anything to you?"

"Oh yes." Margot's voice sounded even quieter, even more frightened.

"He says no one will blame you", continued Erika, "He wants you to promise him you will be brave and do whatever is necessary. He is quite agitated. He wants you to promise. Will you do that? Will you promise?"

"Yes. Yes." choked Margot, "I promise."

Abigail looked round, unable to resist sneaking a glance at the now demolished Margot who lets things go on long enough. To her amazement Margot turned out to be the would- be PhD. So what was it that had gone on so long? The PhD perhaps? Abigail had a friend who'd been doing one for years. It had become quite a joke between family and friends, although they'd never let on to her. Perhaps Margot's dad was sick to death of it. Perhaps he thought she might manage better on another topic. Or perhaps he meant her relationship. The baby bird certainly sounded a bit of a dead loss.

She sneaked another glance round at Margot and was shocked by her ashen face. It must be something much more serious. I don't suppose we shall ever know, thought Abigail regretfully.

"Remember, Margot," boomed Erika, "you have made a promise. A promise for the spirits must be kept. They rely on us."

Erika's mood shifted.

"I've a couple coming through – two women. They're asking for their nephew. Is it Andrew? Alan? Anthony? They're very faint. They're trying so hard. Can't someone here help them? Please. Please."

"I'm Ashley. Might they want Ashley?"

It was the man leaning against the window directly behind her. There was a look of quizzical amusement on his face. A look of someone quarter waiting seriously for a message, but three quarters just wanting to be entertained and to have something to laugh about later on in the pub

"Yes. Yes. I think they do. They're asking about a pet, Ashley. Have you a pet?"

"I've got a cat," replied Ashley. Abigail thought he sounded , quite naturally, a bit surprised.

"They're worried about it. Is it well?"

Ashley assured them all that it was well and couldn't be healthier.

But Erika wouldn't drop it. "I can't quite get to their real worry. I think it might be food. What do you feed it?"

"Tinned stuff usually. Partial to strong cheese with a bit of Dundee cake as well. Eats like a horse, not a cat. Who are they anyway?" There was a growing edge to Ashley's tone.

"I'm getting Hetty and Agnes. Does that mean anything to you?"

"Not a thing." By now Ashley looked quite peeved. He'd obviously come for something a bit more challenging than a discussion about catfood. The two old biddies who ran the Heavenly Cat Refuge must be a bit short on things to do at the moment. Leave it Erika, Get going on someone else, willed Abigail.

Suddenly Erika turned those blazing eyes on her.

"Why are you here?" she boomed.

Abigail certainly hadn't expected anything quite so direct. It verged on the intimidating.

"I'm just interested. I want to know more."

"I can feel your disbelief. You're holding me back. You have no faith."

"That's partly true. But I'm not a sceptic in a hostile way. I'm genuinely trying to keep an open mind. I came to learn. Honestly."

Mercifully Erika relinquished her gaze and transferred her attention to the other side of the room.

"I'm seeing a great cloud of indecision hanging over you," she told a small elderly woman. "You just don't know what to do, do you?"

The woman nodded. "Is my husband there?" she asked, "he'd know just what to do. He'd know."

Erika closed her eyes and flung her arms toward heaven. "I feel he's doing his best to get through," she murmured, "but someone is trying to stop him. Who could be stopping him?" She swivelled round and cast a baleful glance at Abigail, who was trying hard to look like a meek mouse. Then she raised her eyes upward and stretched out her hands above her head.

"I can't quite reach his name," she gasped, as if the man was dangling from a ceiling light with his name round his neck. "What is his name?"

"Frederick. It's Frederick. Fred." The little woman was almost in tears with a madly quivering lip, "Please try to reach him. He'd know exactly what to do."

"I feel him trying to get through," Erika told her. "He's trying so, so hard, but someone is stopping him. Who is pulling him back? Everyone must will him to get through." She glared again in Abigail's direction. But – what a blessing – at that moment good old Fred managed to burst through.

"He says you're to talk to… - I can't quite get the name. Would it be a mutual friend? Am I getting Bill? Does Bill mean anything? No? I'm sure it's a B. Ben? B…?"

"Perhaps he means Barbara, "suggested Fred's wife timidly, "she's Fred's sister. She and he hadn't spoken for years, and she wasn't very nice at the funeral."

"Yes!" was the triumphant response from Erika, "he means Barbara, You're to speak to Barbara. Then you and she can sort it out."

Abigail was beginning to find Erika irritating rather than amusing. What a charlatan you are, she thought. One look at this poor little lady and anyone can tell that, for her, decision making or sorting things out equals megatrauma. She probably needs a long lie down after choosing her books in West Kingscove Library. You don't need psychic powers to work that out.

But Erika was on her case again, fixing her with that evil eye,so Abigail practised looking very meek and very sympathetic. She decided it was time to beat a retreat, so as soon as Erika turned her attention elsewhere Abigail struggled to her feet, with a bit of a hand from Ashley. She was just creeping out when the medium's next words stopped her in her tracks.

"I can hear a baby crying," Erika had lowered her voice. "I've heard it a lot lately. I think it's lonely. There aren't many babies in the spirit world. I think it's lost. It isn't old enough to talk, so it can't tell us what it wants, but I can feel its sadness. It's still crying. Can anyone help?"

Various women began to mutter anxiously, some plaintively. Abigail did not wait to find out who wanted to help it. She fled. It was starting to rain, and a wind had got up. It was turning into an unpleasant evening in more ways than one.

All the way home on the bus her mind was in turmoil. The bus was quite full and there were lots of silly conversations she could have listened to, but the only conversation that interested her was the one going on inside her own head.

Don't be silly, she told herself, a lost baby is the easiest ploy in the world to stir up a load of women - so many babies – the babies we never had, the babies that miscarried, the stillborn babies, and on and on. But this talk of babies had ruined her night.

When she got back to Augustus House she bumped into Hubert in the forecourt, suitably dressed against the elements and off for one of his contemplative walks along the beach. He much preferred the sea in this nastier mood.

"Hello. How did it go?" He greeted her.

"Absolutely stupid evening. Shouldn't have gone. Don't want to talk about it." She snapped, and shot down the steps to her front door.

Hubert looked taken aback, but knew when to leave well alone. He rammed his cap firmly on his head and turned his steps into the wind.

Abigail felt so out of sorts she didn't even realise that she'd been rude. She fumbled, not helped by her cold wet fingers, for her house keys, and after dropping them in the porch twice, she finally got into her flat.

Her first move was to turn on the heating, and then she poured herself a glass of brandy – so out of character.

As she cradled the glass in clammy trembling fingers the heating system began to creak and rumble.

"Oh, shut up and go away, Augustus," she spoke aloud, "I have far too much bothering me now to think about what to do with you."

She sat at the round table in her kitchen for a long time, sipping her brandy and mulling over the night's events. Gradually she calmed herself down. This wasn't a new nightmare. It was something she'd been faced with time and again and she had worked out a pretty good strategy over the years for dealing with it. She could confront it in her own head, but she felt she would never ever be able to bring it into the open… it was just too painful.

Still, she thought , I only have one life, it wasn't my fault, and it was a long long time ago.

Brave talk, which half worked, but still the night seemed to go on for ever.

*

By morning she'd realised how rude she'd been to Hubert and rang him to apologise. Hubert might be pompous but he was a very forgiving soul and she found herself sharing a very nice breakfast in his dining room overlooking the still raging sea.

"Don't worry, Abigail. I didn't mind. I could see you were tired and cold and very annoyed."

"She was such a phoney, Hubert. It's so easy. I could do it with practice. There are two types of people who go to these séances – people who just want a bit of a laugh, and people who are desperately trying to make contact with someone dead, someone they loved and find it hard to manage without. It's alright to con the first lot, but very wrong to make capital out of the second. There was one poor old lady who was really manipulated. I felt terrible. Poor people like her are so desperate for signs that they just keep handing you clues, and they snatch desperately at all your efforts. You can get away with telling them anything."

If he was honest with himself Hubert would have to agree. He had never been sure whether his mother was just very clever at it, or whether she really did have premonitions and make contact. His considered opinion was that she might well have convinced herself in the end. Fake or not, however, she had certainly helped and comforted lots of people.

"Perhaps one can forgive Erika," he said to Abigail, "as long as she makes them all feel better. If that's the case then I suppose there's no harm done. After all, we're going to try to do something similar for Felicity, aren't we?

You know what Trotsky said – the end may justify the means, as long as there is something that justifies the end."

"I have decided I don't want to help with the séance, Hubert." Abigail sounded faltering but looked defiant. What she really wanted to add was - and damn your stupid quotations.

And although she didn't flounce straight off downstairs Hubert could tell that it wouldn't be a good idea to try to change her mind. Not right now anyway.

So he poured her another cup of coffee.

Chapter 8

While Abigail sipped her coffee and tried to restore herself to better spirits Hubert talked to her about his roof garden.

He had one of those classic love-hate relationships with it.

To start with, he was very aware that it wasn't really a roof garden at all. A garden, even on a roof, should be grounded in proper soil, not just pots, even if the plants are so prolific and so close together that the pots become invisible. The eternal purist in him always felt the need to explain this to people, and he always felt bad about it. He would have liked the perfect proper version.

When he'd bought his apartment all that had been there was a flat roof, surrounded by a low wall and a higher fence. It had been a bleak looking site, and was overlooked by a high proportion of the flats in the houses in the adjoining roads. It was a bit like a concrete goldfish bowl. Augustus' father had bought up the back gardens of all those houses when he was extending to build his ballroom, now Hubert's ruined Tower. It had been the Tower, with its associations with Augustus Booth and his fellow Victorian poets, which Hubert had coveted. The only thing that had attracted him about the flat roof was that it was above his bedroom and belonged solely to him- no one was likely to be tap-dancing above his sleeping head in the middle of the night. He would be in control – or so he thought.

After he moved in, he gradually realised its potential. It was a good space, about 25ft by 25, with an easy staircase up to it. In the summer it was an amazing suntrap and very quiet, because most of the rooms overlooking it from other houses were bedrooms.

Hubert had never gardened until then, but had since discovered, like so many others, that the Goddess of Gardens possesses very seductive ways. Soon he was hooked. He did not realise how good it was for him, how it soothed and modified his too correct a temperament What he liked best about it was the challenge of dealing with the extreme changes – in summer, once the sun was high enough in the sky to rise above the ring of tall old houses, it was a baking desert environment, in winter possibly the coldest, bleakest, most sunless spot in Kingscove. So he had to find plants which could cope with both ends of this spectrum, and, being Hubert, he managed, taking to horticultural research in the same rigorous, meticulous fashion that he had employed for his lifelong research into the lives and minds of his beloved poets.

His garden was now a wonderful haven. It seemed much bigger than it really was, because of many mirrors cleverly framed by hardy creepers. He'd established its own mini -climate by skilful planting, put in a tap, and had played very rash by Hubert standards, investing in an outdoor gas heater (his justification was that it paid for itself because he was so inspired when working in his new little summerhouse).

Just to the left, there stood the Tower. Hubert had plans to extend the garden over the surrounding flat roof – as soon as he got round to having it repaired. At the moment that bit of roof was a strictly no-go area – so rotten that one step on it might be your last.

Love-hate was mentioned earlier. It was never plain sailing up there.

Every now and then there are lapses in East Town

manners - sometimes from people, and sometimes from the weather. Hubert's bedroom had a large skylight window which opened up into his garden. One Sunday morning, fortunately in winter, when he kept the window closed overnight, he'd pulled back the blind and was confronted by a grisly sight. Most of the window was obscured by blood and guts. Some bird had come to an awful end.

"So dull, so dead in look, so woebegone;" mourned Hubert quietly. He closed the blind again. He'd have to go up soon and clear the poor thing away. Not the best way to start a Sunday, but he thought he'd better get it over with.

When he started to clean it up he felt there was a familiar smell. The truth dawned – remains of a dead bird, yes, but not in the way he'd thought. It was the remains of a fiery red chicken tandoori. Hubert could only think that an angry drunk had hurled it out of one of the surrounding flats in a late night row. Such are the risks of close urban living.

Hubert and the weather were old adversaries. Salt-laden gales, baking sun and cold dank mists, sometimes all on the same day, could wreak havoc with the plants. Abigail had had quite a surprise up there one morning last summer. Hubert had persuaded her to do the watering while he was away in Barcelona at some conference or other. An unusually high wind for the time of year had rolled up the Channel howling and growling. Just about anything growing on the seafront turned brown through windburn. When she ventured up to water she was so relieved to find that the tall houses had warded off the worst of the storm. To her surprise, a dear little blue and yellow paddling pool sat proudly in front of the summerhouse.

I didn't know Hubert had a paddling pool, she thought, Surely he doesn't steep his feet while he ponders on the mysteries of Francis Thompson?

When Hubert returned he was most indignant.

"Of course it isn't mine," he'd spluttered.

Then Abigail had annoyed him even more by asking if he had a suitable quotation to celebrate the unexpected arrival of a paddling pool in one's garden.

They never did find out where it came from. The wind had been so strong that night that it could have travelled all the way from West Kingscove or even Le Havre. Abigail had this lovely picture of it sailing and twirling across the night sky.

There had been one even stormier night later in the year – the sort when you had to fight hard to open the heavy Augustus House front door, and then work even harder to close it, and when the seafront would echo with hysterical screams of laughter mixed with terror from young women forced by the west wind to sprint unwillingly in their high heels along Regent's Parade towards Hastings at unaccustomed speed. It was the sort of night when all manner of objects would be whirling through the skies and Abigail and sensible people like her went indoors and battened down the hatches.

Lately the love-hate relationship Hubert had with his garden was becoming more of a love-fear experience.

He usually heard nothing after he'd retired for the night, except the occasional nocturnal yowlings of the two very athletic cats from the basement flat next door. He could never work out how they managed to scale what seemed an unscaleable wall, but they did, and they had claimed his garden as their personal territory. Fortunately he liked cats and this was one way of enjoying them without real responsibility. It was quite normal now to find him in his summerhouse, a laptop on table and a cat on lap.

Recently, however, the atmosphere had changed. Several nights running he had imagined weird wailings, moanings, dragging sounds, scuttlings. Was he imagining it? He was beginning to wonder. On the last occasion he'd sighed in annoyance and gone up to investigate. When he pushed up the skylight door at the top of the staircase he could see nothing but mist, and all that could be heard was the drip, drip, drip of soft persistent rain, the distant yowling of cats, and the owl-like sound of the foghorn down the coast. Of course it was imagination, he told himself, and yet he had this feeling that there was someone there.

"Do you think it might be Augustus?" he ventured to ask Abigail.

"I've told you, Hubert, I don't want to talk about Augustus. I don't want to talk about spirits at all," she'd retorted.

He still hadn't got out of her what had caused last night's bother.

When she'd gone he did a bit of reading up, and came up with what he hoped might be a solution. It had to be Augustus, didn't it? The first séance had obviously unsettled him and he was impatient for some action. Abigail wouldn't contemplate another séance so both Felicity and Augustus were going to be let down. Unless…

He remembered, long ago, his mother organising an exorcism in collaboration with the rather eccentric local Anglican vicar. Perhaps he could pick the brains of their very own resident priest? He'd read somewhere that each diocese had a priest who specialised in this sort of thing- perhaps Cedric could point him in the right direction.

*

When Hubert telephoned up to Cedric he got his answering machine. It's really not the sort of thing you can leave a message about – "Hello. We'd like you to do an exorcism."

Now that he had longer to think about it he started to dither. Surely the whole thing was too silly? Yet it is odd how childhood events can grip you for the rest of your life. Deep in Hubert there was still that little boy who'd been fascinated by his mother's exotic way of paying the bills and loved it when she let him dress up and play along.

When he heard Cedric come in, he tried his phone again.

"I'd be very grateful if you could spare me some of your time," he told Cedric, "I want to ask your advice."

Cedric had never seen inside Hubert's flat, although he'd heard about the famous Tower. This was too good an opportunity to miss, so he agreed to go down for a quick drink at 8pm.

He was quite astonished when Hubert explained his problem. He would never have imagined that the man he encountered from time to time in the Senior Common Room of Whitedean University, the strait-laced, straight faced, set-in-his-ways, Emeritus Professor of Victorian Poetry, might have this bizarre side to him.

Cedric regarded him intently over his half spectacles. He had very little self confidence these days, and he wore these a lot, even though he didn't really need them. He thought they gave him a little bit of gravitas.

He was a fair haired man just giving way a teeny bit to fat, possibly in his late forties, and of middling height. He was very nearly handsome. Lots of women had considered Cedric. He had a quiet charm about him, and it has to be said that a dog collar can be a rather powerful aphrodisiac. Strangely,though, something about him had always stopped any of them from giving him the real come on. Sad really, because he was a very civilised man who greatly appreciated the company of women. A lot of nonsense is talked about the love of a good woman, but a soulmate would certainly have helped alleviate Cedric's searing loneliness.

"So you think there is a ghost in your garden." He stared at Hubert, who found himself blushing at what now seemed a ridiculous notion.

"There's definitely something strange happening," replied Hubert, defensively. "I've read that the Anglican Church will undertake exorcisms?"

"Do you think the spirit in your garden is possessed by demons?"

"No. No. He's a very gentle spirit." Hubert sounded very definite about it.

"Well in that case I think attempting an exorcism would be wrong. Opinions in the church are much divided over exorcism anyway. You say this is a benevolent spirit? Why don't you bless the garden and tell the spirit that the Lord God awaits him in love. Then he may well depart to his proper resting place. Where were you when you first conjured up this spirit?"

"In the Tower Room."

"Can I see it?"

They were sitting in the adjacent Sun Room. Hubert slid back the sliding doors to expose the dark, cold, gloomy space with the tarpaulin gently flapping over the central Tower.

Goodness! thought Cedric, no wonder he gets the creeps.

"I think I'd start in here if I were you," he continued aloud. "Bless this room first. Tell everything here that is evil that it is unwelcome. Tell it to go. Tell it cannot flourish here. Then move up to the roof and repeat the process. Bless the spirit and tell it to go towards the heavenly light. Perhaps sing a hymn. See if that works. I'm really going to have to go, I'm afraid. I'm meeting some friends at 9."

Got out of that quite well, he thought as he hurried down the road to the pub. The last thing he wanted was to draw attention to himself in ecclesiastical circles by conducting an exorcism. These things got round, no matter how quiet you tried to keep them. What a silly old fool to go messing about like that and imagining such nonsense. Anyway, Christmas was almost upon them. Who would want to mess about with exorcisms at a time like this. Surely Professor Jeffries was old enough to know better.

*

"Well, the Reverend Wright has more sense than I credited him with if he's put you off an exorcism," declared Abigail. "Tell me again what he said."

"He thought we should bless the Tower and the garden, and bless Augustus. Then sing a hymn and tell him to move towards the heavenly light."

Abigail exploded. She might manage to persuade herself to join in with this pantomime seeing as the purpose was to move Augustus on, rather than to summon him. But there was absolutely no way that she would stand in the Tower singing a hymn - and she could just imagine how Andrew would blot his copybook in that situation.

She made her feelings very clear to Hubert.

"And anyway," she added, "wasn't Augustus rather sceptical about Christianity? I'm sure I read somewhere that he and Francis Thompson fell out over it and were not reconciled for some time. He may not wish to move towards a Christian heaven. Perhaps we should try to construct an alternative ceremony."

"Would you be part of it if I planned something of which you approved?" Hubert ventured.

Abigail grudgingly said that she might.

And so the humanist blessing of the Tower Room, a roof garden, and a young poet took shape. As it was such a nice morning, Hubert and the cats retreated to the garden to plan it. Music, he thought. He must find music which Augustus would recognise. And some readings – poetry perhaps.

Hubert couldn't resist the thought of composing some poetry of his own, perhaps to incorporate Augustus' blessing and valediction. He stayed on the roof until the spring sun went down behind the encircling houses in the early afternoon, and then hurried down to show his plans to Abigail. To his secret jubilation, he managed to convince her.

*

The best thing about constructing one's own ceremony is that one can make up one's own rules. Abigail and Hubert decided that serenity and beauty should be the most important elements and that it would be a mistake to have too many people there. Felicity and Andrew would naturally want to be present, but they drew the line there. They planned the ceremony for midnight – not hoping for a specially dramatic effect at the witching hour, but because the spirit only seemed to be active in the night.

Abigail invited them all to supper and was a little more pressing with the wine than usual. She felt that the success of this ceremony might well depend on a little alcoholic oiling. She still wasn't sure if she should have let Hubert cajole her into taking part. The baby incident was more or less back in the recesses of her mind, but it was still lurking there ready, as always. When, oh when, would she be able to put the past to rest. She knew the answer - probably never.

Hubert left them tucking into the cheese board and went upstairs to put the finishing touches to the Tower for the ceremony. After a few minutes the others followed. During the afternoon, with Andrew's help, Hubert's imposing dining table had been moved into the Tower. It was now set with a rich red velvet cloth, and four large candlesticks holding simple clear-burning candles. He'd borrowed as many other candlesticks as he could, and scattering these around had softened the atmosphere.

Abigail had suggested William Byrd's Mass for four voices as the opening background music because of its tranquillity, and it was now playing gently in the background. Together the music and the candles made the Tower a much more welcoming place than when Cedric had seen it. It was easier to ignore the cold and the flapping tarpaulin and to imagine how impressively beautiful it must have been when Mr And Mrs Booth had held their opening celebration party in 1875.

Hubert had arranged a formal order of service, and there was a copy on the table next to each chair.

He had tried to involve everyone. Andrew had given in reluctantly, but Felicity preferred to leave it to the others.

*

A Ceremony to bless the Augustus House Tower Room and Roof Garden, together with the

Blessing of Augustus Booth, and all others present who strive for a virtuous life.

Saturday, 11th December at 11.59 pm In the known presence of Abigail Josephine Harvey, Felicity Emily Stanton Green, Andrew James Eliot, and Hubert Norman Jeffries.

Greetings – Hubert Jeffries.

Readings : -

Daisy by Francis Thompson. Abigail Harvey.

To Hope. By John Keats. Andrew Eliot.

Exhortation and Valediction. : - Hubert Jeffries

Music : -

Opening – Mass for four Voices – William Byrd.

Concluding – Ode to Joy, from Symphony No. 9, The Choral – Ludvig von Beethoven

- during the playing of which those present will process to bless the Roof Garden.

*

Abigail suppressed her smile with great difficulty – Hubert was in his pompous element. He coughed slightly and stood up. He actually looked quite good, in his finest suit, with a sober dark tie. He'd insisted Andrew wear a suit also. Andrew had objected at first, but eventually dragged out the cream linen one he'd bought on one of his work trips to Florida. He always scrubbed up nicely.

"We are here to give thanks," Hubert's deep voice echoed round the cavernous Tower, "for every part of our splendid building, and for everyone who has ever lived here and helped to establish its traditions and atmosphere."

Abigail wasn't too sure about that bit. What about all those who had given them aggro – not paying their maintenance charges, making such a mess with their rubbish that they ended up with rats in the forecourt cellar, and the people who had kept them all awake with small hours boom-boom music. She'd been more inclined to give thanks when those people had departed.

"We are here to affirm," Hubert continued, "that it is a place of peace, love, and hope. Evil is not welcome. We bring blessings to the building and to all the virtuous people present, living or dead."

He sat down and looked expectantly at Abigail, who stood up hastily to read the Francis Thompson poem.

...The hills look over on the South,

And southward dreams the sea,
And with the sea breeze hand in hand
Came innocence and she…

They'd decided not to read any of Augustus' work. Hubert was convinced that the pieces which had so far been unearthed by various researchers were not final versions. He felt Augustus might object to the reading of something with which he still felt dissatisfied. Hubert was sure there was much waiting still to be discovered in Augustus House.

Instead Andrew read a poem by John Keats which Hubert hoped Augustus might know. Abigail loved the ending couplet.

Sweet Hope, celestial influence round me shed,
Waving thy silver pinions o'er my head.

Then it was time for Hubert. He stood up and paused for effect, looking up into the darkness of the Tower.

Perhaps she was too hard on Hubert. Yes, he was pompous, but this was certainly an evening they would remember. If someone asked them on Monday if they'd done anything interesting over the weekend they would be hard pressed to say no.

"Augustus!" he began, "we bless you, we are proud of you, we have grown to love you, but it is time for you to go. Your happiness is now elsewhere. You are trapped here no longer. We will safeguard the things you cherish, because we too cherish them. But you must go. Your happiness depends upon it."

Then he switched into overdrive intonation and began again with something he had written himself.

Augustus, bid your tears farewell.
Begin your happy progress to the stars.
Have hope. Be strong
The grief has gone – appreciate the song.
Let verse be your immortal legacy. Yours lingers with us still.
Farewell.
Farewell, dear friend, is but a word – and words mean what you will.

Abigail found herself hoping that it wasn't just a matter of time before he forgot where this had come from and started quoting it. She could just imagine it – he would be saying good night to her and out would come 'Farewell is but a word'.

His voice echoed around the huge room for a moment after he'd finished, and there almost seemed to be a duetting rumbling accompaniment - a crescendo of guttural growling and stamping noises up above. It sounded evil. What frightful thing was happening?

Hubert seemed oblivious, quite caught up in his grand moment. He turned up Beethoven full blast, grasped a candle and forged out of the Tower towards the roof terrace stairs.

The other three looked at each other. They picked up their candles, but each was very apprehensive. Was it really wise to go up there, their eyes were asking each other.

Hubert strode resolutely forward, deaf and blind to any danger. If it had been the Christian ceremony he'd really wanted he would have been carrying an enormous cross protecting all their heads. The noise of the growling was so animal, so scaring, that Abigail almost wished that was the case.

He'd reached the bottom of the staircase when even he was frozen in his tracks. There was an almighty wrenching, tearing, crunching noise, together with a voice screaming blasphemies of the foulest kind. Then came a loud crash. They rushed back to the Tower. It was lighter in there now. The tarpaulin had ripped completely and parts of it seemed to have fallen into the room. The moon shone through and cast its light on a body, tangled in torn tarpaulin, and sprawled across the table.

Chapter Nine

Cedric was on his way back from a night at the theatre in London. He could see the flashing lights of an ambulance up near Augustus House way before he reached it, but he didn't pay much attention. Ambulances were quite common on Regent's Parade because of its proximity to the hospital. It wasn't till he was much closer that he realised that the ambulance was actually inside the Augustus House forecourt. He groaned, remembering that this was the night of the exorcism. What had that stupid old Professor Jeffries done, he wondered. Got so worked up that he'd had a heart attack? Or just got so high on pomposity that he'd exploded? He couldn't help grinning.

But as he neared the scene he could make out Hubert, alive, though not exactly looking well, at the centre of the usual crowd of onlookers which gathers wherever an ambulance parks on one of its errands of mercy. Next to him was that busybody, Abigail Harvey. He felt a bit guilty straightaway and half withdrew that idea – she wasn't that bad. She worried him, though. He often caught her giving him very funny looks when they passed in the hall, as if she knew more about him than he knew about himself. Pull yourself together, he thought, what can she possibly know?

Anyway, better put on his clergyman's hat and show some concern, especially as they both looked so anxious. A muffled up body on a stretcher was being wheeled out

"What has happened?" he asked Hubert.

"Someone has fallen through the Tower Room roof." Hubert looked very shaken indeed. "He's still alive, but he must be badly hurt. It's a massive drop. The paramedics seem to think he'll be alright. He came down tangled up in the tarpaulin. They think that saved his life. He was very drunk as well and they thought that must have made him much more relaxed as he fell."

"How can I help?" asked Cedric.

"Could you take Mrs Harvey inside." replied Hubert, who seemed so shocked that he was having to search for words and was talking very formally. "Miss Green is very upset. I think Mr Eliot is making some tea for her in his flat, so perhaps you could take Mrs Harvey there. Could you tell them that the police have gone, but one of them will come back to see us tomorrow."

Cedric began to shepherd Abigail towards the front door but they had to pass the paramedics, who were just preparing to leave.

"I'm a clergyman," he told them. "Can I help?"

"No thanks, sir. His life isn't in danger. We just need to get him admitted and made more comfortable."

Cedric tried not to look too relieved. What he really wanted to do was to get his new shoes off and have a drink himself. He decided to try the fatherly approach, putting his hand on Abigail's shoulder.

"It's not a good idea to stay out here, Mrs Harvey. It's quite cold, and I expect Mr Eliot could nicely do with your help if Miss Green is upset." He offered her his arm.

For once, Abigail gave in quite meekly and let him lead her into the house. The little gaggle of people began to melt away, disappointed that nothing more dramatic was going to happen, and the ambulance departed on its short journey up the road, blowing its siren in a half hearted sort of way.

Cedric deposited Abigail at Andrew's door and, refusing

the offer of tea, retreated thankfully to his flat.

Felicity was hunched up in a corner of Andrew's sofa, clutching a mug of tea. She had been crying.

"I thought he was dead. I thought he was dead," she was muttering for the umpteenth time.

Andrew looked decidedly out of sorts too.

"Abigail, can you for goodness sake tell her to stop trying to take the blame," he pleaded, "it's doing my head in. If an old drunk is stupid enough to fall through the roof how can it possibly be her fault?"

Felicity raised her tearstained face, "Don't be so heartless. It wouldn't have happened if we hadn't been messing about. If he hadn't heard all our noise he wouldn't have come looking. I expect we woke him up. Can't you see that?"

Andrew's retort that he shouldn't have been there in the first place didn't seem to help.

Abigail made a big effort to pull herself together.

"I think the best we can possibly do, Felicity," she urged her, "is to try to get some rest. We've got to be able to make sense when the police officer comes to see us tomorrow."

Much to Andrew's relief she managed to persuade Felicity up the stairs to her own place, where they found a bottle of brandy left by Ann on one of her visits and poured themselves a good helping each.

"At least it's solved one problem." She told Felicity, "Hubert has been so worried about all the strange signs and noises on his roof. It must have been that old man all the time. I could see you thought Andrew was a bit unfeeling, but he's right really – it isn't our fault that the old man was up on Hubert's roof, and he wouldn't have fallen through if he hadn't been so drunk."

Eventually, soothed by a second glass of brandy, Felicity dropped off to sleep and Abigail trekked wearily back to her own place.

The next thing she knew the phone was ringing – on and on. She tried to ignore it. It must be a dream, she thought. But the insistent noise wouldn't go away and she had to answer it.

"Hello," she muttered, her head throbbing with the unaccustomed effect of last night's excesses. It was Hubert.

"Abigail, the police have arrived. Can you come up?"

How typical of them, she thought with annoyance as she flung on some clothes. If it's urgent you can wait around forever for them, but if all you want to do is sleep, sleep, sleep then here they are, banging at the door in the small hours. Then she looked at her watch and realised it was 10.30 on Sunday morning.

She coincided with Felicity at Hubert's door, and Andrew came bounding down the stairs shortly after. At least Hubert had got some coffee going. The police officer was already sipping hers appreciatively.

"The victim is doing well," she told them. "They were amazed at the hospital to find he had fallen so far and just escaped with shock and a few bruises. It seems the roof tarpaulin must have saved him. I gather he got all tangled up in it and brought most of it down with him when he fell. Anyway, he's sitting up in bed eating everything that's put in front of him. Seems to think it's a luxury hotel. I'm sure he'll be discharged very soon."

Nobody said anything, but the looks on their faces showed how relieved they were.

"We know him well," she went on, "his name is Duggie MacDonald and he has a bed in that hostel just behind Regent's Parade. He has such a big alcohol problem that he even drives the other alcoholics mad. They often gang up and kick him out so they can get some sleep. Then I expect he wanders over the flat roofs till he finds somewhere to go on drinking. He must have sorted himself a little corner on your roof, drunk himself to sleep and then been wakened by your noise. Had you been having a bit of a party?"

"Er, that's right," Hubert came in rather quickly there, before Abigail could get her mouth open, He looked at her sternly, defying her to disagree. "Yes. A bit of a celebration."

When the policewoman had gone, closely followed by Andrew on his way to work and a still pale faced Felicity, Abigail reproached him for being economical with the truth.

"Well what did you expect me to say?" he replied testily, "Can't you just see the headlines in the Argus if it got out what we'd been doing? You should know by now that I don't share your leftover hippy attitudes. I care about my reputation."

Abigail pursed her lips and let it go. She was too tired and hung over to argue. This accident seemed to have brought out the snappy side of everyone, she thought ruefully. As soon as she could she went back downstairs. A big part of her wanted to go back to bed, but she knew she'd wake up feeling even worse if she did that. She decided to go out. It didn't seem a bad day and, being Sunday morning, the seafront was really quiet. She walked and walked in a westerly direction. When she got tired she hopped on a bus and ended up having some lunch in Worthing. What a mess. Deep down she felt as upset as Felicity. She knew they couldn't really hold themselves responsible for an old drunk who happened to be hiding out on Hubert's roof – but even so… It reminded her too about how it was becoming more and more important that the entire roof at Augustus House should be properly repaired rather than just patched up.

When she got home she rang the hospital to enquire about Duggie MacDonald, to be told, to her relief, that he had been discharged. So she closed her eyes, fell into an accidental sleep, and woke up feeling much better.

This thing would have floored her for days when she was younger. Alarming how life seemed to have developed an almost callous streak in her, which would have astonished those who thought they knew her well. But not callous enough, she thought ruefully. Some things still haunted her. She could lock them away for a while, but she still hadn't managed to throw away the key.

*

Felicity didn't fare so well. She tried hard to push the episode out of her mind, but to no avail. A picture of the body sprawled across the table in the flickering candlelight kept coming back and back. It really needed sorting.

"Andrew," she ventured the next Saturday night, "you sometimes go to church, don't you?"

He looked at her in surprise. It was about 7 o'clock and they were sitting in a Thai restaurant in St. Peter's Street.

"Well, yes I do. Not very often, though. My parents are

Christians and they sent me to a Christian boarding school. Quite liked it. Sang in the choir. Got into lots of trouble because I used to get the giggles in church – doesn't go down too well, especially when you're reading the lesson. I don't really regard myself as a believer, but there is this niggling little need inside me, so every so often I end up at Mass on a Sunday morning at St. Hilda's. They have great music. I think that's what I like best about it. And I always seem to come out in a better mood. Father Peter is a great preacher. Seems to know exactly what's bugging me – as if he's got a hotline into my heart and his sermon is addressed directly to me. I don't know if he makes everyone feel like that. If he does, then the man is truly amazing."

"Would you take me tomorrow?" she asked him.

*

And so the next morning saw them rushing off through the town to St. Hilda's. Felicity couldn't see why the hurry. There seemed to be bags of time. But when they arrived she understood. Any church service she'd been to in recent years had been rather empty (except for her wedding service). St. Hilda's was already rather full with 15 minutes still to go. It was always quite crowded, Andrew told her, but it would be even more so on this occasion, as the Organist and Choirmistress for the last 20 years was retiring. This was her last service.

The service was just about to start -- you could tell that from the way the organ was crashing and crescendoing – when a figure came catapulting down the aisle. He ground to a halt one pew in front of them, and sank to the ground in a flamboyant genuflection. There wasn't really room for him to sit down, but people magically parted to make space for him. Felicity had not yet seen his face, but something about him filled her with thoughts that she didn't think were at all suitable for the start of High Mass. (When Abigail was regaled with it later in the day she made a sourly sarcastic comment about Ecclesiastical Viagra.)

St. Hilda's was very High Church, with an exuberance of bells and smells. There was a wonderful opening procession with priests in sumptuous robes and masses of vestmented followers, one carrying the cross and another carrying a large ball-shaped object which he was swinging from side to side, producing a heady, almost intoxicating smell of incense.

"I used to do that," Andrew whispered to her.

Felicity had been brought up a Methodist so all this was a bit foreign to her, but very exhilarating. The .organ thundered out the bars of the first hymn. She was overwhelmed – but was it a great spiritual high inspired by St. Hilda's, or was it because she couldn't take her eyes off the tall figure in the row in front, his hair pulled back into a corn gold pony tail in a vain attempt to control it?

She could hear his rather good bass voice. She couldn't wait to see his face.

There came a point in the service where everyone in the congregation shook hands with each other as a sign of peace. His hyper energy meant that he shook hands with practically everyone in sight, and when he turned to grasp hers she found herself caught, riveted in his extraordinary grey-green gaze. If she hadn't been so overwhelmed she might have remembered reading an article once about beautiful people sparking a brain reaction in the beholder. This man was certainly beautiful- his features symmetrical, his eyes clear and flashing, but there was something more which made him what he was, and only time would divulge that something.

Andrew was right about the lovely music. While he went up to receive communion she sat listening to Kodaly's Missa Brevis. The whole service was so dramatic, orchestrated like something in the theatre with three priests in sumptuous robes celebrating the mass. There was a constant flow of people returning to their seats, and through the crowd, almost as if under a spotlight, came once again the golden stranger. With great effort she averted her eyes. He sank to his knees, no doubt thanking God for his recent forgiveness for all the hearts he had broken during the previous week.

Her visit to church had certainly taken her mind right off the old drunk on the roof.

*

Even if you are not a convinced Christian there seems to be something very uplifting about going to church. When you come out you feel much better – so morally superior to all those people still in bed or only just up nursing their hangovers after a raucous Saturday night. Something else about it seems to give you a ravenous appetite and a great thirst – the bread and wine does wonders for the soul but the stomach screams for sustenance of a more robust nature.

So Felicity and Andrew were soon sitting around the

corner from St. Hilda's quenching their thirst at Dr Brookes' Tavern, and waiting with starving anticipation for their lunch. Much to Felicity's disappointment, the figure from the pew in front seemed to have disappeared as quickly as he had materialised. She'd been hoping to get a better look at him as everyone milled out on to the church steps and stood about catching up on each other's news, or trying to grab a word with Father Peter. She saw what Andrew meant about this man's sermons – this morning's had seemed very relevant to her present predicament.

Jeremiah 14.8 – Oh Hope of Israel, its Saviour in times of distress,

Why are you like a stranger in the land, like a traveller who stays only a night?

Father Peter might have been disappointed to find one of his congregation linking his text to the gorgeous man sitting in front of her. He had been trying to focus the minds of his parishioners on far nobler, more spiritual things. Instead, Felicity was thinking, what if he *is* only a traveller and going back to his real world tonight? What if I never see him again?

Dr Brookes', irreverently referred to as Brookes'oes by those in the know, was one of Kingscove's untrendy trendy spots. Rumour had it that it was converted from an old surgery, where Dr Brookes, a local legendary early 20th century figure spent his entire professional life ministering to the Kingscove poor. He'd finally retired in 1948, reckoning that, now they had the NHS, the Kingscove poor could manage without him.

The story could be true. The place had the graceless look and feel of an ancient surgery with ill assorted, uncomfortable old wooden chairs. If you closed your eyes you could easily picture the masses of people sitting waiting, waiting – eventually almost turning to stone in their patient, desperate desire to see the doctor. None of your sparkling glass and chrome here, none of your huge vases of exotic flowers and seed heads. Just bare scrubbed tables and bare scrubbed floors.

Why did people go? Certainly not for this décor, but the drinks were amongst the cheapest in Kingscove and, by pub standards, the food was spectacular, especially at Sunday lunchtime. It was certainly the place to be seen.

There was one particularly noisy group in the far corner roaring with laughter. Felicity looked over to see who was so entertaining. It was him! He was holding centre stage, regaling his table with some long tale. Even though her food had arrived and she was starving, she could not bring herself to concentrate on eating it. Eventually there was one last gale of laughter, then a long round of hugging and kissing. When he swept out into the Kingscove afternoon it seemed to her as if night had suddenly fallen.

She started picking at her food again, but it now seemed tasteless.

"Are you alright?" asked Andrew.

"Yes. I'm just tired. It's been a bit of a week, hasn't it?"

*

Andrew had gone to work and Felicity was sitting by her window looking out over the sea. She couldn't get that man out of her mind. Men who could sing, and men who could make her laugh had always been at the top of her list. She wondered these days how she could possibly have married Dominic. He certainly couldn't sing. She hadn't even heard him trying to until he began murdering 'Love Divine All Loves Excelling' as he stood next to her at the altar rail. Perhaps that explained a lot. And as for making people laugh – the only person he'd made laugh was Ann, and it was because she thought he *was* a joke, not that he ever made any.

This man was stunning to look at as well. She wondered what he did for a living. She couldn't imagine him buttoned into a city suit, toiling over London Bridge every day. There wouldn't be a suit that could tame him.

There was a knock at the door. It was Tracie, clutching a bottle of wine. She and Felicity had quickly progressed from just passing the time of day on the stairs, and were beginning to get on rather well.

"Do you fancy sharing this with me? Martin's gone out." She looked a bit forlorn.

Felicity knew she'd drunk too much already. She'd have a foul head in the morning, but she desperately wanted to talk to someone about this godlike Superman. She wondered if you ever grew up and got over this feeling of being completely swept away. Did Abigail ever feel like this, for instance? Or Hubert? Was that how he felt about Abigail?

She beckoned Tracie in, and went for a corkscrew.

A couple of hours later they were well into their second bottle when the phone rang. It was Abigail, wanting to know if Felicity would witness her signature on a document.

"Of course, come up," she urged her, "Tracie's here. We're just having a drink."

Abigail arrived shortly after, very sober, but with another bottle of wine.

Perhaps there should have been a notice pinned up in the main hall of Augustus House warning residents not to get involved in a little drink with their Company Secretary unless they wished her to find out absolutely *all* their business. By the time the third bottle had been demolished Abigail had learned that Tracie and Martin were going through a very bad patch indeed, that Tracie had a new job, of which Martin did not approve, and she had heard several times over that Felicity had met the most wonderful man.

And he became even more wonderful with every glassful. No, she didn't know his name. No, she hadn't spoken to him, but he was out of this world gorgeous.

Hmmm, thought Abigail, as she went back downstairs, I smell big trouble.

*

Andrew got back from Cyprus on the Wednesday afternoon following the visit to St. Hilda's. It had been a trouble free flight. Gosh! Christmas Day on Saturday, he thought. Augustus House seemed very quiet. Abigail had put up some decorations in the hall, but there weren't going to be many residents around. Felicity, Tracie, Martin had all gone back to their childhood homes, and Cedric was up in London.

Andrew had a shower and a quick walk along the seafront to blow away the claustrophobic effect of 5 hours in a plane. Then he picked up the phone.

His old friend Stephen answered.

"Stephen. It's Andrew. Heard you were back. Then saw you in Brookes'oes on Sunday, but you were right in the thick of it over the other side. Next time I looked you'd gone. How are you?"

"Great to hear you," came the reply, "you should have come over and joined us. It was someone's birthday – it turned into quite an afternoon I can tell you. We must meet and catch up. I've rung you twice . Your messaging didn't seem to be working. Are you doing anything tonight?"

"Not much. I've just got back from Cyprus. Three days off now," he replied.

"See you in The Gayte, then? About seven? That's better placed than Brookes'oes for both of us isn't it?"

The Gayte was in East Town. There had been a pub on the site for at least 100 years, but The Gayte was a relatively new venture, full of the glass and chrome and flowers so conspicuously absent from Dr Brookes'. The previous place had been full of old men crouched all evening over one pint, and had smelt of 100 years of split ale. When it had changed hands there had been an absolute furore. The local paper had hosted a flood of letters with assorted emotive headings :-

Beginning of the end for Kingscove pub life.

Locals ousted from their drinking place.

Profit over pensioners.

Bitter end to The Admiral Gordon.

The Gayte had been open a year or two now, and the dust had settled on this row. It was actually a very welcoming, inclusive place, and had made a big effort to pacify the old clientele by creating a snug to accommodate them, although by now most of them had either died off, or drifted away to other pubs where the beer was cheaper.

Andrew and Stephen had been friends since schooldays. They didn't see much of each other now because they both had the sort of job that made regular meeting difficult – Stephen on oil rigs, Andrew on planes. Stephen owned a vast flat on the top floor of a house in Victoria Crescent. He'd bought it in the days when Kingscove wasn't anything like as trendy and prices were relatively low. Because of his work, he wasn't there much and rented out three of the four bedrooms to longstanding tenants. They were all trusted friends – very important considering his long absences.

Andrew had never seen Stephen so animated. He really began to wonder if his friend was in love, but the real reason soon emerged.

He was back for good, Stephen told Andrew, and he'd just landed the job as Organist and Choirmaster at St. Hilda's.

"I've finally earned enough on the rigs to pay off the mortgage. What with the St. Hilda's job and weddings and funerals, and the rents from my spare rooms I think I'll be able to get by. At last I can just concentrate on music."

When the rest of the usual preliminaries were well over - enquiries after health of family members and close friends, and some old common enemies – Andrew decided to jump straight in with what he *really* wanted to know.

"You seemed to be with a good crowd on Sunday. Didn't recognise any of them," he probed.

"You wouldn't. It was a birthday crawl. I only knew the birthday boy"

"Who was that?"

"The one with the ponytail. Did you notice him? Paul Streetman. Worked with me on the rigs for a while. He's staying with us at the moment - using Tim's room while he's in India. He's back early in the New Year, so Paul will have to find somewhere else soon."

Stephen looked at his watch. It was eight o'clock.

"He was supposed to be coming here at 7.30. But that's him. Never on time."

In fact it was gone nine before the door to the snug burst open and in catapulted the man from church. Andrew had had an hour to get worked up. Felicity hadn't been the only one to be smitten that Sunday morning.

Stephen stood up to welcome his guest.

"Paul, this is my old school friend, Andrew Eliot. Andrew, this is Paul Streetman."

Andrew staggered to his feet and offered a hand so clammy that he was sure it would give the game away. The flashing eyes met his. He couldn't think of anything to say, and stood there, almost quivering. In the nick of time he remembered his father's unfailing remedy in nearly every tricky situation.

"What will you have to drink?" he managed to croak.

Chapter 10

A couple of weeks later Andrew drove his ancient Mazda back from the DIY Superstore into the forecourt of Augustus House. He finally managed to open the door against a burgeoning January wind. It looked as if there might be torrential rain any minute. Better get all this stuff in before he got drenched. At times like this he wished he'd bought that place he'd looked at in Redhill - much nearer Gatwick, definitely less windy and cheaper too.

Felicity had been agonising over whether to go to her art appreciation class on such a wild night. Cezanne and Picasso had just won and on her way out she met Andrew on the stairs humping up tins of paint. There was another pile of tins in the entrance hall.

"Don't tell me you're going to finish doing up your spare room at last," she teased.

"Yes," he puffed, trying hard to sound nonchalant. "Friend of a friend needs somewhere to stay. I said he could come for a week or two."

He carried on up the stairs and she forced herself out into the Force 8.

Andrew had not been able to believe his luck at The Gayte - first of all Paul turning up like that, and, secondly, needing somewhere to live.

He'd been surprised when Stephen had tried to warn him off. While Paul had gone to get in a round he'd said, "Look Andrew, don't get too involved. He's very attractive – draws people like flies to a candle – but he can be bad news as well. And there's definitely something up this time. I reckon he's on the run. I don't mean it's anything criminal, but there's something strange. He always ends up in Brighton when he needs a hideout. Just play it carefully."

Andrew hadn't taken the warning seriously. He'd even wondered if it was sour grapes – perhaps Stephen had fancied Paul and hadn't got anywhere. He certainly seemed to be making a big deal out of it.

I'm only being charitable and giving Paul a temporary roof over his head, aren't I? Andrew told himself, That isn't getting involved, is it?

He couldn't even admit to himself just how very excited he really was. Instead he was channelling all his energies into doing up the long- suffering second bedroom.

He had been threatening to do this for such a long time that it had become an Augustus House joke. If he'd been able to think straight now he would have realised they would all sense that something was up.

Paul had to be out of the borrowed room by the coming weekend, and it was Tuesday night already. There was masses to do. Perhaps he could persuade Abigail to give him a hand tomorrow? After all, she'd done most of Hubert's dining room for him while he just did his usual - spouted quotations, lifted the odd brush, and made the coffee.

Andrew had actually begun a few months ago – cleared it out, got rid of the very ancient bed his mother had passed on to him, and put a first coat of white on the walls. Then he'd got bored.

However, it was going to need at least two more coats to obliterate the awful dirty mustard that had covered the place and given the game away about its 1970's origins.

He'd better get his hair cut as well. He looked at it ruefully in the hall mirror. What could he do about all that greying at the temples? He was only 33, dammit. No good Felicity telling him how distinguished and attractive it made him look. He was very fond of Felicity, but it wasn't her he fancied, so he wasn't really bothered whether she thought his grey streaks were fetching or not.

He could hear the rain pounding against his windows. It certainly wasn't the weather for going out again, so he thought he might as well make a start. Because there was an urgent reason it seemed easier this time and he got the second coat on surprisingly quickly. He looked at his watch and to his amazement it was 11.30. Better call it a day. After all, he had been up since 3.30am, and had travelled back from Malta, as well as to and from the DIY! He was just washing out the roller when there was a jaunty rap at the door. Andrew grimaced in irritation. Who on earth was this? Now he'd stopped he suddenly felt so, so tired. All he wanted was just to fall into bed.

He decided to ignore the knock, but after a moment there it was again, this time more urgently. Reluctantly he opened the door. There stood Paul, waterlogged and bedraggled, a dripping bag at his feet. His wetness seemed to have no effect on his usual exuberance. Instead, it seemed to have extra- fuelled it.

"Thank goodness you're in," he beamed, "I thought I was going to have to sleep on the stairs. Been pressing your buzzer for ages. Must be broken. I was lucky someone else was coming in and took pity on me."

He grinned engagingly at Andrew, who was trying to find some words – any words.

"I… I thought you weren't coming till the weekend," he

eventually faltered, "I'm still doing out the room. There's not even a bed there yet."

Paul took off his sodden jacket, slung it on the hall floor and started to unbutton his shirt. He turned those flashing eyes, full of amusement, on Andrew.

"I'll just get out of these soaking clothes. Never mind about the bed. I'm parched. Put that roller down and make me a cup of tea, there's a love. And then I'm sure I'll think of something."

Andrew suddenly didn't feel tired at all, but falling into bed still seemed a very inviting idea.

Chapter 11

Felicity had got pretty wet as well. It hadn't been her who'd let Paul in, but they must have only just missed each other on the front step. She'd been for a drink with her art classmates.

The storm had lessened a bit but it was still far from calm out there and she found it hard to sleep as the wind whistled through her old and badly fitting windows. Finally she got up again, made herself a drink and sat in her window seat staring out to sea. As her eyes grew accustomed to the darkness she began to make out the vast breakers rolling in in great white curls and beating on to the shingle beach. She could hear their regular insistent noise. And she could just make out a familiar figure walking up the sea side of the road. What was Tracie doing out at 1.30am? That girl was going to pieces, Felicity thought, and she was growing fond enough of her to worry about it.

Since that Sunday, the man in church had scarcely been out of her mind. She finished her drink, drifted back to bed, and fell into a sleep of sorts. It would have been an even worse sleep if she'd known what was keeping Andrew awake downstairs.

*

Felicity found it very hard to get up next morning. If she hadn't taken a cab she certainly wouldn't have caught her train. Rushing into the milling station with just a minute or two to spare, she was pulled up sharply by the sight of an unmistakeable corngold ponytail bobbing and weaving its way through the commuters in the station hall, head and shoulders above a great many of them.

She groaned to herself. What awful luck. What a dilemma – he wasn't even going in the same direction. They were announcing a Portsmouth train and it looked as if that was what he was heading for. She actually considered ditching all her morning's appointments, ringing those involved to say she was ill – "I've just got to the station and I feel so faint I don't think..." – but a lifetime of responsibility, combined with a big dose of timidity and cowardice pushed her in the direction of the London train.

"Grow up," she told herself. It was a rotten start to the day. She spent the whole journey lamenting lost opportunities, trying to console herself with the observation that he hadn't had a bag with him, so there was a strong possibility that it was only a day trip. What could she have done about it anyway? Got on his train? Sat opposite? Drooled at him so much that the poor bloke had to move? Yes, that would have been really successful, wouldn't it?

Or taken the bold line – Excuse me, I saw you at Mass in St Hilda's and I just can't get you out of my mind. Can I spend the rest of my life with you?

And what about her mortgage? She needed these clients to survive. Paying the mortgage loomed quite large in Felicity's life, so she forced herself to make a success of all her morning's appointments. However, by the time it got to the afternoon's strategy meeting with Ann at her flat by the Thames her resolve was dwindling fast.

It was an unusually mild day and the doors from the vast living space were open. Felicity stared across to Tower Bridge while Ann droned on about this and that.

No, that wasn't fair, she tried to tell herself. Ann was very business- like. She took a long drink of water, sat up straighter and tried harder.

You couldn't fool Ann that easily. She put down her pen, took off her specs, and stared hard at her colleague. "Felicity Green! Something tells me that I might as well just give up and put the kettle on. *What* is wrong?"

Ann always had a sharp sarcastic side, but underneath it lay a very warm nature. Felicity usually didn't let the outer layer phase her at all, but today, to the dismay of both of them, she burst into tears...

Unrequited love does seem to have a terrible effect on the waistline. Several chocolate digestives later she felt a little bit better.

"It's not a crying matter at all," declared Ann, "I thought half of you had died for ever when that blasted Dominic went. This is the first man you've shown any interest in since then. I think it 's wonderful. You're on the road to recovery at last. Au Revoir, Dominic. May you rot in oblivion, where you deserve to be. Let's have some champagne." And she passed the chocolate biscuits over again.

By the time Felicity took the train back she felt quite a bit better, although a lot of that might have been due to three very nice glasses of fizz.. Perhaps Ann was right. It was a very long time since she had been able to fancy anyone. It just needed keeping in proportion – in lust, really, not in love.

"Enjoy it," Ann had said, "wish I had someone on hand I could fantasize about."

There was no sign of Paul on Brighton Station when she returned, but that would have been too much of a coincidence. As she sat on the bus for the last part of her journey home she remembered that first evening when she'd sat behind the two old ladies and wondered if life would ever let her slot back in. Perhaps that time was growing closer.

"Quite a spring in your step tonight," said Andrew, as they passed on the stairs.

"Funny," I was just thinking the same about you," she replied.

Chapter 12

Abigail was surprised to find Tracie ringing her buzzer, especially as she could have sworn those were tearstains on her face.

"I've locked myself out," Tracie told her, "have you still got our spare set of keys?"

"Come in. I'll get them for you. You look frozen. Would you like some coffee?"

Tracie nodded gratefully. "Please. I've been sitting on the front step wondering what to do. Kept hoping someone would come home and then at least I could get through the outer front door and be warm. Eventually I remembered Martin once saying he'd given you some keys."

When Abigail came back from finding them in her writing bureau she was pretty sure she had been right about the tears.

"What's wrong, Tracie?" she asked her gently.

The silent tears gained a trembling voice.

"Martin's gone. We've had a huge row. I don't think he'll come back."

"Then perhaps you need something stronger than coffee? How about a brandy?"

"You haven't any vodka, have you? Brandy always gives me a such a head." Tracie looked so very forlorn.

Abigail nodded, and went off again to find it.

They sat in silence while Tracie gulped at her drink.

After a minute or two she seemed a bit more composed and began to recount the sorry tale.

She'd grown more and more to hate her job with the

council –hated having to get up and go to the same place every day - hated watching the clock all day because she found her work so very boring. Like so many before her she'd come to university in Kingscove, fallen in love with the place, and not been able to bear the thought of leaving after she'd graduated. She'd taken a job, any job, so that she could stay. Martin had done much the same, but he'd been luckier. His job had turned out to have real prospects, and he enjoyed it.

Abigail had heard a lot of this already on the night she'd gone up to get Felicity to witness her document and found the two of them deep in that soul searching drinking session.

"I'd given a lot of thought to what I might do instead, but the way out finally turned up by accident," Tracie continued.

Apparently, one day, in a charity shop in George Street she'd found this dinky Teddy Bear suit .She couldn't resist it. It had such a lovely little face, and it was only £9.99. A friend was having a fancy dress party and she'd thought it would be ideal. She'd even wondered if she might be able to persuade Martin to go as Goldilocks. She gave a desperate little laugh.

They didn't have a bag big enough for the suit in the shop, so she'd brought it home over her arm. Then she'd bumped into a friend, who'd invited her in for a cup of tea, and it hadn't taken much for him to persuade her to try on the suit.

Tracie looked at Abigail. "He'd got this old recording of the Teddy Bears' Picnic, and just for fun I started dancing around to it. He joined in and I grabbed the tea towel from his kitchen and started smacking him on the rear with it. At first we were both laughing our heads off, but suddenly he went quite funny and backed off. I was really puzzled. After all, it was only me in a fake fur teddy bear suit, with a wet tea towel. It had obviously had an effect on him, though - sparked something off. He wouldn't explain, said I was imagining things. I found myself thinking about it all that evening."

She was quite friendly, she reminded Abigail, with Rosie, the dominatrix who lived in the house next door. They sometimes invited each other in for coffee if they met on the forecourt. The next time she'd seen Rosie she'd shown off her charity shop acquisition.

"I told her about my friend's odd reaction. I was really surprised by what she said, Abigail. She wondered if my friend had suddenly realised that he was enjoying the fun a bit too much. She thought he might have decided it wasn't a good road for him to venture down."

Abigail was a bit surprised too, but Rosie was, after all, an expert in these matters. When she thought about it, though, she'd always had reservations about that song – perhaps not quite the sweet little song it made itself out to be – you'd better not go alone, safer to stay at home… And just think of all those people who still cherish their Teddies long years after they have reached adulthood. She also found herself speculating on who this friend might be. Tracie seemed over coy about naming him.

"Rosie suggested, half joking, I think, that I might have found my new career. She knew I'd always been fascinated by what she did for a living," Tracie continued, "she gave me some tips, I bought my own copy of The Teddy Bears Picnic, and gave it a whirl. I've discovered there seem to be an awful lot of men who thoroughly enjoy being chastised, or mothered in an aggressive way by their childhood teddy."

She stopped suddenly, biting her lip. "But you don't really want to hear all this, do you, Abigail?"

"On the contrary, it's fascinating. Go on." urged Abigail. And she meant it. What a strange place the world was. She even found herself wondering if Hubert had a need to be mothered, chastised, dominated. Don't be an idiot, she told herself, Hubert gets his kicks out of doing the dominating every time.

"So what was today's row about?" she probed.

Tracie filled her in on the details. Martin had never shared his secret with her, so she'd started playing him at his own game. She'd given in her notice and rented a small studio in West Kingscove where she now had paying clients. She called it The Porridge Pot. She really enjoyed it - partly because the clients enjoyed it, and partly because she got quite a kick out of it herself. When she put the suit on she became a different person, an anonymous but powerful person.

"And I can make in 45 minutes what would take more than a day at that boring office," she confessed, obviously still amazed at how easy it all was. She went on to explain that when Martin found out quite by accident that she had moved jobs he was furious, particularly when he discovered what the new job entailed.

"I just find him so hypocritical," she exploded, "I'm supposed to accept *anything* he does – even though I find it very difficult- but he thinks what I do is disgusting and won't even try to see it differently. It's not as if any of my clients lay a hand on me. It's just role play - horse play.

I discovered what he was up to by accident at that party – he discovers me in West Kingscove, again by accident – what's the difference?"

She couldn't help smiling through her tears at this point.

"It was quite funny. He came to give an opinion for a planning application at the house where I rent the studio, and we met on the stairs. I don't know which of us was most taken aback.

I've been trying really, really hard to take his foibles on board. After all, we must have been sleeping with this Roberta woman hidden in a suitcase under the bed for years. How does he think that makes *me* feel? Tolerance, for Martin, does seem to be a one sided coin."

She'd told him that she had no intention of giving up her new venture, they'd ended up doing a lot of shouting, and he'd packed some things and stormed off. She'd needed a walk to try to clear her head, but had been so upset that she'd forgotten her keys.

She looked at Abigail. "You are being very nice, but really you must be thinking I'm disgusting."

"Not at all," Abigail regarded her seriously, "not many of us are pure enough to pass judgement on others. I admit your new job wouldn't be something I'd want to do, but it takes all sorts. You're obviously fulfilling a need for your clients. You don't seem to be hurting anyone else, and you're happier than you were in your last job. It certainly pays the bills. I think I'd rather just leave the jury out on it for now."

But Abigail felt she knew why Martin was so very upset and she made an effort to explain. Martin was deeply involved and concerned because he loved Tracie far too much to be indifferent. After all, hadn't Tracie been blazing furious when she'd first found out about him? If it had been a friend who'd turned out to be the transvestite might Tracie not just have smiled tolerantly and said, ' Well, after all it *is* Kingscove'? It is much harder to be tolerant when the problem is so near to home. It was the same situation now. They'd had very high standards for each other, almost worshipped each other, and now that they had both crashed off their pedestals neither could cope.

Tracie looked at her watch and gasped.

"I must go. I've got a client this evening. By the way, I haven't seen Professor Jeffries for ages. Is he alright?" she asked Abigail, trying hard to change the subject while she hurriedly gathered her things together.

"He's in Malta," Abigail told her, "doing detective work about one of his blessed poets. Having a wonderful time, I gather. Are you going to be ok?

"Yes. Just walk up the steps with me, will you?"

Tracie looked even smaller than usual, and very sad. "I don't think I can ever forgive him for not telling me right at the beginning," she confided. "If he had, I think I might have managed to come to terms with it. I was crazy about him - but not having the guts to tell me – that sort of took away a lot of my pride in him, and he's never done anything to get it back. It makes me so sad."

Sad wasn't a strong enough word, Abigail decided. It was almost tragic. The things that these two used to find most attractive about each other seemed to have backfired on them. Tracie had always loved the gentle, almost feminine, side of this big, strong man, and he had loved her feisty, independent, inventiveness, crossed with a surprisingly motherly streak. These once treasured things seemed now to be what were causing their downfall – making them almost despise each other.

As the two women said goodnight, Andrew was crossing

the forecourt with another man. Rather a stunner, Abigail noted. This must be his new lodger – but one look at Andrew's face and she knew he was more than a lodger.

When Abigail said goodbye to Tracie she discovered it had turned into a beautiful evening, so she stretched her legs along to the Pagoda and back. When she returned she found Andrew pacing the forecourt. He looked very relieved to see her.

"Abigail, you have a visitor. She's got your name wrong, but I'm sure it's you she wants. I've put her in my flat to wait because she said she'd come a long way. May I bring her down?"

"Yes, of course," Abigail was startled.

"I've made her a cup of tea," continued Andrew, "so just give us five minutes for her to finish it and I'll bring her down."

Must be bad news, thought Abigail, nobody arrives unexpected at ten o'clock at night unless it's bad news.

A few minutes later Andrew shepherded in a disagreeable looking bustling woman, probably in her early eighties. She peered anxiously at Abigail.

"Lorna, Lorna Turnbull is it you?"

Abigail nodded, horrified. Nobody called her Lorna Turnbull now. Who was this woman?

"A've been looking everywhere for yuh, pet."

Suddenly Abigail realised, and cold fear juddered through her .

"Is it Mrs Milburn?" she asked, resting her hand on the bookcase to steady herself against the shock.

"Why aye. Of course it is. A haven't changed that much,

have a?"

In a more composed mood Abigail might have been thinking – no I don't suppose you have changed. You were an old nasty woman when you were young, and I expect you still are. But the awful shock had stopped Abigail's flippant aspect dead.

"I expect you're wondering why I'm here. I don't travel much these days, but this is important."

"We'd better sit down, Mrs Milburn. Have you had anything to eat?"

It turned out that she hadn't, so Abigail made her some more tea, and a cheese and pickle sandwich. It was a good way of playing for time and when she came back with the tray into the sitting room she had prepared herself for the worst.

"Freddie died last week," said the old woman matter of factly.

"Oh dear, I'm sorry." To be honest, Abigail didn't care at all about what happened to Freddie, but she supposed she ought to try to feel sorry for Mrs Milburn. It must be dreadful to lose a child – even a grown up one.

"How old was he?" she asked, trying to say the things Mrs Milburn would expect.

"Only 64," replied the old woman, "he had lung cancer. Smoked himself silly most of his life. Never got over that day, you know. When he was dying he returned to the church, thank God. The priest came every day."

Abigail couldn't understand why she had come all this distance to find her and tell her this. Perhaps it would come out in a minute – and it did.

"You must be wondering why a'm heeya," said Mrs Milburn, "a promised him on his deathbed. He confessed to the priest, and the priest told him to make amends. A couldn't believe it. Thought he must be having fits or something, but eventually he convinced me. He said he was jealous of her. Said she'd spoiled everything – and a had to agree with him."

"I did wonder," replied Abigail, "after all, I knew I didn't do it."

"Well why did you confess, then?" The old woman's voice went up and down in the familiar northeastern lilt.

"Because Freddie said John did it. And John just dried up, he was so frightened, and so young. And I was supposed to be looking after him. He wouldn't say anything at all. Part of me felt he couldn't possibly have done it, but he did have a terrible temper, so part of me was thinking what if he had done it. I was only a child myself. I was so worried. So I said I did it."

"Well I don't know why you didn't just let your brother take the blame. Everybody knew he wasn't all there, and he could be a nasty little bugger. They would have locked him up, and your mother would have probably been relieved. He drove her mad every day.

Anyway, it wrecked my Freddie's life," Mrs Milburn was looking almost accusingly at Abigail, who had been struck speechless. "He was never the same again. He smoked too much, and he drank too much. It broke him."

"And what do you think it did to me?" Abigail was at last roused to anger," I spent years in an institution for young offenders, my mother scarcely spoke to me again, my father died of a broken heart. Don't talk to me about wrecked lives."

"Aal reet, aal reet," Mrs Milburn was getting worked up as well, "a wish a hadn't come. A only came to save my

Freddie from damnation. You can't blame me for what happened – you shouldn't have been such a silly bitch as to confess. A can't stand this. A'v got to watch me blood pressure. You don't want me on your conscience as well, do you?"

"Well what have I got on my conscience? You've just told me yourself that Freddie did it."

"But you told a lie, didn't you?"

I want this woman to go, before I do her serious damage, thought Abigail, she seems to think that lying is in the same league as murder.

"It's getting quite late. What are your plans?" she asked Mrs Milburn, "I could find you a B and B if you have nowhere to go."

"No need to put yourself out. You haven't changed. You were a stuck up bitch when you were a little girl. I'm staying with wor Norma for a bit. She lives at Shoreham now. They picked me up at the Coach Station and a said a wanted to get this over with straightaway. They're in the car waiting." She rummaged in her handbag and gave Abigail a letter.

"The priest found out where you lived from Mrs Evans - I didn't know she used to come and see you in prison - and then he wrote this for you, and Freddie signed it, asking your forgiveness. He was too ill to write it himself. Now you've got it Freddie can go to heaven. It was easy for me to forgive him. That baby was a terrible burden to me. I really don't know why he was jealous of her – I always loved him best and I hated her. Once I got over the shock it was a load off my mind."

She realised she'd said too much.

"Oh well, it's all water under the Tyne Bridge now," she

said, putting on her coat and picking up her handbag, "I expect you forgot about it long ago."

After she'd gone, Abigail felt like throwing all her most treasured possessions around the room and jumping on them. She was shaking. The woman was nasty, yes, but what got Abigail most was how illogical she was. She seemed to blame Abigail for ruining Freddie's life. Abigail remembered him as being as nasty as his mother. If his life was ruined surely he only had himself to blame. She wept tears of anger and frustration. What a good job I don't believe in hell, she thought. Otherwise I would be praying for Freddie to rot in it for ever, and hoping that his mother would join him there very shortly.

For over 50 years she'd relived that awful day in 1951 again and again. She was the oldest – just – at 11 and usually got the difficult job of being in charge. Mrs Milburn was usually keen to get rid of her children to Abigail, and as she and Abigail's mother were great friends, Abigail didn't have much choice. It was during the holidays and she'd been told to take them all for a walk. Her favourite was right along the cliffs to a little sandy beach near Smugglers Cliff.

. If she'd got any pocket money left she would bribe them to behave, and then, depending on the weather, they'd share a bag of chips or an ice cream from the little café down by the beach.

It was hard work looking after them – pushing baby Mary's pram, old and rickety, with Dot, the fox terrier's lead tied to the pram handle. Freddie was always tormenting John, who would usually lose his temper in a way that could be quite frightening.

She was bringing back the bag of chips to where they

were sitting on the cliff top, and was just in time to see Mary's pram disappearing over the edge.

The next hours were awful. Freddie had turned on John in well acted anger," You did it. You did it. You killed me sister. Bliddy morderer!"

John had stood frozen. He did not speak for days. Abigail just couldn't decide. Perhaps it *was* him. She was sure he would never have meant to kill the baby, but perhaps in a fit of anger he'd given the pram a push and…

She didn't dare take the risk – she was meant to be looking after him.

"I did it," she told the policeman, "we were just larking about. I wanted to watch it roll over the edge. I forgot it was so far down. I thought it would land on the sand. I didn't think it would kill her."

Really stupid, of course, but she was only 11 years old and doing the best she could. By the time she'd realized she'd been really stupid it was too late. They all believed her first explanation and thought she was now just trying to wriggle out. Child criminals were not treated so carefully and sympathetically then.

They'd locked her up and the lives of the whole family changed. Her mother and father had to sell the shop, because people boycotted it. Her mother persuaded her father they should emigrate, and they took John to Australia on the £10 Assisted Passage Scheme. Abigail never saw them again. One kind neighbour, Mrs Evans, used to visit her , and she brought the news that her father had died in Australia, of a broken heart she'd thought. Apparently he hadn't wanted to go. He had loved his little girl, but had never been able to stand up to her mother. Abigail had always wondered if he had committed suicide.

In spite of what she'd told Mrs Milburn, Abigail did have a conscience about it all. How could she have suspected poor dear John who only lost his temper when people bullied and tormented him.

He could be very irritating, she knew, but it wasn't a deliberate thing. She suspected now that he'd sufferered from a mild form of Asperger's Syndrome, but nothing was known about that affliction all those years ago. Was he still alive? Was he happy? She would probably never know.

She deliberated tearing up Freddie's letter but somehow didn't have the energy. She stuffed it in a drawer in her desk.

It was going to be a long miserable night. She found herself wishing so much that Hubert was in residence upstairs, but he wouldn't be back for another week. If she still felt like this tomorrow, she told herself, she'd fly out to Malta. She'd have to risk his taking it the wrong way, but he was the only person in whom she felt she could confide.

Chapter 13

Hubert was pursuing Augustus across Malta on a bus. The wonderful old yellow rattletrap was full of holidaying couples. One or two looked ok, but some seemed trapped in a living hell, constantly snapping at each other. They had hoped, no doubt, that a few days in the late autumn sun would make them happy, but unfortunately they seemed to have brought all their relationship problems on holiday with them.

What goes so wrong? Hubert asked himself. Perhaps Abigail was right after all, and one shouldn't risk a good friendship with a bad marriage.

He'd spent time recently in various libraries in London and Oxford, researching Emily's family, the Stantons, because he'd come to a complete dead end on Augustus and the Booths.

He'd discovered that Emily's father had been a military engineer. Colonel Stanton had been stationed in Malta from the late 1870's helping to mastermind the building of a series of fortifications, the Victoria Lines, across an east – west high ridge in the north-central part of Malta. The island was becoming so important for British trade since the opening of the Suez Canal that the British Government was determined to improve its defences.

What if, Hubert had thought, Colonel Stanton's family had joined him in Malta after Emily fell ill with the tuberculosis that was to kill her? What if they were hoping that the kinder Mediterranean climate would work a miracle? What if Augustus, her fiancé, had visited?

He'd shot the idea past Abigail.

She'd thought it was certainly worth investigation. Privately, she'd felt that poking around in new libraries in lovely places would be a great holiday for Hubert whatever the outcome, and a bit of Mediterranean sun wouldn't go amiss for him either. She'd helped him track down on the internet a very reasonably priced apartment.

Naturally, on his first day he'd made straight for the National Library in Valletta and spent a happy age sifting through old newspaper records. Now he was on his way to Gharghur, a village by the Victoria Lines. His hunch had been right –he'd found a newspaper account of Emily Stanton's funeral in the Anglican Cathedral of St. Paul's in 1882, together with the information that the Stantons had been resident at the time of her death in the Governor's House in Gharghur.

He changed buses in Valletta leaving behind the grim faced bickering couples to spread their gloom around town. The next bus was pretty full, but they were all locals – Gharghur wasn't on the tourist trail at all. It was a pretty little place, and quite unspoilt, with plenty of the traditional Maltese houses with their distinctive balconies, complete with their religious statues and menacing carved faces, designed to ward off the evil eye.

Hubert didn't linger to admire them. He was anxious to find the Governor's house. He knew it was right on the edge of the village, on the way to Madliena. He turned a corner, and there it was, perched at the highest point in the little community – almost like a fortress itself. The only means of direct communication with the world was through a somewhat forbidding heavy door. All else was enclosed and hidden behind a very high wall, which extended so far that it must have contained a very large garden. All the rooms looked inwards into this garden.

Poor Emily must have died here. She'd probably had good days and bad days in her illness. On good days she'd be wheeled out, he imagined, on to that large high roof terrace he could glimpse over the wall, to enjoy the air and the view over the sloping countryside down to Madliena and the blue Mediterranean.

Hubert felt ashamed. He knew that he could be a grumpy old man, yet what had he to moan about compared with what poor Emily must have gone through? Thank God it was now much more possible to treat tuberculosis. So many young afflicted Britons at that time had, just like Emily, sought out the sun or the high mountains, desperately hoping for a cure. But nothing then could treat the scourge, and it demolished rich and poor alike.

The road down to Madliena and the sea was lined with small fig trees, their few leaves and the odd remaining figs shrivelled. The branches were white and stark, almost as if they had been struck by lightning. Yet when he looked more closely there were fresh buds, just about to break open.

From the fig tree learn its lesson, he quoted St. Mark to himself, *as soon as its branch becomes tender and puts forth its leaves, you know that summer is near.*

He must remember to tell Augustus that.

There was something specially uplifting about the sea today. It was very blue, but a blue of many shades, with streaks and pools of ice blue, deep blue, grey blue and black blue. Long tails of soft clouds in white, blue grey and purplish grey dappled the sky, and over it all a very warm early afternoon sun shone benignly.

The whole village was so so still, clinging to the traditional idea of siesta from noon till four. He loved this tradition, with the certain daily calm it delivered, and he savoured the quiet walk back to the centre of the village. The limestone church of St. Bartholomew stood golden yellow against the blues of the sky. Next to it was parked a large fruit and vegetable open sided van. Stacked in blue plastic crates were pumpkins, turnips, and the largest cauliflowers Hubert had ever seen. Several women were milling around it, buying and passing the time of day, breaking the siesta silence with their loud, companionable laughter.

Hubert went into the church and sat down, head in hands. It was so silly, he tried to tell himself, to get so overwhelmed by a tragedy which was over one hundred years old, but he knew that it was because, through poetry and through Augustus House, he had forged a link with these people of an earlier age. The human predicament does not change – their hopes and fears were as his own.

A loud bumping noise forced him to sit up. A man and a woman were struggling to move a large potted plant into a new position near the altar and he went over to lend a hand. The man thanked him, telling him it would have taken ages if he hadn't helped. "Are you a tourist?" he asked.

"Yes and no," Hubert replied, and he explained his purpose in visiting Gharghur.

"I will explain to my sister," the man replied. "Her English is limited."

The woman was obviously very interested. She held a really excited conversation with her brother, who turned again to Hubert.

"My sister is sure that her father in law will be able to help you. He only lives across the road. He's almost ninety, but he's a formidable old man. His memory is sharper than mine, and he can get the better of me playing dominoes any day."

They left the woman in the church cleaning brassware and crossed over the square to an old sunbaked town house. They had to wait a while before their knock was answered.

"He has quite bad arthritis," Marco explained.

Then a surprisingly young looking ninety year old appeared.

"Marco!" he greeted the younger man with an affectionate smile.

After an animated conversation they drew Hubert into the dark and cool house where Marco once more began to act as an interpreter.

"He says he can certainly help you in your quest," he began, "as his grandmother worked for the Stantons. They didn't live here long – perhaps 18 months. Miss Stanton was ill for all of that time, but her condition grew steadily worse. He knows a lot about this as his grandmother brought him up after the death of his mother. When he was a little child she told him the story again and again. She told him also about Miss Stanton's handsome, shy fiancé, Mr Booth. He came out twice while she was ill, and on the last occasion stayed until she died. The family were devastated, and so was his grandmother. She'd become very fond of them, and they of her. They left the village very shortly after Emily's death. They couldn't bear to remain where they had endured such sadness. He thinks the Colonel applied for – what would you call it - compassionate leave? He remembers his grandmother telling him that they'd gone back to England. Until her own death in 1935 – she made a journey each year on Emily's anniversary to lay flowers and say prayers at the grave in Ta'Braxia cemetery in Valletta.

When they left, the family gave her a very generous bonus, which she used to start buying this house. She never forgot them.

The old man said something to Marco and hobbled out of the room.

"He has remembered," Marco told Hubert ,"that he has things belonging to Miss Stanton. He is getting them to show you."

He returned with a large old leather folder and spoke again to Marco.

"Miss Stanton gave these watercolours to his grandmother," Marco relayed to Hubert, "and when she was clearing the house after the family's departure she found these scribblings which she thought belonged to Mr Booth. She knew she should probably have tried to return them, but she did so want something as a keepsake. He thinks she kept the things safe hoping the family would come back. He is happy for you to borrow and copy them, as long as you swear to return them before you leave Malta. He has left them in his will to the National Library in Valletta."

They enjoyed a sociable glass of wine and then Hubert left, solemnly promising Carmelo, the old man, that he would visit again to return his treasures before he left Malta.

Hubert should have been elated. In his hands he possibly held the missing last poems of Augustus Booth, but he could not celebrate. He could not yet bear even to look at them. All the way back on the bus he was reliving Emily's last sad journey along the same road to Valletta for her funeral service in St. Paul's Cathedral – four carriages – the coffin in the first, the second with the Stantons and Augustus, the third with army colleagues and their wives, and the fourth with Carmelo's grandmother and other local friends – the whole journey in a terrible bereft silence.

Abigail would have made him snap out of it – It's life, Hubert, she would have said, if you let it get you too worked up it will destroy you."

How he missed her.

Chapter 14

Hubert was on his way back to his apartment. He was in a splendid mood as he'd had another satisfying morning in the National Library in Valletta, first researching, then photocopying the precious bundle he'd been lent on the previous day, rounding it all off with a late lunch in early spring sunshine, at a pavement café. One of the things which was endearing Malta to him most was the accommodating way that this Maltese weather seemed to be bypassing winter and sliding straight into spring. The Maltese folk he spoke to usually shook their heads and muttered something about biting winds still to come, but to a sun-starved Brit it was wonderful.

Even though the old yellow bus was excelling itself for bumpiness he felt himself nodding off, returning to the world with a jerk every time the bus braked violently, or tore joyfully, on two wheels he felt sure, round a corner. Just a bit further, then a nice cup of coffee and a proper snooze before he sorted out all the notes he'd made this morning.

He had left the bus, and was walking the short distance to his apartment block when he noticed a figure slumped on the wall outside it. The figure seemed familiar. No, it couldn't be. But as he got nearer he was increasingly sure that it was.

"Abigail?" Hubert spoke in total amazement. He moved closer and a greyish-yellow crinkled face half looked up at him. His main reaction was one of alarm. He could see that it would be useless to ask her what was wrong, useless to ask her anything. Gently he guided her into his apartment, and as he closed the door behind them she collapsed, sobbing, upon him – sobbing the pent up tears of years and years.

Hubert helped her over to the sofa. He tried to go to make her a cup of tea, but she clung to him. He thought the sobbing would never stop. He sat there, stroking her hair and forehead, rocking her like a child, and mopping the cascading tears until gradually she calmed and fell into a troubled sleep. When she awoke about an hour later Hubert was still stroking her hair and was singing to her. It was so calming that for a few minutes she pretended she was still asleep.

"Down by the sally gardens," sang Hubert, "...but I was young and foolish, and now am full of tears."

Like Felicity at St. Hilda's, Abigail was a sucker for a nice voice. If she had been her usual self she would probably have been thinking that a choral quotation from Hubert made a very welcome change. She let go of Hubert at last and he went to make that tea.

When she'd drunk it he tried to look at her sternly.

"Now, Abigail. I really do think I deserve an explanation. I am so worried about you."

So she told him, haltingly, with several stops for yet more tears, the whole sad story, starting with Mrs Milburn's ghastly visitation. When she got to the bit about her parents having to sell the shop Hubert murmured sadly, *"You have made us the derision of our neighbours and our enemies laugh us to scorn."*

He listened intently, his own eyes brimming.

"My dearest girl," he said eventually, "how long have we known each other? At least ten years? Why haven't you told me this before? I've always known that something must trouble you deeply. You forget my bedroom is just above yours. I have heard you having nightmares. Why, in God's name, have you tried to carry this all by yourself? I would have been so willing to have shared it with you. You should have known I would understand."

"I thought you might not believe me," she gulped, "I just felt so ashamed. I think I'd almost convinced *myself* that I'd done it, that I was guilty. In the end I'd told so many desperate lies, changed my story so often, that I could scarcely remember the truth.

After I came out of the Institution I changed both my names and moved right away. Again and again I thought I'd buried it all, but it would always come sneaking back when I was tired, or upset about something else. And, as you know, I had such nightmares – poor little Mary was always rolling off the cliff in her pram. Then I used to start on the If onlies - if only I hadn't left them and gone for the chips, if only... But I used to thank God that John had disobeyed me and let Dot off her lead. If she'd gone over as well it would have broken his heart. Dot was the only one who never tormented him, who loved him unconditionally. Then I'd feel guilty for thinking more about a dog than about Mary. And I'd hear her crying in my dreams. And then the medium heard her crying in the séance in West Kingscove – that's why I was so upset and..." The words were just tumbling out amid tearful torrents.

"Listen to me Abigail. And look at me. Now." Hubert took her face between his hands, desperately willing himself to find the right words, "You were only a little girl, and Fate dealt you a chilling hand. I am so proud of how you coped, so proud of how you protected your little brother. So proud to be your friend. You are going to have to learn to be just as proud of yourself. You could not have behaved better.

Now get up, go and wash your face and put your things in that spare bedroom. Then we're going for a walk by the sea to try to blow this away. You are far too strong for it to defeat you. Don't shake your head like that – it is the truth. After that we're going out for some dinner – you must be starving."

Of course, it isn't possible to wipe out fifty years of sadness in a couple of hours, but it was a start.

When they got back from dinner, Hubert made coffee and told her to put on some music. He'd brought on his trip an extremely old personal CD player and a couple of tiny speakers. They produced a very tinny sound, but it was still very pleasant to listen to Brahms and Sibelius before bed. She was nosing around to see what else he had brought when, to her amazement, she found right at the bottom of the spool Help! And Abbey Road.

"Hubert," she said, astonished, "I didn't know you liked the Beatles."

"There's probably a great deal you don't know about me, Abigail," he replied, poker-faced.

They talked long into the night. Very late on he realised that he hadn't told her of his findings in Gharghur. By then he was as exhausted as she was. It could wait. After all, they had another five days here together.

"Leave your door ajar," he almost commanded as they finally retired for the night. "I want to be able to hear if you have nightmares. We're going to nip them in the bud."

But Abigail slept extremely well. Perhaps it was exhaustion, or the sea air and the wine, or perhaps it was because she was beginning to feel that one day she really might vanquish her demons.

Chapter 15

Abigail woke up to the sound of Hubert washing the previous night's cups and

glasses. It promised to be a beautiful day, he told her, as he brought her in a cup of coffee.

"I think we should go to Gozo. This might be the best day we get," he decided.

And a beautiful day it was. Gozo - only a half hour ferry journey, and yet a wonderful world away. They climbed up the stepped street to the ancient Cittadella in Victoria. For centuries, whenever there was fear of invasion by the Turks or attacks by pirates the local people had fled up the same street. Abigail felt them still there, rushing past her breathlessly, tugging a few precious belongings, the air throbbing with their cries of fear and alarm.

As she and Hubert walked round the tranquil Cathedral deep in the Cittadella , Abigail was reading little chunks out of the guide book. There was a bit about how they'd run out of money before they'd capped the Cathedral with the obligatory Maltese Dome. So what? They painted a trompe d'oeil on a flat roof instead.

Abigail and Hubert stared up at it – unique and beautiful.

There was a little café tucked into a high corner of the battlements, bathed in the spring sun, with views out over the limestone walls. In all directions there seemed to be small hills topped with towns, the towns topped with tall churches. The scale seemed somehow all out of proportion, and yet it worked, and was beautiful.

They sipped strong coffee and nibbled sumptuous home-made fruitcake at an outside table while Abigail carried on broadcasting from the guidebook.

"I didn't realise that Calypso's cave was here on Gozo. It says this is where she seduced Ulysses and kept him enthralled for seven years, I don't believe that, you know. You can't keep someone enthralled that long. The first few weeks – yes – overwhelming, all-exclusive, awesome – but then stuck in a cave for seven years? No. It must have been going downhill long before that. By the end, it was probably downright boring, perhaps even sour. That's why I never want to be married again, Hubert, - imprisonment till death, not just seven years."

He really surprised her then - telling her that since he'd been in Malta he had come round to the same point of view.

"I think our relationship," he went on, "is too precious to be risked."

She couldn't decide if she was miffed or relieved.

"And I think," continued Hubert, "that people should concentrate on tailor-making their own relationships. They may not include sex at all. I think our interaction last night was memorable, but sex was the last thing on our minds."

Abigail wondered if she was hearing right.

"Yes," she forced herself to admit, "there was only one person I wanted a couple of nights back after that ghastly Mrs Milburn had departed. You were the sole person I felt I could turn to."

Immediately she was annoyed with herself for saying such an unguarded thing. She changed the subject to something more mundane.

They'd intended to have supper on Gozo, but when they

checked the ferry timetable they found that the boats and buses stopped earlier in winter, so they weren't able to do that. They ended up back at base quite hungry. Their apartment block was owned by the hotel next door, so they drifted into the bar to see what was on offer, and ordered a selection of Maltese antipasti and a couple of glasses of wine at the counter. An Elvis lookalike was providing evening entertainment. He was rather good, and seemed to have attracted quite a crowd. There was only one free table left, by the entrance. They soon realized why the table was still free - it was a bit chilly right by the open door - so Abigail popped up to the apartment for a jacket.

When she got back, Hubert wasn't there. She assumed he'd gone to the gents – and then she realised – Hubert was on the dance floor! He was dancing with a woman of about Abigail's age, but rather better dressed and certainly slimmer. What's more, he seemed to be enjoying himself.

The food arrived, and she decided to start without him. After all, why wait when he might be ages yet reliving his youth. Elvis, however, finished his session at that point, and Hubert delivered the woman chivalrously back to her table and her friends.

He saw Abigail had started eating.

"Is it good?" he asked.

"Yes," she replied shortly.

"Will I like it?" he tried again, sensing he was in the doghouse.

"Don't know."

"What shall we do tomorrow?"

"Don't know." She knew she was being very silly, but she

just felt so put out.

"Abigail," he looked directly at her, "you're annoyed with me."

"Of course I'm not."

"Well, you're managing a very good imitation. What's wrong?" He suspected, with growing amusement, and perhaps even pleasure, that he knew.

She couldn't contain herself any longer. "Of all the time I have known you," she exploded," you have *never* asked me to dance."

"Abigail. I don't think I've ever been with you before in a suitable place for asking. You and I usually find ourselves together in a library, or in a DIY shop buying paint. I'm not sure how you'd react if I fandangoed you through the fiction, or salsa'ed past the sinks."

He knew it would have been better not to have shown how funny he found it, but he couldn't help it.

"Oh, stop it!" she snapped, "you know what I mean. I didn't even know you *could* dance – I just turn my back for a minute and there you are – off with a strange woman, and…" She looked at his face, and the silliness of it all hit home and she gave up semi gracefully. What was she thinking of? Particularly after all that high falluting talk on Gozo about open relationships. If she didn't know better she'd have said she was jealous.

"*She* asked me, as it happens," he confessed. "It would have been rude to have refused, wouldn't it? As for knowing how, we had dancing lessons at school. Didn't you? I would ask you now, but Elvis seems to have gone home."

They managed to laugh it off, but for the second time that day Abigail had been rather miffed. Alarm bells were sounding. It was one of those classic – I don't think I want you, but I certainly don't want anyone else to have you – situations that a lot of us get into, and shouldn't.

You definitely sailed into the north of your lady's opinion there, Hubert told himself, better get it sorted soon.

*

From then on time just flew. He'd told her on the ferry to Gozo about his successful search, so now she had to see the Governor's House at Gharghur, and to meet Carmelo to take back the papers, and see St. Paul's in Valletta, and finally to go to Ta'Braxia Cemetery to see Emily's resting place.

They took two bunches of flowers with them.

"These, Emily, are from us," said Abigail, as she laid the first bunch upon the grave, "and these, are from Augustus."

*

I'm thinking of writing a book," said Hubert. He was cooking in the apartment for Abigail on their last evening there, trying to use up all his leftovers.

"What on?" she asked, "Maltese poetry?"

"No. Although I have become very interested in that, you are right. No. This would be a cookery book – something along the lines of '100 ways with a red baggage and a cab of shallots.'

"I've got that wrong, haven't I? Must be that little

aperitif we had. Anyway, back to my book. I bought a beautiful red cabbage and a normal sized bag of shallots days before you arrived. The more I use, the more I seem to have left. I could do a nice line in feeding the five thousand. It must be staying here right by where St. Paul was shipwrecked that puts me in this biblical frame of mind."

Abigail sat there, helping drink up their last wine, and visualising a red baggage getting out of a cab full of shallots. Her grandmother would have said she must have come over on the last onion boat.

Abigail really was not sure how to take him these days. She still hadn't got over that woman trying to poach him the night they came back from Gozo. As if that wasn't enough irritation he was still aggravating her in the old ways. She'd heard him on his balcony that morning, hanging out his smalls and muttering one of his favourite quotations about Hope while the wind blew and the rain threatened.

Hope, indeed! Some hope of them drying, she thought. He's so like my grandma. She would look up at a thunder-black sky and say, Oh, I think it'll get out.

Fools both of them. I must not get any deeper involved with this very dear, very irritating, quite ridiculous man.

But when they came back from their day out and he harvested his bone-dry washing she'd had to wonder.

*

Andrew pulled open his bedroom curtains very late on Sunday morning and looked out towards France. It almost wasn't Sunday morning. They'd been to dinner last night with friends of Paul, and then on clubbing. He was still tired.

Abigail and Hubert were just getting out of a cab. Abigail was hunting for her keys, and Hubert was paying the driver. Andrew chuckled loudly. So that was where she'd got to. The dark old horse – she'd left a hasty scribble saying she was off for a day or two, but he'd worried a bit, what with that unexpected visitor...

He must tell Felicity what Abigail had been up to. Might amuse her. Felicity was worrying him. She seemed to be acting very weirdly ever since he'd introduced her to Paul.

"What are you making all that noise about?" came a muffled groan from under the blankets.

Andrew smiled to himself. He'd discovered that the golden boy wasn't quite so golden first thing. It was a relief to find he wasn't completely perfect.

"We've missed church," he said, and went to put the kettle on.

Chapter 16

Felicity could hear 'Night on the bare mountain' playing again and again, ever louder.

"Answer it, answer it," she tried to persuade herself, turning over in bed and fumbling for the mobile hiding upside down in the blackness on top of the cardboard box that was still her bedside table. Just as she thought she was getting the situation under control, it stopped ringing. It must be one of life's irritating new certainties. If there were still prophets descending from the South Downs with truths engraved on tablets of stone there it would be – *'Just as thou shalt finally unearth thy mobile the caller shall ring off.'*

She looked at the time and groaned – 2am. She could nicely have done without this. Ever since Andrew had introduced her to Paul the other day she'd been having bother sleeping, mainly because of extreme pique and jealousy. This was the first night she'd got off to sleep without any bother. It might be an emergency, though – better keep looking. She was still fumbling for the light switch when the phone started up again.

"Good evening, madam. Am I speaking to Felicity?" It was a female voice, but she didn't recognize it. "Yes. Who is that?" she replied, anxiety mounting.

"I'm PC Whittington ringing from the local police station. I'm trying to track the next of kin of Tracie Taylor. Are you a relative?"

"No. A friend. What is wrong?" The shock in Felicity's voice must have been very apparent.

"Perhaps I could come to see you?" suggested the policewoman.

"Yes. Yes. Come now." Felicity was desperate to know what had happened. Was Tracie alright? She'd told her again and again she thought she was in a dangerous business. Had one of her so-called clients attacked her? All sorts of horrific explanations were crowding through her head.

"I need your address. I only have your mobile number. I got that from Ms Taylor's mobile."

"Look," Felicity was getting quite worked up," You must tell me what has happened."

"I'll be straight round. Easier to explain face to face. Augustus House, you say, Green – top buzzer? I seem to remember visiting there a little while ago." The line went dead.

Felicity found her dressing gown in the wardrobe and put the kettle on. The policewoman, good as her word, was pressing the buzzer pretty soon. It was the same woman who had helped deal with the 'body through the Tower roof' debacle, but Felicity was too worried about Tracie to care what she might be thinking.

PC Whittington smiled and nodded in answer to the offer of tea.

"No sugar and hardly any milk, please. How do you know Ms Taylor?"

"She's a neighbour. She lives in the flat underneath. If you're looking for next of kin it may be difficult. I know her mother is dead. She hasn't seen her father for years – they don't get on – I think he works in Hong Kong. She and her husband are estranged. Look, you must tell me what has happened." Felicity had been getting more and more wild-eyed.

The officer paused, trying to decide how much she should

tell, then she straightened her shoulders as if she had made up her mind, and proceeded.

"She has had a bad accident, and is unconscious. I thought you said she lived here? We found her at a house of converted flats in West Kingscove."

"Er, yes." Now it was Felicity's turn to work out how much she should say, and to make it sound convincing, "I think she rents a small place there – started when she and her husband were quarrelling a lot and she needed some space." She could tell the woman didn't seem particularly convinced. What a weird bunch she must think they were at Augustus House.

"What sort of an accident?" Felicity asked.

PC Whittington, still treading carefully, told her that they weren't yet exactly sure what had happened. She'd been found at the bottom of a flight of stairs with a head injury.

Felicity was all for going to see her there and then, but the officer dissuaded her.

"Get some sleep now and ring in the morning, Ms Green," she advised, "hopefully she'll have regained consciousness then and you'll be much more use to her if you've had some rest. Oh – one last thing – Do you know of anyone who might have wanted to harm Mrs Taylor? And how I can get in touch with her estranged husband? I think you said that they quarrelled a lot and she had to move away?"

Felicity shook her head again – this time really emphatically.

"Martin wouldn't hurt her. He's the mildest man. They only quarrelled with words because they were so upset. I don't know where he is. Possibly at his mother's. I don't have his phone number. I imagine Tracie must have it in her mobile. I can't think of anyone who would want to injure her. She's not the sort of person who makes people angry. She really isn't." Felicity was on the verge of tears.

'I'm just bashing my brains out against a hysterical woman here,' thought Ms Whittington. She ascertained that Felicity would be around Kingscove the next day if they needed to talk again and trekked out into the blackness of a very early morning to consider her next step.

Better see if there is a Martin in the mobile, she supposed. There did seem to be rather a lot of men's names there… And that outfit she was wearing… hmmm… The wind was getting up yet again, and what had been quite a gentle rain earlier was turning into something much more wetting and insistent. Kingscove weather never behaved moderately. Either it was heavenly, pretending it was the Cote d'Azur, or it was like this – quite definitely disgusting. What did they say about a policeperson's lot? She stumbled into her car and drove back to the station.

*

Felicity did try to go back to sleep, but it was quite useless. Her head was spinning. She'd been born with the half empty gene. Even when things were going well she always suspected that the worst was just around the corner, so now that she was faced with something that really might be mega-serious she found it quite impossible to stay calm. She got up and went to make some more tea, and stood staring out of the kitchen window at the thrashing sea and pouring rain.

'I hate, hate, hate Kingscove,' she muttered to herself, 'Full of show-offs. Full of people with more money than sense. I hate Andrew. How *could* he steal Paul from me? You just have to look at them to know he's not the lodger. How could he? I hate Paul as well. He can't have any taste. How could he possibly fancy Andrew, that dithering useless character. And how *dare* he be gay! I hate bloody Kingscove weather – this bloody foul pissing wet and windy weather going on and on and on…' She tailed off. She was so upset that, by her normal standards, her language was quite out of character.

She remembered that Ann had warned her. "Bet it's not idyllic in the winter," she'd said.

Felicity brightened a bit.

'That's it. I'll ring Ann,' she thought. Ok, so it was 2.30am, but Ann never went to bed early, and she wouldn't mind being woken up anyway. This was an emergency, and Ann liked Tracie.

Felicity disapproved of Tracie's new job, but she had a sneaking feeling that Ann almost envied it. She rang Ann's mobile. It was switched off, so she left a message and rang the landline. No reply.

This was to prove an even greater pity than she thought at the time. Ann, ever the purveyor of common sense, ever able to make one see and accept the obvious, would have pointed out that Andrew hadn't stolen Paul away from her- she'd never had him. And had she ever told Andrew how much she fancied Paul? No? So how could she blame him? She was just jealous. Nothing wrong with being jealous, as long as you remember that's what it is and don't go round making poor Andrew out to be the arch betrayer. And Paul was obviously predominantly gay so it seemed pretty unlikely that she'd ever been in with a chance anyway. Andrew dithering? Had she looked at herself lately?

Yes, Ann would have said all this, then poured them both a stiff gin and started getting her to make plans for what might be a difficult day ahead.

But Felicity could only leave another message – this time a long anguished panicky one about Tracie, asking her to ring, telling her that if she wasn't at home she'd be at Stella's (an art class friend whom Ann had met) but forgetting to give Stella's number.

She looked at her watch again. 2.45. Even in her present state she could see it was a bit late to ring Stella. She took her tea back to bed.

In these situations the final straw is always just offstage, waiting. Often it is something quite small which might be hilariously funny at any other time. Then again, it might be something really bad, more of a landslide or an earthquake than a straw. Some psychologist has probably devoted an academic life to classifying these on a sort of Straw Scale. The one on its way would be about 5 out of 10 - quite bad enough to do the trick considering the lead up and the person.

Felicity's tea was having some effect, calming her a little, until she noticed that the bed around and beneath her seemed a little damp. Had she spilt the tea? She didn't think so. Must be her imagination. She shifted slightly, so that she could put her tea down and reach it more easily. If she had clumsily spilt it she did not want a repeat.

And then... A large drop of very cold water landed on the

edge of her nose, and another… and… She looked up at the ceiling and beheld a soggy bulging protuberance. Her ceiling wasn't particularly white at the best of times, but this huge canopy bending precariously towards her bed was of a filthy greenish grey. There were three minor bulges within the main one. Each had a hole which gently swelled, then sank as water seeped through, forming great quivering globules, then depositing them upon Felicity and her bed. .It was as if a great grey-green evil three-nippled goddess was looming above her. She stared upwards, transfixed in horror at the malevolent sight, but when the goddess' skin began slowly to rip and the immortal one began to haemorrhage at a growing rate she screamed and ran from the room.

What could she do? She must get help. Where could she go? Not to Tracie's. Could she call James, their builder? He was a lovely man- he would come when he heard the state she was in – even at this time of night – but what could he do? Nothing till morning, and even then only if the storm abated. He'd been trying to get them to have major roof repairs for ages. Abigail was always saying it would take a catastrophe to get them all to agree and cough up. Well here it was. She tried Ann again. Still no luck there.

She couldn't go to Abigail. Apparently she'd gone up to Newcastle of all places, goodness knows why. And Abigail had told her that Hubert had gone to visit an ancient aunt in the depths of East Anglia. She didn't know the Reverend Cedric well enough. That left 'the dithering useless one' two floors down. She'd have to swallow her pride. She was desperate.

Normally, of course, Andrew would have been her first

port of call, but now... especially as he might be with Paul. At least he would be at home because she knew he was on standby from 6am that morning. She stumbled down the two flights. She couldn't see straight for tears, and she'd left her specs upstairs, which made it worse.

There was no reply to her hammering on Andrew's door. Was *everyone* away tonight? She was getting hysterical and could scarcely see at all through her tears. Eventually she realized that the door had opened. A wet steamy figure half wrapped in a towel Stood there. She flung herself upon him, gibbering about Tracie and roofs and ceilings and water. And then she realized – it wasn't Andrew. Paul drew her in, and closed the door.

*

Bit by bit he got the story out of her, clucking sympathetically in the right places, wrapping a blanket round her shoulders, patting her hand. But when she got to the bit about the ceiling, even without her specs, she could detect a quivering at the corner of his mouth. He looked just like Andrew when he was trying not to laugh.

"Oh, come on," he tried to encourage her, "a leaking roof's not the end of the world. Haven't you lived anywhere before where there's been that problem? No? You *must* be posh. I was brought up on leaky roofs. What they say is true, you know, it'll all seem much better in the morning. Andrew's not here. They called him unexpectedly and he agreed to help them out with a Tenerife trip. He won't be back till this afternoon. You can't go back to your own bed, so why don't you get into his and go to sleep. I'll wake you at eight if you're not up, and then you can phone to see how your friend is. I bet she'll be sitting up by then. And then you can ring the builder."

There hadn't seemed much rush to get a bed for the second bedroom, so he retired to the sitting room sofa.

Felicity tossed and turned. She just could not sleep. Paul couldn't sleep either. His great length did not fit comfortably on a sofa. There wasn't even room there for him to toss and turn. He heard her go to the bathroom. He gave her a minute after she was back in bed, then called softly, "Are you ok?"

"No," came the faint reply, "it's no good. I can't sleep."

"Neither can I. Shall I come in and we can talk?"

It was a large bed, and a cold night, so it seemed quite sensible for him to slip into it, particularly when he told her that he'd been on the sofa. And, after all, he was gay, thought Felicity, so where was the harm?

Paul had the knack of putting people completely at ease and making them talk. He heard all about Dominic, folded his arms comfortingly around her, and encouraged her to have a really good cry.

Of course, she should have called a halt when she felt the first tinglings from his exploring fingers. Unfortunately, by then she was enjoying it too much. As the storm raged on, the comforting moved up a gear.

*

Perhaps Felicity should have made Cedric her first port of call after all. It might have taken his mind off his own troubles. There he was, three floors down, having one of his regular, emotionally draining, "decision" evenings. These seemed to be coming round ever more frequently. He was beginning to wonder if he shouldn't just write them up in advance on the engagement calendar in his kitchen – Tuesdays – 9pm till dawn on Wednesdays – Agony Session.

The script usually went like this - Shall I give up the church? I hate what I do. I don't believe in what I do. But what else can I do? I'm not that badly paid. I've got a pretty comfortable life. But I'm a hypocrite. I end up preaching sermons extolling all the virtues. What virtues have I got? Why can't I have the sort of job where people wouldn't care what I got up to? I'm so bored that I get a kick out of dancing around with a fake Teddy Bear slapping me with a wet teatowel. What does that say about me?... Shall I give up the church? I hate what I do. I don't believe in what I do… Round and round and round and on and on and on…

He would sit on his big white sofa, drinking much more than was sensible, and finally he'd slump there in a fitful drunken sleep.

It had been an even more agonizing session than usual tonight, as Cedric had had quite a confusing day. Normally, as he dropped off to sleep he'd be thinking, Yes – yes, I'll do the right thing. I'll resign in the morning. Of course, in the morning life would be just too busy and he'd decide to give it one more go, and so on. Today, however, it was more complex. He'd had a visit from an old friend – an old friend who mixed these days in highish ecclesiastical circles. The friend's excuse was that he'd had to visit Eastbourne and that it seemed near enough to look in on Cedric his old buddy from college days. After a while it became obvious that this wasn't strictly true. He'd been sent to sound Cedric out – to float an idea in front of him. The idea one third astounded Cedric, one third titillated, and one third horrified. Apparently his name was being bandied about in the aforesaid highish places as a possible future bishop.

"You're wasted here in university lecturing and chaplaincy work. Anyone could do this. Admittedly not as well as you, but it doesn't make best use of your skill and dedication. There's talk of you as bishop material. What would you say to that?"

Cedric had absolutely nothing to say to it, as he was temporarily struck dumb. Inside his head he felt they must be jolly hard up for talent if they were looking to him to help guide the church through the years ahead, but he at least had the sense not to say so out loud.

How on earth could the powers-that-be have got it so wrong, he thought. The truth, however, was that he was being very unfair to himself. He had lost all sight of his own worth long ago. Despite his private crisis of faith, Cedric was a very conscientious and dedicated priest who made quite an impression on all who met him at the university. It had been the same in his parish work. He had hated it, because he'd found it so draining and had felt so lonely, but in spite of that he had done invaluable work and been greatly loved and admired. It's not that uncommon in any profession. You can be very good for the job, but the job's not good for you.

"You'd need some more experience, of course," continued the emissary, "you've done a good stint in parish work already, but perhaps we could now get you a spell as Rector of a major city parish, How would that appeal?"

Cedric had shuddered at this point.

"Perhaps then you could be Dean of a Cathedral? There are one or two possible places coming up. I seem to remember you as quite a good admin man."

At this point Cedric had made a bit of a mistake. The idea of Dean was so much better than the first suggestion that his face had become slightly more animated, and the friend had interpreted this as enthusiasm for the whole idea.

"I'll report back, then, that you are not unminded to consider this," he'd said, as he got up to leave. "Great to see you, old chap. I think someone will be in touch."

And he was off before Cedric had really found his voice. Thus are Deans and Bishops made?

Consequently, this evening's agony session was proving more complicated than usual. He had spent a lot of time wrestling with the sins of Pride and Lust. Part of him quite relished the idea of becoming a Dean. If the Dean had to devote much of his time to administration then perhaps he could concentrate on doing a great job on that. Then people might not notice the shortfall on Faith. But where on earth had that idea of Cedric as a good admin man come from? He was a hopeless organizer. Mistaken identity here for sure.

Then, of course, the Dean, not the Bishop, is in charge of the Cathedral. That really appealed to him. No more need to cowtow to Vice-Chancellors and Professors, or even stroppy students. He would be the boss, and with a beautiful house in a Cathedral Close with luck. So Pride would win for a while.

But then Lust would take over – living in a Cathedral Close must be like living in a goldfish bowl. They'd probably want him to get married and lead a blameless life. He'd never met anyone he'd like to marry, and a lonely blameless life didn't sound his style at all. Even less could he imagine anyone who might like to marry *him*. So Dean Cedric Wright would be condemned to a lonely boring life of celibacy. All of this made the following fitful sleep on the sofa even more troubled than usual.

To cap everything, today was the anniversary of his much loved mother's death. She had suffered a painful, lingering illness, which had distressed him much more than it had bothered her. She had confronted it full on with a blind faith which he had found he could not match. Ironically her stalwart strength had been the last straw in his own struggle. It had happened a few years back, so he had more or less come to terms with it now, but whenever the actual date came round again he ended up reliving the whole thing and taking refuge in the bottle. Tonight he had excelled himself in that direction. What an aching head lay in store for him tomorrow. He tossed and turned on the sofa and it was almost a relief when PC Whittington's call jolted him back into half consciousness.

"Surely they can't be in touch already," he muttered as he fumbled for the phone. He was surprised how normally his voice came out. Indeed Ms Whittington thought it was by far the nicest voice she'd heard so far from Tracie's men friends.

Cedric was horrified by her news.

"Yes. I know both Tracie and her husband very well. How is she? Can I see her?"

So the officer had to go through it all again. No. Not now. Ring the hospital in the morning.

She wasn't sure if she really wanted to go rushing off on

another interview in this storm, even if he did sound rather nice. He might be just another of these gluttons for punishment who lived on the windy seafront. What she really needed to do was to run this husband to earth.

"Do you know, sir, where I might find her husband?" she ventured.

"Isn't his number in her phone?" Cedric sounded puzzled, "I would have expected it to be there."

Then he had a thought. "Is there someone called Sailor? That's his nickname – you know – Tinker, Tailor, Soldier, Sailor."

There was a pause at the other end – then –

"You're right, sir. Thank you. Just found it. I'll leave you in peace. Sorry to have rung so late."

And when he'd assured her that he'd be around tomorrow if needed she rang off, and went looking for Sailor Taylor.

*

Cedric was definitely too worked up to get back to sleep now that he had another big worry on his mind. He decided he might as well do some tidying up in case this police officer decided to pay him a call in the morning.

The sitting room certainly needed a good clean up, and as for his study! As usual, the whole room was knee deep in bits of paper, mostly failed sermons and failed lectures. So the Dean had to be a good admin man, did he? Then Cedric hoped the Dean's study would have a fair bit of floor space, as that's where all his admin seemed to get done. No – that was wrong – where his admin got not done. At least he was on his knees, and that was surely a holy thing for a Dean.

He found a large cardboard box, and started shovelling the papers into it. There's nothing of interest – chuck it all away, was his attitude. He'd read somewhere that if you ignored paperwork for a year then there was rarely any need to take action on it, as everything would have become irrelevant.

The Tracie situation was uppermost in his fuddled brain and guilt began to build it up out of all proportion. Surely he should have used more influence to persuade her not to get involved in this new venture of hers? All he'd done was laugh and find it funny. Worse still, if he was honest, he'd found the whole thing rather titillating. From the way the police officer was talking Tracie's condition sounded critical - and he had almost egged her on. If she died it would be on his conscience, wouldn't it? As if there wasn't enough weighing heavily there already. He was a total disgrace to his calling. How in all conscience could he *possibly* go any further with this suggestion about the future direction of his ministry. He was a complete failure. What would his poor mother think of him if she was here now? Her last words to him had been, "Never forget, I love you dearly and I am so very proud of you."

What was there for her to be proud of now? A faithless priest with flagging standards.

Earlier in the evening he had just begun to think that a brighter chapter in his life was about to unfold. Suddenly everything seemed back in crisis again. Torrents of guilt and grief had drowned all trace of sense and reason in his being. The walls of his flat were crushing in on him. He needed to get out. He desperately needed some air.

Tired, drunk and totally demoralised, he staggered through his front door and down the stairs into one of the wildest Kingscove nights in living memory.

Chapter 17

Ann was in a black cab on her way back to Shad Thames. She'd been out on yet another disappointing CitySparks date. Although she always hid it well she suffered from a problem which plagues many people who work long hours from home – loneliness. Consequently, she really valued Felicity, her closest woman friend. However, what Ann really wanted was a man – a man who didn't have an over-inflated ego; a man who, even occasionally, asked how she felt and listened to her reply; a man a bit out of the ordinary, with interesting ideas, who made her laugh; a man who wouldn't be phased by her seemingly spiky exterior; a man who inhabited a different sort of world, not obsessed with finance.

That appeared to be expecting too much of one person, she reflected sadly, as the cab lurched the last few cobbled streets to her loft. She was almost inclined to agree with that woman Abigail who lived in the basement at Felicity's place. She needed three men, she'd confided to Ann and Felicity one night over a drink – one to talk to, one to dance with, and one to go to bed with. Ann had been quite surprised – but then she'd got to thinking about it. Unfortunately she never seemed to come across one of these men, let alone three. Even if she had thought it sensible to combine business with pleasure, all her clients were women. That was the nature of her business- helping money-rich, time-starved women stash away their wealth.

Rather furtively, she'd joined an internet dating agency for City workers – citisparks.com - but all it seemed to throw up were boring blossoms like the one she'd met tonight.

At least, she consoled herself, she loved where she lived and was always glad to be back. The phone in the hall was flashing. It was Felicity's panic stricken message. Ann didn't need to think twice – two of her friends in difficulties. She looked at her watch. Too late for a train. She bundled what she'd already stacked on her desk for dealing with the next day into her briefcase, picked up the overnight bag she had ever ready, together with her laptop, and rushed down to get the car. She was always organized, almost to a fault.

As she left the underground garage she opened the window to get some air to liven her up for the drive, and shivered. There was quite a wind coming off the river. That meant there would be a positive gale in Kingscove, she was sure. Still, the road would be quiet at this time of night. Most things still on the move would be returning from Kingscove to The Smoke. She proved right. She'd hit the M23 before she knew it, and was bowling down the last stretch towards Kingscove Pier in double quick time, in spite of the cross wind which was doing its best to blow her on to the hard shoulder. It made a change from having to negotiate one's way through lots of weaving streets to avoid the seaside jams.

When she turned left at the pier she could feel that the storm was on its last legs, halfheartedly blowing itself out. There was no reply from Felicity's buzzer, so she assumed she'd gone to Stella's, but she had a set of keys so she was soon in, preparing to rifle the gin and tonic before, hopefully, getting her head down for two or three hours in Felicity's bed. She wasn't prepared for the awful sight. What chaos! Felicity hadn't mentioned this in her message. Hopefully she knew about it. Otherwise, thought Ann, it will finish her off. The worst of the dripping seemed to have stopped, but a large piece of damaged ceiling paper flapped dangerously, and Felicity's beloved snowy white bedlinen would never be the same again. Ah well! She closed the door on the dismal sight. Thank goodness Felicity had got round to buying a sofa. That would have to do.

Unfortunately, like everyone involved that night, even though she was very tired, there was just too much going on in her head for any chance of sleep. She looked out of the window. Things had settled down outside even more now. All the galloping raging white horses were slowing to a canter. The sea wasn't exactly smooth, but she was sure a walk along the beach would no longer be dangerous. It turned out to be rather lovely down there. There was just enough light from a pale moon scudding through the clouds. An old man who was walking a lively dog nodded companionably. The young couple that she passed further along only had eyes for each other.

Then she realized that there was one other person, sitting on a pile of driftwood - someone hunched up, disconsolate.

Leave him, she ordered herself. She was pretty sure it was male. You're never short of lame ducks. You don't need this one.

She walked on past, down as far as Abigail's Pagoda perched high above. By then she had realized how chilly it was, and Felicity's sofa was beginning to call to her. She retraced her steps. He was still there. The old man and the dog were in sight, playing what was obviously a well practised game of fetch the stick, so she felt it would be quite safe to talk to the crumpled stranger.

"Are you ok?" she asked tentatively.

"I suppose so," came the muffled reply.

"I'm going back up to Regent'sParade. Why don't you walk with me? Then you can tell me about it."

"What makes you think there's anything to tell?" he mumbled.

"Well, people don't usually sit by themselves, wet through, on the beach, in the middle of the night, looking half dead, unless there's something to tell. Come on! Get up! It's going to start raining again."

She didn't think it was, but she thought the threat might move him.

"I'm soaked already," he groused. However, he did shamble to his feet and began to follow her to the steps up the cliff, shuffling a few paces behind her, like an elderly disgruntled dog.

When they reached the road Ann had more light to look at him properly. He'd obviously had a really rough night. He looked as bad as Felicity's bedlinen – just as wet and dirty, and just about the same ghastly smell and colour. In spite of all this he looked vaguely familiar, though she couldn't place why.

"I think we should get you home and you should have a hot shower," she told him, "and I need a cup of tea." She had decided he was too far gone to be any sort of a threat. There was something sadly appealing about him.

He nodded meekly. He was shattered in every sense and needed someone bossy to take his situation by the scruff of the neck

When they arrived at the front door of Augustus House he turned, preparing to enter. She finally realized why he had looked familiar.

He couldn't find his keys. "Must have got swept away in the sea," he muttered.

He was still too shell-shocked to find it strange when Ann opened the main front door with Felicity's keys. His own front door was ajar.

"Doesn't always lock properly," - he seemed more talking to himself than to her.

What a pigsty, thought Ann, as she glanced around, this man truly needs taking in hand.

Later, with Cedric in dry clothes and a blanket, and when they'd moved on to something a bit stronger than tea, she started to get the story out of him. It wasn't easy – a bit like drawing teeth.

"I get the main drift of it, I think. Something's plunged your life into crisis and you just gave up. So how come you didn't manage to drown? You look as if you tried hard enough. Do you think, perhaps just think a tiny bit, that deep down you might have wanted to stay alive?"

He looked at her pitifully. "Tide must have been coming in. Sea just kept tossing me back. I read somewhere the sea and the gallows refuse no one, but I'm obviously so useless that even the sea won't have me. I was just thinking about walking to the end of the pier and having another go when you came along and started to bully me, thank God."

"So what is this crisis? How can I help you if I don't know? Come on. Out with it. I'm only bullying you for your own good." Ann was enjoying herself.

But Cedric had fallen asleep. She brought the duvet from his bed to cover him and found, to her delight, that he had a spare bedroom. Better set her phone alarm for 7. If Felicity wasn't back by then she'd go up to the hospital herself to check on Tracie.

*

"Well, you gave us quite a fright last night. You must be very tough to shake it off this easily." A cheerful nurse was tidying Tracie up a bit. She hadn't given her a mirror yet. She'd decided it would be better to let her come round a bit more before she saw what a truly dreadful mess she looked.

Tracie's first words had been, "I'm starving." She was now gobbling her way through a bowl of cornflakes.

"Don't eat them quite so fast," the nurse warned, "you might be sick. Are you well enough to see the police? There's been a woman officer champing at the bit half the night, but I can put her off for longer if you like."

"Can you ask her to hang on for 15 minutes or so," suggested Tracie, "I just want to pull myself together a bit more."

What she really meant was that she wanted time to sort out her story. To her relief, she realized she'd be able to tell 90% of the truth – there was just the odd crease that might need ironing over.

"I can remember most of what happened," she told the officer shortly afterwards. "I was carrying this huge imitation bronze urn down from my place to an artist friend's studio on the ground floor. I know I should have got someone to help, but I couldn't find anyone and I thought I could manage. My friend's been commissioned to do a Gothic style mural on a huge garden wall for a couple of well-off types revamping their flat, and he wanted to borrow it to do some preliminary sketches. I'd promised him that it would be outside his door by first thing in the morning , and I suddenly realised I'd forgotten. The last thing I remember is tripping and dropping the urn – that stair carpet really needs repairing. I suppose then I must have fallen on the urn somehow as I tumbled over and over down the stairs. It has big spikes sticking out all over – looks a bit how they used to draw landmines in the old comics. I think it must have well and truly spiked me. I hurt all over."

"You were dressed somewhat unusually," observed the policewoman.

"Oh, the Teddy Suit! I bought it a while back for a fancy dress party. I want to wear it again, but I've put a bit of weight on. I was just seeing if I could still get into it when – as I told you – I remembered the urn. Good job I was wearing it. It probably kept the spikes at bay a bit."

Tracie decided to bite the bullet. "I'm surprised you are here, Officer, investigating something like this. It's not as if someone pushed me down the stairs trying to do me in. Is that what you thought?"

She looked carefully at the officer's face and realized that that was indeed what had been suspected. 'Heavens,' she thought, 'I must really look a mess.'

PC Whittington ignored the question and posed another of her own instead. "What do you do in West Kingscove? I understand your home is on Regent's Parade."

"I do counselling. I've got a degree in Psychology." Tracie crossed her fingers under the sheets. Well, she thought, my clients feel better when they leave and I did do that Psychology module in my Foundation Year.

Hmmmm, WPC Whittington thought again. There *was* a large urn lying in the hall, and the stair carpet had indeed looked past repair. I'll ask the doctor whether her version could account for those wounds, and get forensic to have a look at the urn. She certainly isn't behaving like someone recently brutally attacked . And if she hasn't been attacked we've no need to be involved. I'll run it past the boss and see what he thinks.

Felicity and Ann were just arriving as the police officer left. They'd only met outside, so they'd not had time for any catching up. Ann thought Felicity looked *very* interesting – absolutely done for, but oddly glowing, all at the same time.

The state of Tracie's face horrified them, but she seemed in surprisingly good form considering, and thoroughly enjoyed regaling them with her story.

"Thank goodness you're ok, Tracie," said Felicity when she'd finished. "We were so worried. We all seem to have had a bit of a night." She went on to tell them about *some* of her own nocturnal goings on – especially about the ceiling.

"I'm going to have to leave you to Ann," she ended, "I've got James, the builder, coming in half an hour to try to patch the roof. You should see my bedroom," she trilled, and whirlwinded out.

Positively euphoric, thought Ann, what is going on?

Felicity was scarce out of the door when she leapt into action to try to find out. "Come on, now. Spill the beans! What really happened?"

"Exactly what I told you. Very mundane. I really did just trip, and there was no one else there. Sorry I can't regale you with a tale of kinky high passion. It must have been some trip, though. I feel crushed to bits, and I think I've done something to my neck, and both my ankles are giving me hell," she grimaced.

"What did you tell the policewoman about the costume?"

"Just that I was trying it on for a party when I remembered the urn. I don't see why she shouldn't believe me. I had a client coming, but he wouldn't get any reply from my buzzer as I was unconscious. I expect he just went away disappointed, poor man. What worries me most is that that woman has been prowling through my mobile phone book. She obviously got Felicity from there, and I gather Martin has phoned, and another friend, about whom I'm specially worried because I don't want to have him mixed up in any of this. He's in the sort of job where it wouldn't go down at all well."

The nurse popped her head round the curtain. "There's a Mr Martin Taylor here. Says he's your husband. Do you want to see him?"

"I suppose so." Tracie pulled a face at Ann. "Ask him to hang on a minute while I tidy myself up, please. Have you got a mirror, Ann?"

Ann's heart sank, because, of course, when Tracie saw the dreadful state of her face she didn't feel quite as chirpy. She had to bite back the tears. Ann couldn't think of anything to say that would help, but Tracie gave herself a mental shake.

"Well," she said, "I imagine this will all heal eventually. Till then I'll just have to wear the Teddy suit all the time to hide the damage. Do you think they'll let me into Waitrose in it?"

*

When Ann got back, Felicity was on the flat bit of the roof with James, so she took the opportunity to look in on Cedric. She decided she'd better start by explaining her connection with Augustus House.

"I kept thinking I should know you, but I was so drunk I thought I must just be imagining it," he told her. "Do come in." He seemed much improved in spirits.

"I'm so glad to see you, because I need both to apologise, and to thank you," he continued. "I thought you'd done a Cinderella on me, without even leaving your slipper. Wouldn't have blamed you – couldn't have looked much like a Prince Charming crouched on that rock last night – more like some large sea-dwelling frog, and I bet I smelt rotten."

"I won't argue, but you do seem to have improved - even the smell. Any reason? Your problem can't have just gone away."

"Well," he began, "I was completely out of control last night, as you know, and I do apologise again. I still feel worked up and worried but I'm a bit more able to get on with it now. For one thing, I'm sober. That makes an alarming difference. I've decided I've got to sort out my drinking. And don't you find that daylight nearly always improves a grim situation? Things are still bothering me, but at least I can think straight now. There's a hymn 'New every morning' all about that. I've had some good news, as well. I was desperately worried last night about a friend who'd had a dreadful fall, but when I phoned the hospital this morning they said she had regained consciousness. So - New every morning - naff or not."

Stop! Stop! He was telling himself. Are you sure you're not still drunk? Why are you telling this woman all these things?

"Not altogether naff," replied Ann, "after all, it's an old traditional hymn. You'd expect to find a bit of wisdom in it. It wouldn't have survived this long otherwise. I don't go along with it all, though. What's that bit – the trivial round, the common task, will furnish all we ought to ask. I think I'd go mad if I thought that was true."

Cedric was staring at her, half amused and half amazed.

"I may be a heathen now, but I wasn't brought up a heathen," she protested in mock outrage, "I know my hymns."

Then she looked at him more seriously.

"You're a clergyman, aren't you?"

He nodded. "What makes you ask? My droning on about hymns I suppose?"

"No. Much simpler. There are two battered clerical collars on the floor in your hall. You do live in a tip, you know. Are you going to put the kettle on? I really need some tea. And what have you got to eat?" she prompted. She could usually go for ever without eating, but this morning she felt starving.

He managed some toast from a couple of bin ends of bread. As she munched her way through it she couldn't resist teasing him.

"Yes. It's a big relief that Tracie's out of danger, isn't it? I've just been to see her."

Cedric had been coming to sit down with his toast anyway, but he ended up doing it very suddenly. He looked at her in amazement.

"How did you know it was Tracie?" he asked.

"I'm not really sure what I know about all this, but I'm sure of one thing – you really do need to talk about it. We've been through a lot together since last night," Ann looked at him seriously. "I don't tell many people this, but my father is a priest. I understand how sacred confessions are. Whatever it is, it won't shock me and it won't go any further."

Cedric hesitated. He liked this woman. He felt instinctively that he could trust her. What did he have to lose? He so much needed someone to talk to: someone to help him find his way through this maze of confusion. Out came the whole sorry tale.

"Well," Ann replied finally, "what are you going to do about it?"

"Not much I can do, is there? Leave the country? I'm serious. I only rent this place so, if necessary, I could start again tomorrow somewhere far from Kingscove. That's not unknown as a clerical way out. Train for something else? Or I could ride it out? It usually passes. I usually manage to put it away and carry on. Only you and I know how silly I was last night."

"You're leaving out the best solution," she reminded him, "you could face it out. Look it straight in the eye and defeat it. Perhaps try to repair what you used to have. I'm sure loss of faith isn't uncommon among priests - and that is what's right at the root of all this, isn't it? - something precious which you feel has gone for ever. Confront its loss. Otherwise it'll just come back and back and you will never be truly happy again."

He sighed. "You're right, I know. And I get the feeling you're going to make me do it. But it'll have to wait just a while. I don't think you will last long on that toast, and my head is still too muzzy for serious thinking. Let me take you out to brunch. You know more about me now than is good for either of us. Perhaps I can find out something about you that'll even things up a bit. And then I really promise I'll take action."

A man, wanting to talk to me, about me, thought Ann, as they walked down the road. Perhaps she'd been looking in the wrong places all this time.

Chapter 18

All the old excitement was flooding back. Abigail was a little girl again, peering out of the train window, while John danced around on the seat opposite and their mother, tight lipped and sharp tongued as nearly always, did her best to control him.

Suddenly, there they were – Durham Cathedral and Durham Castle standing side by side, proud and invincible before her, just as they had stood there for hundreds of years.

She and John had always looked for them whenever they went to Darlington on the train to see their father's brother, Uncle Ernie. It was always a great day out. His wife was a wonderful cook with a matching wonderfully sunny nature. Abigail had once accidentally overheard her father telling his brother that he thought Ernie's wife must have got double rations of optimism and warmth when things like that were being doled out, whilst his own wife must have joined the queue too late. She remembered being a bit shocked to hear her Dad talking in that way.

Then he'd lowered his voice even further, but Abigail was still sure he'd said, "I wish to God I'd never married her."

She stared at the cathedral from the train window, luxuriating in its uplifting effect and craning her neck to keep it with her as long as possible. When even an ostrich could have seen it no longer she sat back and closed her eyes. Well, that was the easy part over. If only the rest of this long overdue trip was likely to go this well. She bit her lip in apprehension. She shouldn't have let Hubert persuade her to make this journey.

What a hard time she had given him in the process.

"I'm sorry, Hubert, I really don't want to talk about it any more," she'd snapped angrily, "it just upsets me too much."

He had waited a week after they got back from Malta before he'd started working on her, but it wasn't long enough. The truth was that she didn't think any time would be long enough to cleanse her heart of the evil Milburns. The silence in his sitting room after her outburst had been overpowering. But Hubert had gritted his teeth and tried again.

"Why is it so difficult to talk about it to a friend? It's what you've needed to do all these years. It's sitting inside you heaving and boiling about like one of those volcanoes that never really burns itself out. It will eventually destroy you if you don't get in first."

Abigail had rested her elbow on the arm of her chair and used her extended hand to half prop up her thumping confused head.

"I have tried, Hubert. I've tried religion, and I've tried therapy."

Neither had worked. Christianity hadn't helped at all because it required her to forgive, and she didn't want to forgive. The Milburns had taken everything from her. Everything. Her youth. Her family. Her future. Her happiness. Why should she forgive?

So, once again, Hubert had had to give up on it.

"Alright," he'd conceded, "I promise I'll not mention it again tonight. I'm starving. I'd no idea it was so late. Shall I see what I've got to eat?"

He'd only promised, of course, not to mention it again that night, and as was so often the case, he had got his way in the end. Here she was, on a train, soon to be whipping through the inner suburbs of Newcastle.

She sighed. She supposed she would just about have time for a coffee and a bite to eat before she went to visit Mrs Evans.

*

"Lorna, pet. I am so pleased to see you again. How many years is it? I was hoping and hoping that you would come." Mrs Evans stretched out her arms from her wheelchair, her pale, thin face breaking into a warm smile. Abigail remembered that everyone all those years ago had regarded Mrs Evans as very stuck up and above herself. At the time she had never understood why because Mrs Evans was always really nice to Abigail and her brother.. She didn't shout, and she didn't say spiteful things. She could see now that that was probably why her mother and Mrs Milburn disliked her. They were suspicious of anyone who remained aloof from all their catty gossip.

There had never been any of that malice in Mrs Evans. She had been the only person who had regularly visited Abigail in the institution for young female offenders to which she was sent. It was she who had brought the news about the family emigrating. Abigail's mother had only gone once or twice, then she'd stopped completely and she'd banned her husband as well – a sweet man, but totally unable to stand u to his domineering wife.

The old lady now lived in a care home on the edge of town. Abigail was very relieved to find her happy and comfortable. To her great shame, they'd more or less lost touch. When she had been released she'd wanted to close off that part of her life for ever. She'd started using Abigail, her middle name, and conveniently been able to ditch her surname when she married. Mrs Evans and the parish priest had done really well to track her down.

"I'm sorry it was such a shock, pet. Neither Father Murphy nor I expected her to act so quickly and just turn up like that. She's certainly not the nicest woman to have landing unexpectedly on your doorstep. Perhaps she has more of a conscience about it than I thought. But I felt it was important for you to have the whole true story from her own mouth. I'm sure you still think about it and it still upsets you. I thought if you knew what really happened it would help wash it all away.

Abigail shook her head vehemently. "Nothing," she said fiercely, "will do that. I still hate them both."

Mrs Evans had always been one of nature's psychologists. She looked hard at Abigail.

"I'm not talking about your feelings for them," she told her. "I'm talking of how you feel about yourself. Hate them if you must, but is it worth the effort? Freddie's dead anyway, so anything you try to do to him is a waste of energy. And his awful mother is old and more broken up by his death than she lets on. Time and their own actions have done for both of them. But you've still got years ahead. Wouldn't it be good to enjoy them? Lorna, you're punishing *yourself*. How daft is that? It's like giving the Milburns a big present. You're letting them win. Be good to *yourself*, Lorna."

Sparks would have flown if Hubert had tried to talk to her like that, yet here she was taking it meekly from a frail little old lady in a wheelchair. Deep down she knew Mrs Evans was right. She'd reverted to being a little girl in her presence. Mrs Evans had always been like a favourite auntie. She used to talk to her about all the things she couldn't discuss with her mother. What a pity, she was thinking now, that she hadn't told her the truth about that awful day on the cliffs. Things might have turned out so differently, but, as it was, she did not want to let it go. Hating the Milburns seemed to help her cope and keep her sane –but deep down she knew it did not keep her happy.

She was rescued by the arrival of the afternoon tea trolley. Abigail had bought a carrot cake on her way up from the station and they munched their way companionably through a large chunk each while Mrs Evans filled her in on some of the changes the town had seen in 50 years, with news of some of the people still around..

"Now don't leave it another 50 years before you come back again because I just might not be here," she'd ordered Abigail as she hugged her in farewell.

What a wonderful woman, thought Abigail, as she walked back to the Metro Station, how lucky she was to have known her. On the way she stopped off to buy two lottery tickets, as requested, with the cash Mrs Evans had given her.

"One is for you, and one is for me," she'd told her, "But if you win I shall expect half, and if I win I'll give you half. I play every week. It's one of my silly treats. I forgot to ask my carer to do it for me today."

What a waste of money, Abigail had thought, as she stuffed them into the wallet section of her purse. She could just imagine Andrew's reaction of amused amazement if he'd seen her buying them. Little did she know that nothing would have been funny enough to make Andrew smile that night.

*

Andrew was so enraged that he was literally spitting out his words. Felicity watched, terrified and mesmerized as his showering droplets of saliva glistened in the rays of the sun slanting through his sitting room window.

"It really is lucky you're a woman. Just get out. Clear out. Now. Before I forget myself completely."

Ann was right. She shouldn't have told him. Sometimes confession is more for your own benefit, Ann had suggested, because you don't like carrying the pain of your guilt. If you confess, you move the pain across to the person you've wronged. But is that fair? Andrew was pretty distraught already. Paul had gone – along with his handful of possessions. He'd left a scrappy note saying he'd had an urgent phone call, had taken a morning flight from Gatwick to Marseille and wasn't sure when he'd be back. Wasn't that enough for Andrew to cope with?

Ann had done her best, without being too cruel, to stop Felicity thinking he'd gone because of her. You just had to look at him, she'd insisted, to know he would have no difficulty playing one lover off against another. He must wriggle in and out of scraps like this all the time. Felicity certainly wouldn't phase him so much that he'd make off to Marseille. No. It must have been something much bigger.

"Watch my lips!" Ann had ordered, "*don't* tell him."

But Felicity was always so moral. She was one of the 'Tell truth and shame the devil' school. She was certainly regretting it now.

“Please don’t get so angry, Andrew,” she pleaded, “you’re frightening me.”

“So how do you want me to behave then? Ooo, what fun, Felicity, how exciting for you. And in my bed! I can’t wait now to get into it myself – I’ll get such a frisson, won’t I? A sort of surrogate shag. Perhaps we can exchange notes about his performance?

“Oh, Andrew, please,” begged a tearful Felicity, “stop being so coarse. You know that’s not what I want. I didn’t mean it to happen. It just sort of …got out of hand,” she ended lamely.

“Me? *I’m* coarse? So your behaviour’s been really refined, has it? Good mannered Felicity – butter wouldn’t melt in her mouth Felicity. And I thought we were real friends. Seems you’re much more worldly wise than you let on. Just get out – now!

And the whole house seemed to rock as Andrew vented his anguish and frustration by hurling a suitcase repeatedly against his bedroom wall.

Eventually he pulled himself round enough to turn his mattress and change his sheets, but whether he could bring himself to get into that bed ever again remained to be seen.

*

Since schooldays, when things went wrong Stephen had turned to Andrew, and Andrew to Stephen, so it was his natural next step to phone him.

“I did tell you to take care,” said Stephen sadly, when

they were established in the snug at the Gayte, "I reckon he'd go after anything that moved, you know. He's just a sexaholic. Do you remember my telling you that I was sure he was hiding out in Brighton, that something was up? I've found out what it was. He's been having a rip roaring affair in London with an opera singer – a huge and handsome young tenor - and seeing to the bloke's mother in Chichester at the same time. He's made the mother pregnant. Naturally it's got a little complicated. Someone must have warned him that the opera singer was on his case. I expect he's on a ferry to Tangier by now. You really don't want to get involved, Andrew."

"I *am* involved," Andrew muttered, "I've never been this involved in all my life."

"Lots of people have been in the same boat," went on Stephen, "they called him the Sheikh of Shags on the rigs. He really is a serial practitioner. I suppose that's why he has to go to St. Hilda's every Sunday, for Absolution. I could probably write a Cantata about it to be performed by all those he's taken for a ride– we'd have enough voices, male and female. I could call it "The Passion of St. Andrew and St. Paul the Divine."

Andrew winced.

"Oh come on. I'm just trying to shake you out of it. Do you really want to be tied up with someone like that? This woman's done you a good turn. Let me get you another drink."

Andrew sat hunched in the corner just coming out with the odd monosyllabic reply, so Stephen felt compelled to keep going with a virtual soliloquy.

"She'll be telling the truth," he assured Andrew, "it won't be her fault. She wouldn't be expecting it. He doesn't take women very often, prefers men, but I gather when he does then he takes them completely by surprise – real sweet seduction stuff. Gets them talking, gets them crying, turns on the old comfort thing. Up till then it's just how any self respecting gay man looks after a close woman friend who's upset – but then he moves it on too far – and he's very good at it – really puts his charms to work. Suddenly they don't want him to stop. Not really much different, I suppose, from how he deals with us, but perhaps a bit gentler."

Andrew looked sharply at Stephen, "You seem to know a lot about him."

Stephen flushed. "Well, like I said, most of us have been there."

A pinched sadness briefly crossed his face: "Try to remember that everyone wouldn't treat you so badly."

He laid his hand on Andrew's.

When he got back to Augustus House Andrew felt the place had the same sad, forlorn look that everywhere had had for him that day. Hubert had recently discovered a portrait of Augustus in the library of the poet's old Oxford college. He'd persuaded the Fellows to let him have a copy made and it now hung in the common entrance hall, just at the foot of the stairs. Andrew could feel his eyes being drawn towards it. It seemed as if Augustus was looking at him. It was partly a look of sympathy, but there was something else in his expression. Andrew thought it might be alarm, but he could not think why.

I hate this place, he thought. I'm going to put my flat up for sale.

Chapter 19

Andrew wasn't the only one to notice Augustus' disquiet. Poor Felicity, tossing at night on her sofa, (her bed still drying out) guilt and grief stricken, could feel him pacing around her flat each night. He hadn't done that for a very long time. Next he would go wandering down the stairs to the old servants' quarters, now Abigail's flat. If she had been at home she would certainly have heard him down there.

What was agitating him? Perhaps he was just upset by the vibes of unrest pulsing through the house. There certainly wasn't much feeling of wellbeing amongst the residents left in Kingscove - Tracie, still in hospital, and having to psyche herself up just to look in the mirror; Felicity, in emotional terms, just as bruised; and Andrew equally battered, with only his seething anger keeping him going. The only happy one seemed to be Cedric, who was going around with a surprisingly unfurrowed brow, and the merest hint of a half smile.

When Abigail returned a couple of days later she could feel the atmosphere as soon as she opened the front door. It was just like a Saturday night in St. Peter's Street, she thought. You could stand at the bottom of the street at dusk, sniff the air, and know straight off what sort of night the street was going to have. Most nights you sniffed a fun evening, but very occasionally the air of foreboding could be quite overpowering and the next morning there'd be news of a vicious fight, or worse.

The atmosphere at Augustus House wasn't heavy with quite that sort of foreboding, but the feeling of sadness was very, very evident. Abigail went straight into action the next morning, starting with Andrew. It wasn't long before she'd prised the sorry tale out of him. What a mess, she thought. It would have to be mended, though God knows how. It was too small a house to have all that hate lurking in the common ways.

"Don't worry," Andrew had assured her, "I'm going to sort it. The flat's going on the market today. I'm leaving Augustus House."

Of course, that made Abigail feel worse, so it wasn't long before she was tapping on the door of the top floor flat. There was no reply, but she persevered because she was pretty sure that Felicity was in there. Eventually the door opened a few inches and a pale, exhausted face peered out. There was a look of relief when Felicity realised it was Abigail, and she opened the door wider to let her in. Abigail heard the whole tale again, but with a slightly different slant.

"Ann was right. I really shouldn't have told him," wept Felicity. Abigail thought for a moment, then shook her head.

"I'm not sure that's true," she consoled. "There's a lot to be said for being honest. The truth will usually out in the end anyway. Although I do agree it's had a terrible effect in the short term. Do you think things will improve if we give him time?"

Felicity shook her head ruefully. She was pretty sure she had messed it up for good, and the thought made her desperately sad. She felt she'd suffered a double loss. She'd fallen overboard for Paul the first time she'd ever seen him at St. Hilda's, but Andrew had become like the brother she'd always wanted - and now she'd lost them both.

"I don't think he will ever forgive me," she said, "I can't

bear to stay here. I'm going to sell my flat."

"Take your time," advised Abigail, managing to hide her horror. "You're not going to get far with a sale while the roof's in such a mess. And by then I bet he'll have stopped bleeding, even if he hasn't healed. Why don't you try to go away? Didn't you tell me your parents lived in Hampshire? Might you be able to work from home there till things calm down? It must be really difficult for you both having to live in such close proximity at the moment. You've got the excuse about the damage to your flat."

*

William Blake was quite right," announced Hubert, as he carefully uncorked their bottle of wine and stood it on the sideboard to breathe, "It is easier to forgive an enemy than to forgive a friend. One expects to be let down by an enemy - but a special friend - that is so different - one has given them a part of oneself, and to feel betrayed after that must hurt very much."

One effect of the recent upset was that Abigail was almost glad that the roof had fallen in. Initially she had been horrified to find Felicity's note telling her about it. A note from James had followed, together with his bill for the temporary patch up. He'd told her he couldn't guarantee the work at all - come the next storm things would probably be even worse. But now she began to regard the ailing roof as a lifeline. No way were these two going to get far with selling their flats until it was repaired, so she had a bit of time to try to get the rift healed.

"Surely they'll both have seen sense by then," she said to Hubert, "surely they're not going to put their lives through such major disruption just because they've fallen out over some sex maniac. It certainly sounds as if Paul was the real villain. There's nothing they can do about it now - they're really just punishing themselves. Why are you looking at me like that?" she ended sharply.

Hubert just shrugged his shoulders, but Abigail knew what he was thinking.

"How can you compare forgiving someone who has gone to bed with your philandering boyfriend and forgiving someone who got you sent to prison for murder?" she blazed.

"I didn't think you were talking about forgiveness, Abigail. You seemed to be saying that Andrew would be a fool to sell his flat and change his life completely. You said he'd be punishing himself. I know you suffered a much greater wrong, but the same applies - there's nothing you can do about it now, so why not let it go? I'd better change the subject, hadn't I? What are we going to do about this roof?"

Abigail told him sulkily that she'd got James coming that afternoon to estimate for a thorough repair. Hubert was a bit surprised. "James is coming to me as well," he told her, "while I was away I decided it was time to get the Tower Room roof repaired before someone else fell through."

Abigail couldn't think of a good reply, but she paused in the hall on her way back downstairs to look at Augustus' portrait.

"Did you hear that?" she asked him, "Try not to look so miserable. Things are going to get better."

*

The Tower Room had been constructed in 1872 - part of Mr and Mrs Booth's long term plan for their Regent's Parade house. They were both extremely sociable, hospitable people. Their roots were in the West Country but Henry, Mr Booth, had made a large amount of money in London in millinery and hatting. Their fondest dream was to be accepted by what they thought of as "society", but the London scene scorned them for making their money in trade - hence their move to Kingscove. Mr Booth travelled up to town most days on the wonderful new railway, while Mrs Booth worked hard to establish them in the best Kingscove circles.

It wasn't easy for them in Kingscove either. Henry had decided that standing for the local Kingscove Council might be a way in, but snobbery held strong sway there too, and references to him in the local press invariably began with - 'Mr Councillor Henry Booth - the well known hatter.'

They'd decided that the way forward might be to cultivate their artistic sides. They both loved music and had long since developed a habit of employing a singer or a violinist to entertain while they dined on anniversaries and other special occasions. They decided to expand this practice, but although their dining room overlooking the sea was quite large, once one imported a grand piano, a pianist and a soloist, space ran decidedly short. They needed somewhere with much more style and size.

Mrs Booth persuaded her beloved Henry to expand. At the rear of their home was a smallish garden, surrounded on 3 sides by other gardens. It was before the days of stringent planning laws and Henry decided to make his neighbours offers they couldn't refuse. Four gardens became a building site in the early 1870's, and out of the chaos a towered concert hall slowly climbed.

Mrs Booth herself had been in her youth an accomplished pianist, and she now built up an address book of comparable and better musicians. Word gradually filtered round the town that, even if the Booths were hatters, they held wondrously good concerts and were genial hosts. On the surface, at least, the Booths were accepted. Then, when Augustus went up to Oxford and mixed with the likes of Oscar Wilde his love for poetry really took off. Gradually the Booth concerts became mixes of music and poetry, and the talk of Kingscove cultured circles.

Hubert had pieced together all this after he'd bought the huge ground floor flat at Augustus House and had become so interested in Augustus' poetry. The Booths had been gone more than a century now, and since then disuse, misuse, the fickle Kingscove weather, and the old tramp had taken their toll. The fabric of the once beautiful private concert room was in need of major restoration.

*

"To be honest with you, I wouldn't know where to start," James stood stroking his chin thoughtfully, "I can repair the main roof - no problem - but this..." he threw up his hands towards the Tower, clothed in its gloomy tarpaulin, "this is a different ball game. I think it would be worth your while to consult an architect I know. I'll give you his number."

He looked up at it again and smiled, "But I would really like to restore it under his guidance. Just imagine how marvellous it will look when the tarpaulin comes off and the room comes alive again. I love old buildings. They seem to sing," and, for once, James did not despair of Hubert when he came back with the inevitable quotation.

"Yes! Yes! What was it Rostand said? *Architecture is frozen music.*"

Hubert gave James the usual answer - he'd talk to Abigail - and James rushed off to his next appointment. He'd already discussed the roof with Abigail, but was having an "estimating" afternoon. On the way out he bumped into the vicar chap who lived on the first floor. He was fair bouncing down the stairs, looking smarter than usual, and with an overnight bag.

He looks pleased with himself, thought James.

*

Cedric stared in exasperation at his ensuite shower room. This would teach him to get cheap hotels off internet sites. It was impossible to imagine how it could be any smaller. He usually cadged a room from his old friend Robert when he was up in London, but Robert had his mother and father staying this week.

Of course it is perfectly possible to get back to Kingscove after an evening up in town, but Cedric wanted this evening to be faultless. He didn't want to have to rush off.

The room itself was not too bad - clean and central - but

this ensuite, really!!

He'd read a story, he remembered, when he was young, called The Borrowers, about tiny people who lived under the floorboards. This was obviously their ensuite, although he thought that even they might have found it a tight squeeze.

His ablutions were going to need very careful planning. It looked as if the only way to use the toilet would be to leave half of oneself behind in the bedroom. It would be just impossible to get right in, close the door and perform any necessaries, unless one was very agile indeed, and acrobatics had never been his forte. Things like teeth cleaning would also involve standing in the bedroom and gingerly tilting one's head in towards the miniscule washbasin, the shape and size of a box for children's shoes.

As for accessing the shower, there was no easy way in at all - not even for half measures. Perhaps that was why it looked so sparkling clean and factory fresh. The only way, even for a very slim person, would be to climb over the lavatory. Still, needs must. He felt very hot and grubby, and tonight he specially wanted to make a good impression. He'd been invited to take a guest to a reception at Lambeth Palace to welcome a visiting Anglican dignitary from abroad. Cedric had rung his contact, the one who had sounded him out about his future career, puzzled.

I've never had this sort of invitation before. What is happening?"

"Nothing much," replied his friend airily, "I expect some of the people who don't know you want to look you over. You *are* going to bring someone, I hope? A woman? Make sure she's suitable."

Cedric had been looking for a good excuse to invite Ann out properly. This was heaven sent in every sense of the phrase, and now here he was, up in London for their first proper date, having spent a small fortune on the sort of gear an aspiring cleric should wear to impress at a posh evening at Lambeth Palace.

That was why he was economising on his room.

There were no two ways - he had to have a shower. He lowered the toilet lid and left his phone on a ledge created by some pipe casing, because he hated missing calls. Then he flung off his sweaty clothes, gingerly mounted the lavatory seat, and crossed over carefully into the cubicle. The shower would only get about 1 out of 10 marks for spaciousness, but fortunately ratings for power and effectiveness scored much higher. Cedric felt quite restored.

Renewed with vigour and misfounded optimism Cedric almost leapt from the shower. He was quite confident that he could easily negotiate the obstacle between himself and his bedroom floor. Unfortunately both his feet skidded, and he found them shooting far above his head, sadly in different directions. Then his body began to turn. In a move which demonstrated either remarkable agility or, more likely, terrible bad luck, Cedric descended to earth at speed and found himself very tightly wedged between the loo and the shower. His legs were spreadeagled skywards. His right one pointed accusingly at the shower: the other waved aimlessly towards the bedroom, a bit like a computer mouse that goes round and round, refusing to find its target. His behind was contained in a smaller space than he would have thought possible and his arms were neatly stored there too. He could not move. He could not bear to think what he must look like, and he was certainly right to think like this.

His elegant and fastidious friend Robert was wont to say that everyone looked ugly without clothes. Cedric knew that in his present pose he looked much much worse than even everyone. And even more worse, he could not see how he was going to lever himself out of this mess. If he had practised for days he could not have put himself so completely into this tight spot.

Dear God, he thought, what *am* I to do? Here he was, outwitted by over optimism and confidence. Ann would be getting ready now. Soon she'd be waiting for him to collect her. She was going to have a very long wait. She'd never agree to go out with him ever again. Cedric was reminded of the saying that one's whole life passed before one's eyes when one was drowning. He was finding something similar now, stuck in the ultimate undressed state, with his head practically down a lavatory, legs high in the air.

Time was ticking on, and he'd promised to pick Ann up in a cab at her loft at 6.30. If only he could move just one leg that would be a start, but no. Then he found he could move his left hand a little if he wriggled slightly sideways. He noticed that his phone had been knocked off the shelf by his fall. It had slipped on to his towel, but no matter how he tried he could not reach it.

He swivelled his head back and forth as much as he could manage, looking for implements to help - if he could only tip over that loo brush and its container then he could nudge them along and use them to pull the towel near enough for him to get his phone. After what seemed a lifetime he managed. When he looked at his phone he was horrified to find that the process had taken him half an hour.

He'd decided it would be best to ring Robert. He lived within walking distance, and Cedric knew he would happily come to the rescue, if only to get a good laugh. Once he'd done that he rang Ann. There was no way he could be at her place by 6.30 now so, full of apologies, he arranged to meet her outside Lambeth Palace, promising to explain later. Heaven knows what he'd tell her.

Then he settled down to wait for the humiliation of being pulled free by Robert and someone on the hotel staff. He certainly wouldn't be able to come back here tonight. He'd give his things to Robert and go back to Kingscove after all when he'd taken Ann home.

*

"You did *what*?" demanded Ann incredulously, when they were in the cab going home after a really successful evening .

"I got stuck getting out of the shower. Really stuck. I couldn't move. They had to take the shower door off to get me out." - he'd decided to tell the truth. "Robert came to rescue me, with the Polish Duty Manager."

"What a good job he brought someone to help if they had to take the door off." suggested Ann, trying hard not to laugh..

"I suppose so," Cedric agreed reluctantly, "it's just a pity the Manager was a woman. I don't know which of us was more mortified. Robert swears he couldn't stop her. He says she didn't understand when he tried to tell her how embarrassing it would be. She certainly found out."

Ann began to quiver and very shortly she was just

helpless with laughter.

"It isn't funny," he complained, "I thought you'd be sympathetic."

She pulled herself together for a minute, but then mirth took over again.

"I wish I'd been there," she gasped.

"I'm jolly glad you weren't. You would never have taken me seriously again."

The cab stopped at traffic lights in a busy street. It was light enough for her to look into

Cedric's eyes, and she was sure that he was trying very hard not to laugh himself. She took his hand. It was a long time since she'd wanted to practice her powers of seduction, and she wasn't all that sure how to start.

"I have to take people seriously all day - people who take themselves far too seriously" she told him, "what I really love is people who can make me laugh. Are you coming in for a nightcap?"

Chapter 20

Cedric hadn't been able to resist taking up Ann's offer, but now he was through the door he felt so jittery. He could see quite clearly, he thought, where this was leading, and half of him would be very happy to be led there. At the same time he was scared out of his wits. It seemed like years since a woman had shown any interest in him. Were his skills out of date? Come to that, had he ever had any skills? Ann couldn't want *him*. He must be misreading the signs. Sometimes people did, didn't they? If they got it wrong they ended up, at best, looking like gropers, at worst like would- be rapists.

Perhaps she fancied everyone - what was the word? -a nymphomaniac - that was it - a glutton for sex with anyone or everyone.

But how could he even consider such a thing? Of course he was wrong - and he must have misread the signs anyway. There was no way that she might fancy him. She was so poised, so sophisticated, so rich. He was quite out of her league. The dress she'd worn tonight was so simple, yet so right. She'd been such a success at the party - everyone there had loved her company, loved her wit. But now here he was, sitting in this vast living space with its state of the art furniture and glorious modern paintings. How could you compare her huge loft with his rented converted flat, even if it *was* on Kingscove seafront. It would almost fit into her hall. What a fool he was to entertain the idea for one minute - she would never settle for him - except perhaps for one night if she was really bored.

Come to think of it, she must have been really bored all evening amongst all those earnest clergy and clerical

WAGS. She'd just hidden it because she'd been nicely brought up in the vicarage.

He couldn't bear to have just a one night stand. He was beginning to think he might want her forever - to wake up every morning to her commonsense, to her sarcastic quips which made him laugh so much. He fiddled nervously with his coffee cup. He really ought to go, before he made a first class fool of himself. He knew only too well how good he was at that. He could see her looking at him in such a nervous way. She must know what he was thinking, she was worrying that he was about to leap on her. He was sure she was horrified and that she wanted him to go.

*

Ann *did* feel very nervous. She wanted this man so much. She loved his shyness and his awkwardness,

but she felt sure that there was much more than that to Cedric - those eyes often sparkled with humour in spite of themselves. She already knew that his own opinion of himself was pretty mediocre, but she thought he'd got it all wrong.

She'd realised a while back that if they were to get anywhere she'd have to do the seducing, but that

could be such a chancy thing. Had she read the signs right? She'd had such bother with many of the men she'd met through CitiSparks. They'd read her signs completely wrongly. None of them thought she was looking for someone really long term, with a soul and a bit of sensitivity, someone with hopes and dreams.

But Cedric... She wasn't usually poetically inclined but

she found herself remembering what Yeats had said about the pilgrim soul. She was beginning to love the pilgrim soul in Cedric - his sensitivity, his gentlemanly almost old world touches. She wanted to help him face his agony over his loss of faith, and all the rest of his perceived shortcomings in himself.

She'd really enjoyed this evening, loved talking to lots of people who were interested in other things than just making money - perhaps it was a case of 'Once a clergyman's daughter'?

So should she make a move? Did he really fancy her? Had she read the signs right? Looking across at him she really couldn't decide. He seemed extremely nervous, playing about with his coffee cup. That was a bad sign - he must think she was going to jump on him. He would have had an alcoholic drink if he'd been hoping for them to make moves on each other, surely? After all, he wasn't driving. She *must* have got it wrong. He couldn't possibly fancy her.

But it was now or never. She might never have such an opportunity again. Should she pounce? She didn't dare. He'd think she was a nymphomaniac. He'd run a mile. That would be that. He'd be gone for ever.

She sat miserably, clattering her coffee cup nervously, looking at him.

Cedric put down his cup.

"I'd better go," he gabbled, "I'm going to miss the last train. Thank you for coming with me this evening." And off he rushed.

Ann was so upset. It was her old problem, she told herself - too pushy, too sharp, too available, too sarcastic. No pilgrim soul for her to love. The last train to

Kingscove wasn't for another couple of hours. She *knew* - she'd been on it enough times. He just couldn't wait to get away.

The tears welled up and began dropping in splatters on the low glass table in front of the sofa. She'd been looking forward so much to tonight. She'd thought of little else for the past week. She'd spent most of today in a state of delicious apprehension, deciding what to wear, trying on this, trying on that, pirouetting like a girl in front of the mirror. And she'd thought everything had gone so well. How wrong one can be, she mourned. She picked up his coffee cup and flung it in furious frustration across the room. Its contents painted the pale rug in muddy streaks while she sat sobbing.

It was a while before she realised that the continuous noise in the background was her entryphone. She didn't answer it at first, but it went on and on, so eventually she had to.

"It's me," came Cedric's muffled voice on the intercom, "can I come in?"

He must have come back to gloat, was all she could think. I expect he knows he's made me cry. But when he arrived at her door he didn't look in gloating mood. He was drenched.

"Pouring out there," he muttered, "I'm nearly as wet as the night you and I first met. I've lost my wallet. I can't get home."

He looked in astonishment at her crumpled wet face and she looked at his. Simultaneously they made their moves - caution swept away by longing and lust.

"You'd better get out of these wet clothes," she murmured.

*

Cedric rolled over in a very comfortable bed, and stretched happily. Ann had gone to make them a cup of tea. Robert was right, as usual, he smiled to himself. He'd given Cedric a lift round to Lambeth Palace after the ensuite rescue, and Cedric had confided his worst fears.

"Don't worry, old chap," Robert had reassured him, "it'll all come back to you. You never forget - just like riding a bike."

Something else came back to him as he was sipping his tea, and he began to beam.

"I didn't realise I made such a good cup of tea," she teased, "what's up?"

"I've just remembered where my wallet is."

Ann looked horrified, "I'd forgotten all about it. We were going to report it and stop your cards last night, but I guess we got a bit waylaid."

"No need to worry. Robert's got it. It was in the jacket in which I travelled to London. I was in too much of a rush to remember to transfer it. I didn't miss it last night because I'd already put enough money for the cab in my dress jacket pocket before my momentous shower."

"I think you did it on purpose. It was a good excuse to come back and have your evil way."

"*Me? On purpose*?" he replied. Then he grinned, "But you're partly right - I did desperately want my evil way."

"And you a clergyman," Ann tut-tutted, "We'd better both go to St. Hilda's on Sunday to apologise to God."

Cedric informed her that he had to go anyway - "Father Peter's on holiday. I'm preaching."

*

Ann was in two minds whether to go to St Hilda's or not. Cedric was, after all, officiating at a serious religious service. She wasn't sure if she'd be able to think of it like that. She hadn't ever seen him decked in the splendour that a St Hilda's priest wore for Solemn High Mass. She could imagine how worked up this might make her. She really did have quite enough to confess already, but when the time came she just could not keep away. She slipped into what she hoped would be a quiet corner with a good view of him, but where she herself wouldn't be on display.

She couldn't believe how happy, how excited this relationship was making her. She and Cedric had discussed it yesterday, as rationally as they could manage because they were at that stage where it was difficult to keep their hands off each other.

"We're behaving like a couple of kids. We must try to keep it under wraps till we're absolutely sure," they told each other. But each of them knew how absolutely sure they were, and behaving like kids felt wonderful.

What was worrying Cedric most was that he would have to preach. This wouldn't normally bother him at all. He was acknowledged as a fine preacher but there must be few things more testing than preaching a sermon in front of one's brand new lover. He almost found himself hoping she would not come. On the other hand he knew this was one of the things he usually excelled at, something where he could really look good, and part of him wanted to show off.

All in all, Cedric had a lot to sort out before Sunday. Ann was given strict instructions to stay out of the way in London until he had written his sermon and had let Stephen the choirmaster know the hymns in good time for the Thursday choir practice.

*

Andrew too had slipped quietly and early into St. Hilda's and was now sitting on the same side of the church as Ann, but right at the back. Getting a good view of the preacher wasn't high on his list. If he was honest, he didn't really know what was on his list - apart from Paul and Felicity - the first because of the big aching hole Paul had left in the very centre of his being, and Felicity because of his righteous indignation over what he saw as her seduction of *his* lover in *his* bed. These two topics had been rolling through his mind night and day for more than a week now.

What really should have been at the top of his list was giving thanks for good friends. Stephen had spent almost every evening with him that week, either at home or in The Gayte, patiently listening to the same story again and again.

Stephen had long since perfected patience to a fine art. He saw it as an essential skill of his trade. If you wanted to get a piece right, he would say, you might need to go through it countless times. You would only get the best out of your choir if you stayed smiling and patient, at least pretending that you were full of hope and enthusiasm.

Eventually, though, even Stephen's patience began to flag. He found the view of Felicity as the great seductress laughable.

"Andrew," he remonstrated, "it's time you stopped this. Paul is a serial seducer, a mega seducer. I've only met Felicity once, but I do not think there is even a remote possibility that she could have seduced Paul. She's not in his league as far as that sort of thing goes, just as you're not, and I'm not. Don't look so bloody hurt. It's a fact of life. Anything that went on that night went on at his instigation, I'm sure. I don't think anyone has *ever* seduced Paul. They would never have time. He would *always* get in first. Face facts. Paul is addicted to sex, you weren't there, he needed his night time dose, and Felicity just happened to come knocking conveniently at the door. I don't know how you can keep this up. Your pride is hurt and you've found a scapegoat. Do you think you perhaps need a dose of St. Hilda's? Why don't you come on Sunday and I'll treat you to lunch afterwards. Now there's an offer you can't refuse!"

He hoped that some of the spiritual atmosphere which St. Hilda's had in abundance would wash away all this hate.

Andrew, as much as anything because Sundays are the loneliest days for miserable people, had agreed, and was now kneeling, head in hands, listening to Stephen doing what he possibly loved best in life - improvising on the mighty St. Hilda's organ. Suddenly he realised that the people in front of him were standing, and that Stephen's improvisations were settling into the very familiar tune of the processional hymn - Oh worship the King. The great ecclesiastical extravaganza that was Solemn High

Mass at St. Hilda's was underway.

*

It was certainly much more High Church than her father's services had been, thought Ann. She couldn't remember his ever having worn such magnificent robes, such beautiful green chasubles encrusted with gold embroidery. The three priests looked strangely like triplets in their identical robes and black tricorn birettas. It actually took her a moment to work out which one was Cedric. His biretta even hid that tiny bald patch on the back of his head that she was beginning to love so much - the one whose existence he vehemently denied. She really needn't have worried about thinking ungodly thoughts - the music, the robes and the atmosphere seemed to have combined to change him into a different being. Ann relaxed and concentrated on the hymn. She loved singing and, my, this organist was good.

*

You had to hand it to St. Hilda's, thought Cedric as he brought up the rear of the procession. The presentation of a service here was as carefully executed as a top West End production. The whole thing was precision choreographed - no leaving anything to chance here, no shuffling aimlessly around. It was all so gracious and ordered, so ceremonial, the collection of hats from the priests each time they sat down and reallocation when they rose, the bowing in thanks of the congregation as the heady aromas of the incense were wafted over them by the ornate silver thurible. And then there was the all-enveloping beauty of the music. It was impossible not to become totally involved.

After thinking long about the hymns he had decided to pick ones which would give the congregation scope to play their own major part. I am so so happy, he'd thought - I'm going to make this Sunday into a veritable Joyfest. I'm going to see to it that we all come out afterwards dancing down the seafront.

He took as his text for his sermon the first verse of *Psalm 47 - O clap your hands, all ye people; shout unto God with the voice of triumph.* When he finished he knew he had done well. He could feel the atmosphere of optimism welling up and filling the huge church. He often had this effect on congregations when he preached and usually felt a fraud because he'd had no effect upon himself. But today it was touching him as well. He felt like cartwheeling back to his seat.

When the service was over he stood in the church doorway with his two priestly colleagues greeting the members of the congregation. He and Ann had agreed not to let on that they knew each other, so there was just the briefest of electric handshakes and she was off to wait for him in his flat. He would be a while because there was tea and coffee in the church hall and he always enjoyed talking to the people with whom he had shared a service, seeing it as an important part of his ministry.

*

Stephen usually continued to play after the service while

people stood around talking at the back of the church. Many, including Andrew, stayed sitting in the pews, enjoying the music.

When Stephen finally came down from the organ loft to collect Andrew for lunch he passed a young woman still on her knees in the opposite corner of the church. He was pretty sure she was crying.

"Is that Felicity over there?" he asked Andrew, "it is, isn't it? She looks very upset. Shall we take her to lunch?"

"No, grunted Andrew, "I'm starving. Let's go."

"I have had enough of this," snapped Stephen, his patience finally spent, "You should see yourself!" He strode back across the church and tapped Felicity gently on the arm.

"Hello. I'm Stephen, Andrew's friend. We'd like you to come to lunch with us."

She started to blurt out an excuse, but he took her arm. "Come on," he insisted, "before all the tables go."

Even though he was sure it was the right thing to do, he was already regretting it.

What a bundle of laughs this will be, he thought.

*

Fortunately, Brooksoes' was particularly heaving and even noisier than normal. They had to sit with lots of other people at the long refectory style table which ran down the middle of the bar. The laboured silences weren't quite as noticeable as they might otherwise have been.

Stephen was ready for his lunch. There'd been a rather long drawn out emergency choir practice before the service, because the choir had had a bit of bother with the Introit - a lovely piece, but very intricate, and new to them. He was damned if he was going to let these two miserable people put him off his food, and he tackled his meal with gusto.

Felicity and Andrew sat opposite him, halfway down the long table. Between mouthfuls he would aim a question at one or other of them, which would bring forth either a surly monosyllabic reply from Andrew or a gasping apologetic whimper from Felicity. Just bank the Brownie points, he kept telling himself: Blessed are the peacemakers and all that. Think of all the bad things you've done this week and regard this lunch as a bit of useful penance.

Fortunately, halfway through this near-Trappist experience, one group of people finished their food and left the communal table. Immediately a gang of Stephen's and Andrew's acquaintances piled in, and the situation defused itself. Paul wasn't amongst them, thank goodness. There had been no sightings of him in Kingscove since the morning after the storm.

Kingscove had now been blessed with wonderful freak weather for a couple of days - almost motionless seas and cloudless skies joined together in a clear, distinct, straight line - above the line a clear azure sky, beneath a deeper blue sea, its stillness just disturbed here and there by tufts of sparkling foam from a few speedboats,

Kingscoveians were getting browner by the hour. Parading along the seafront had temporarily become the city's favourite pastime, so the diners decided to walk off their large lunches by doing just that.

"Thank you, but I really can't ," said Felicity, when asked to join them, "I've promised to go to see Tracie at the hospital. We're hoping she'll be able to come home tomorrow."

Stephen was somewhat relieved. After all, even virtue has its limits.

*

"They're being really awkward," Tracie was almost in tears. "They won't let me come home unless there's someone there to keep an eye on me. I can't bear to stay here any longer. I'm feeling fine. They don't know what it's like being cooped up in this hellhole when there's nothing wrong with you." Tracie's voice was rising hysterically.

Felicity put a consoling hand on her arm. After her own traumatic lunch she was quite glad to have something like this to occupy her mind.

"Don't get in such a state. I think we can sort it. I still can't stand the sight of my bedroom ceiling, so I'm off to stay at my parents' place for a while. They're away on holiday. Would you like to come? You'd approve of the house. I know how you like really old places. Do you remember my telling you it used to be the Stanton family home – you know, Emily, Augustus' fiancée. We'd have the place to ourselves, except for the cats. Hope you like cats. Do you think they would let you out if I said I would look after you?"

When the charge nurse came round they pounced on him to enquire, but he thought Tracie would have to wait to see what the doctor said the next morning. Apparently she would need some of her many facial wounds monitored regularly as there was still considerable risk of infection. He thought it would probably depend on how easily this could be arranged at a local hospital.

Tracie decided she would move heaven and earth to make her escape possible, so she and Felicity began to plan.

It was a mutually beneficial good idea of Felicity's - Tracie always managed to boost Felicity's wavering self-esteem, and Felicity's mother hen approach would be really useful in the present situation, as Tracie might well feel a lot less confident out of hospital than she imagined.

At the moment she was egging Felicity on to be less agonised about Andrew, which was just what was needed.

"Is he still wingeing then?" she asked, "He needs someone to take his mind off it all. Do you think I should offer to put him through his paces. Would he appreciate that, do you reckon?"

Felicity put on her schadenfreude face and tut tutted in mock horror. "I think another man would

suit him better. You just have to take one look at that lovely Stephen to see he desperately wants Andrew, but Andrew's still obsessed with Paul and thinks I'm the villain. You're quite right - he'd feel much better for a good seeing to. You have a really bad effect on me. I only talk like this when you're around, Tracie."

*

Abigail was sitting on her steps in the sunshine, reading

a Sunday paper, when Felicity came back from the hospital.

"That's wonderful," she told Felicity when she heard the news. Then her face suddenly changed. "Felicity," she continued in a much more urgent vein, "will you forgive me if I duck inside? I've just seen Hubert waiting to cross at the traffic lights. I'd rather avoid him right now. He's trying to get me to do something I don't want to do, and I can't face another argument with him at the moment," - and she was off down her steps before the lights changed.

I really must sell this place, thought Felicity, everybody pestering everybody else, trying to tell them what to do. It gets a bit tiresome.

*

Abigail was really annoyed with herself. It was so weak of her to worry like this about what Hubert thought. She was sick to death of his trying to persuade her to let go of her hate and resentment - but the real reason it made her so angry was that deep down she knew he was right. Of course it was stupid to hold on to all this anger - it wasn't hurting the people responsible at all. What was it Mrs Evans had said about Freddie Milburn and his mother? - *Time and their own actions have done for them both.* The only reason they still had this stranglehold on such an important part of her life was because she let them. She just couldn't find a way of finally despatching them to oblivion.

.But thinking of Mrs Evans reminded her that she hadn't rung. Abigail had decided to make a habit of telephoning her every Sunday so that they would not lose touch again. She made some coffee, put her feet up, and prepared herself for a pleasant few minutes.

The telephone voice seems to be the last part of our being that shows signs of age. Mrs Evans' voice came over strongly. She seemed so excited.

"Isn't it wonderful about the ticket?" she asked.

Abigail had no idea at first what she meant. Then it dawned. She had forgotten all about the lottery tickets. Her snobby side hadn't wanted to be bothered with them so she'd put them in an envelope and sent them north.

"One of them was a winner," the old lady continued, "not the big one, but definitely much better than nothing. We've won almost £30,000."

Chapter 21

Felicity had decided that Abigail's idea of decamping to Fordham for a while was inspired, so as soon as Tracie was given the all clear at the hospital she started to organize the trip.

For some reason she suddenly thought about Ann. Perhaps she should ring her - tell her the good news that Tracie was coming out of hospital. Ann might even like to join them in Fordham for a day or two. She must have been working very hard recently because every time Felicity had rung her she seemed to have no spare time at all.

There wasn't a reply on the landline, and when Ann answered her mobile she sounded far away, as if she was daydreaming. Quite unlike her, thought Felicity.

"That's great. She was getting so bored, wasn't she?" replied Ann when she'd come round a bit. "I think she'll improve more quickly out of the hospital environment. How well will she cope with the journey, though? I seem to remember it's a bit complicated by train. She's probably not anything like as strong as she thinks she is."

Felicity admitted she was a bit worried about that. She thought she might have to hire a car. She didn't really want to because her father's car would be waiting for them in the garage as soon as they got to Fordham, so it seemed a waste.

"Let me have a think about it. I'll come back to you," promised Ann.

"I'll drive you there," she announced when she rang back, "I fancy a jaunt into deepest Surrey, and I'll take up your offer of staying the night, so we can all catch up. I've neglected my friends a bit lately, haven't I?"

Felicity would normally have demurred, protesting it was too much bother to bring the car all the way from London, but she didn't because it was such a welcome solution. Unbeknown to Felicity, the car wasn't in London anyway. It was parked on the Downs at Beachy Head, where Ann and Cedric were enjoying a late afternoon picnic in a world of their own.

Cedric pulled a face when she told him. "Do you have to? I've got tomorrow off."

She pulled one back. "Yes, I do. What an uncharitable clergyman you are. Come with me if you like."

He shuddered "Not likely. I can only imagine what you three are like when you get together. Are you going to tell them?"

"Thought I might. Felicity will get really peeved if she finds out accidentally. Every time I open your door I keep expecting to bump into her on the stairs. Just pray we can get away with it one more night. She said she's going back up to the hospital tonight so we can perhaps sneak in then.

"Anyway, that's later. No need to waste time on it now." She returned to the serious task in hand - feeding him strawberries and cream on a long silver spoon .

Between his mouthfuls of strawberries Cedric stared out over the sea into a calm and beautiful distance. He was so, so happy. Just a week or so back he had been a sad and nervous wreck. Now here he was, so relaxed that he was almost falling asleep – partly of course because of the lovely spring weather, but there was something much more - a deep contentment, a springing optimism, and an ever-growing resolve.

I have been given a second chance, he rejoiced. What shall I do with it?

*

Ann brought the car round at 12 noon the next day as promised. Tracie had already been collected from the hospital by taxi and was sitting on her bed giving last minute instructions about her packing.

Half of Augustus House seemed to congregate to see them off - a sort of farewell colour party. When she'd got Tracie and Felicity into the car, together with what seemed like a year's supply of luggage, Ann went round doing her farewells - a handshake for Hubert, a bit of a hug for Abigail, and finally a somewhat overplayed farewell for Cedric, who took it with the deadpan face they'd previously agreed.

"That'll get them all going," she murmured in his ear. She leapt into the car and was off, and Cedric made off along the seafront to meet a friend for lunch, giving a nonchalant farewell wave as he went.

Through the right hand wing mirror Ann could see Abigail looking shell shocked, and through the main mirror she could see Tracie in the back seat looking much the same. She could only imagine what Felicity's reaction must be. How nice to have a cast iron excuse to keep one's eyes straight ahead.

Tracie was the first to break the silence.

"Well you're a dark horse! How long has this been going on?"

The corners of Ann's mouth puckered slightly.

"Oh, a while," she replied, still keeping her eyes steadfastly on the road ahead.

"Did *you* know, Felicity?" went on Tracie.

"No. I didn't." Felicity sounded possibly just a little bit miffed.

"Come on, Ann. We want to know all about it," Tracie demanded. Her day's activities so far had sapped her energies more than she'd expected and this was just the perk up she'd needed.

"You'll have to wait," Ann was definite, "I'm concentrating on the driving. I'll tell you all about it when we get there - so you'd better get navigating for me - the sooner we get there the sooner I talk."

Felicity knew she was playing games. She was quite capable of driving and talking. Fancy not letting her in on it. *She* always told Ann *everything.*

*

After a while Felicity and Tracie had both given up trying to get anything out of Ann about Cedric. Tracie had dropped off to sleep on the back seat. She wasn't too tall, so her knee high plaster fitted there quite comfortably. Ann and Felicity talked about work. Even with Ann driving quite carefully so as not to wake Tracie it was less than a couple of hours before they were driving down South Street, Fordham.

Felicity always greeted this place with mixed feelings. Fordham was a lovely town, so picturesque and elegant, but Felicity had been one of those children who couldn't wait to leave childhood behind, who became much happier as an adult. She'd been a weekly boarder at a girls' school between Fordham and Haslemere, and she'd hated it. There had been a group of girls in her year who'd enjoyed tormenting anyone they thought was a bit different. She'd been so glad to leave. Her Fordham home had been a refuge at weekends and in holidays, but there was always the lurking spectre of the return to school, so even lovely Fordham had been coloured by her worry. She had asked her parents time and again to take her away, but they had refused because her father was convinced such places were good for character formation. He was wrong. It had turned her into the timid, pessimistic, somewhat naive adult she'd become. Although she loved him, she had never quite forgiven him.

Perhaps this time, with her parents elsewhere, and the light hearted Tracie as company, home might turn into the sort of place home should always be. They were at the gate now.

"Wow! I'd no idea you were so well heeled. This is magnificent," marvelled Tracie.

Felicity laughed. "I think the family was quite rich a couple of centuries back when the Stantons were here, but not any longer. My parents can't afford the upkeep. It needs masses doing to it. They've got it on the market. What the place needs is a rich stockbroker who will restore it."

She had opened the wrought iron gates which enclosed a small courtyard garden and a parking area in the front of the house.

The house stood in the main street of the little country town and was one of a row of many stately and beautiful early Georgian houses. Although they were all of the same basic design - each house was adorned with wonderful individual touches - all similar, yet all different. Felicity's home was the only one in the row with a front courtyard.

She closed the iron gates behind the car.

"I'm parched," she announced, "let's have a cup of tea before we do anything else. We can unpack the car later. I want to hear all about this Cedric business... now," - arriving on home territory seemed to have made her more assertive. They helped Tracie up the path to the front door. Tracie was a bit disappointed - she'd almost expected Felicity to get a huge rusty key out of her trouser pocket, but it was just an ordinary Yale and a mortice.

Felicity opened the black front door, which was flanked by two huge terracotta pots of gently fading hydrangeas, with evergreen shrubs flourishing in a small unpaved strip against the house walls. Brick cobbles had been laid in a curving pattern on each side of the path up to the front door. There was an iron boot scraper to the left of the door, and to the right an ancient bell push smoothed to a patina by nearly three centuries of use. On the wall to the left was a faded sign – Wisteria Lodge. Ann was able to be a bit more blase about Wisteria Lodge. She'd visited before, and had been brought up in an old Georgian rectory which was quite similar, but Tracie was enchanted.

Felicity's parents had only left two days previously and a neighbour had filled the short gap for feeding the two Persian cats. Nevertheless, the pair came rushing into the hall to greet them. They were both black, and both extremely furry.

"These are Freud and Jung," Felicity introduced them. "When you get to know them you'll be able to tell them apart. There's a loo just through the kitchen if anyone wants."

Felicity's mother had left plenty of basic supplies behind for them, including an enticing home made fruit cake. Felicity brewed a pot of tea and carried the laden tray through into a beautifully proportioned room. She was right, however - it was desperately in need of refurbishment, as was the whole house. In spite of that, the two sofas were pretty comfortable, and Tracie and Felicity dug in, ready to cross-examine Ann.

"So where did you meet him? On the stairs?" Felicity kicked off.

"No. I met him on the beach - quite a normal thing in Kingscove, wouldn't you say?"

"I can't imagine Cedric on the beach. Seems totally out of character," a disbelieving Tracie told her.

"Ah well," said Ann breezily - "it just shows how little you know him."

Eventually she relented and told them half of the truth.

"It was that night when your roof fell in, Felicity, and you rang me. By the time I got down you'd disappeared. I got really worked up when I saw your ceiling. There was no way I was going to get any sleep. The storm had calmed down so I decided to have a stroll on the beach. Cedric was down there sitting on a big piece of driftwood. He'd needed a bit of fresh air as well. We got talking and it just went from there. You know what a sucker I am for a dog collar."

"I don't think you're telling us the full tale," snorted Felicity as she went out to make a fresh pot of tea.

Ann shrugged nonchalantly.

*

Ann left straight after breakfast the next morning. Her excuse was work, but the real reason was she just didn't want to be away from him.

"It must be what they call chemistry," decided Tracie after she'd gone.

"No," replied Felicity gloomily, "it's more of a case of 'another good woman bites the dust.' I've never seen Ann like this. It really must be very serious. I find it quite depressing. Better change the subject - did you sleep alright?"

Felicity had assumed that Tracie would prefer to sleep on the sofabed in the downstairs study, but she'd had other ideas.

"I can go upstairs quite easily on my behind," she'd declared. So she'd bumped her way slowly up the very grand staircase - wide and weathered, a good solid banister rail at each side, and a large plain brass chandelier hanging above. It led, after a couple of turns, to a three-windowed, creaky floored landing, looking over South Street, with three large square bedrooms leading off.

"I don't know how you can take all this for granted," Tracie told Felicity. "Doesn't history have any effect on you?"

Felicity had replied that she'd always been much more interested in Maths and Science. Even when quite young she was hooked on numbers and most other girls at school had thought her weird because of it.

"But surely just because you prefer numbers doesn't mean you have to ignore the past?" suggested Tracie.

Felicity knew this really and had actually been wondering if it was a subconscious attempt to stand apart from the beautifully old Augustus House so that selling her flat would hurt less.

Ann had spent the night in Felicity's parents' room, which looked out over the back. Tracie's room was the one next to that, slightly smaller, with two windows and folding shutters. Like Ann's room, it looked down over the lovely rear garden.

Felicity's had a view over the street. She had only been a small girl when her Great Uncle Peter Stanton, who had lived in the house all his life, left it to his nephew, her father. She had been given a choice between the front room and the smaller of the two rear bedrooms. She had chosen the front. The light from the street lamps had been very comforting as she drifted off to sleep on winter nights. The rear outlook over the garden at night had always seemed black and threatening to her.

Tracie asked if her parents would be sad to go.

"Yes and no, I suppose," Felicity told her, "it bleeds them dry financially. There's always something that needs doing, and it can be freezing in winter - the central heating is woefully inefficient. Sorry. Forgot to ask. Did you sleep alright?"

Tracie assured her she'd slept wonderfully - much better than in hospital where there had been noise all night. All she'd heard here was the occasional shriek of a fox, and a couple of cats fighting.

"That reminds me," she went on, "there are these notes posted all over the house - quotations from Freud and

Jung. I thought they were the cats?"

Felicity rolled her eyes. How could she explain it without giving the impression that one of her parents was barking mad? Her mother had taken an Open University degree a while back and had become very interested in Psychology. She was now doing a PhD about the connections and disconnections between Freud and Jung. She posted quotations everywhere so that she could keep her mind working on their ideas while she did the household chores.

"She's not mad," she'd assured Tracie, "just a little zany"

"She doesn't sound mad to me," Tracie assured her. "Sounds quite resourceful. I get the feeling she and Professor Jeffries would get on pretty well. Which came first- the quotations or the cats?"

"We already had the cats when she started her PhD, but they were just rescued kittens then called Scrap and Fluff. As they got older they seemed to develop serious sides and Mum decided such lightweight names no longer suited them. She felt it was a bit like calling the Archbishop of Canterbury Basil Brush. Because they were always squabbling and falling out, like Freud and Jung, she thought that's what she'd call them." Felicity looked at her watch, "I suppose I'd better get Dad's car out. Hope it starts. We've got to get you to the hospital in Guildford for 11.30."

*

Life decided to treat them very well that morning. The car started, and the hospital turned out to be very efficient.

"Your wounds must like the Surrey air," said the nurse who looked after Tracie, "they're definitely doing well. The doctor doesn't think you'll need to come daily after all. Can you make an appointment for Thursday at 11.30 on the way out. See you then."

The Appointments Desk was at the far end of the Outpatients' Hall, just where it linked with the Accidents and Emergencies Waiting Room. Felicity idly cast her glance over the people sitting in A and E while she waited for Tracie who was at the Appointments Desk.

Suddenly she stiffened and put her hand on the counter to steady herself. It couldn't be, could it? Yes - she'd recognise that corngold pony tail anywhere. Paul was sitting crouched despondently in A and E. What on earth was he doing there?

As she watched, a nurse called his name. He stood up, obviously in considerable pain, and walked slowly towards the nurse. Felicity could see his face now. It was swollen and bruised, with both eyes quarter closed. He must have had a terrible accident, she thought, her heart starting to go out to him.. Tracie had finished her business at the desk and was also looking at him.

"Well," Felicity heard her murmur, "he's finally got his just deserts, has he?"

"That's a bit cruel, Tracie. Look at the poor man," remonstrated Felicity.

"Poor man, my foot," replied Tracie," You must be the only person in Kingscove who doesn't know what he's been up to. He's been knocking off a bloke and the bloke's mother at the same time. I think she lives near Godalming. I reckon the bloke must have popped down unexpectedly from London to see Mum and caught them at it. You only get in a state like that if you've been beaten up. You've got to hand it to him, though, he's always game. There he is looking like a badly treated giant panda and he can still put on the charm. Just see the way that nurse is dimpling at him."

She was right - Paul seemed to be coming up to top form in spite of everything.

Tracie looked at Felicity. Felicity looked at Tracie. They just managed to get outside before their self control went haywire. Tracie gave way first and began to giggle. Felicity tried hard not to, but Tracie's laughter was so infectious. She could feel the sharp pain that one gets in the corner of one's mouth when one tries hard not to laugh. She fought it as long as she could, but gave in eventually. A wonderful wave of hilarious relief washed all over her as she and Tracie laughed helplessly. Everytime she managed to stop she'd catch Tracie's eye and off she'd go again.

"Come on," she eventually managed to get out, "let's go and find somewhere to eat."

"I didn't realise you knew him well," said Felicity as they drove home hoping to find a nice pub for lunch on the way.

"He was in my year at Uni. He and Martin had Philosophy lectures together. Martin did joint Theology and Philosophy. Apparently Paul made two or three passes at Martin. Martin always said he held him off. Who knows? Paul was notorious even then - mainly men, but women close seconds. I didn't want to say so when you told me about your encounter. You were upset enough as it was. Bet it's done you good to laugh about it."

*

"I'm really intrigued by these cats," announced Tracie, pouring herself another cup of coffee. They'd had a very good pub lunch and were now finishing it off at home with coffee and cake in the back garden.

The back of the house was almost as grand as the front. If you stood half way down the central garden path you had a splendid view of the rear facade, perfectly flat, perfectly proportioned - almost like a dolls' house for giants.

It was a very cleverly designed garden. Two separate paths invited one to explore, each seeming to stretch forever. The path down the middle was broad and sunny. One could imagine walking on and on down it until one just disappeared into the distance. The other was more of a secret path, going in exactly the same direction but hugging an old high bricked wall, with ancient espaliered fruit trees, their branches knotted and intertwined and now overgrown by a tangled layer of thin rope-like ivy branches.

Freud was lying in the sun next to Tracie, rolling over and over in lazy slow ecstasy. Jung had gone prowling stealthily down the secret path.

"It's a good idea to call them after psychoanalysts - stroking them is immensely therapeutic," went on Tracie, stroking Freud gently behind his ears.

She'd decided not to tell Felicity about his other therapeutic intervention because it's not polite to let your hostess know that your sleep has been anything less than perfect. She'd had a very restless stage in the small hours. She'd been lying worrying about the state of her face. She wasn't specially vain, but the fear of being badly scarred for life did, unsurprisingly, bother her, and at night things can get so out of proportion. There was a limit, she kept telling herself, to how much of her life she could spend hidden inside a Teddy Bear suit.

At the height of her tossing and turning she'd felt a light stroking on her face. At first she'd assumed it was her imagination, but when she'd switched on the bedside light there was Freud, staring anxiously at her, carefully washing a paw, then gently stroking her face and lulling her into a calm and dreamless sleep.

*

When they'd drained the coffee pot Felicity decided she'd better make a start on what she'd been putting off. She'd promised her mother she would clear all her childhood junk out of the attic ready for selling the house.

"I can fix up the swinging hammock for you out here, and you can read or have a doze while I get on with it. Jung seems to have done a bunk, but Freud will keep you company."

Tracie preferred to bump her way up to the attic, via the second floor with its five smaller unused bedrooms.

"You're going to wear the seat out of those pants," laughed Felicity.

Right at the very top, up a final steep flight of narrow stairs, was a huge dust-encrusted, junk- infested attic.

Someone, Felicity's mother most likely, had made a start on clearing it, but there was certainly plenty more to keep Felicity busy. Several attic rooms stretched right through the roof space. Felicity decided to begin in the room she'd always used most. Tracie hauled herself into an old chair which looked as if it had stood in the same place for at least a hundred years, and prepared to supervise.

Jung was nowhere to be seen, but Felicity was sure he must be there, watching them, deeply enjoying knowing that they could not watch him. There was something decidedly creepy about Jung, she always thought. Her mother reckoned that if it wasn't for the fact that Freud and Jung occasionally appeared together she would think they were the same cat, and that Jung was Freud's shadow, his alter ego - but Felicity felt that this was just because this would fit so well with Jungian ideas.

There were some old rickety shelves which seemed to be piled with vaguely familiar looking books. She started looking through them and making piles for disposal. The piles grew very slowly because she kept getting sidetracked by the hoardings of her childhood - old photos, letters and sprigs of pressed flowers , which kept fluttering from between the pages. .

Tracie and Freud had both gone to sleep. It was very still up there. Felicity began to feel ill at ease. It was as if there was another invisible presence, not just Jung - as if some poor soul had been dumped there along with the dusty old files and books a long, long time ago.

This is daft, she told herself, a cup of tea is what's needed. She looked around. Where on earth was there to put a tea tray? There was a duster lying on the bookshelf where she was working and she used it to clean up the top of a table standing nearby, ready for the tea things.

When she came back up with the tray she temporarily set it down ahead of her on the floor just inside the attic area while she hauled herself in up the few last steep steps. She looked into the room. Freud and Tracie were still asleep, but Jung had at last appeared from hiding.

What *is* he doing? she wondered. And then she realised. He was intently rubbing himself against and around someone's legs in that way cats have – except that there was no one there. He lifted his front paws off the ground, nudging his face against someone's stroking hand - but there was no one there. Finally he looked up and began to communicate with someone in a string of knowing miaows. There was *definitely* no one there.

She picked up the tray to put it on the table, but she couldn't, because the space which she had carefully cleared was full. She *knew* that nothing had been there when she'd gone downstairs to make the tea.

She just managed not to drop the tray, but Freud and Tracie were both awakened by her cry of unnerved amazement.

Chapter 22

"It merely confirms what I've always felt about cats. No wonder the Ancient Egyptians revered them." Hubert paused to take an appreciative sip of the Assam tea which seemed suddenly to have become Abigail's new passion. He must ask her, he thought, what had become of her addiction to coffee..

They were in the kitchen area of Abigail's sitting room, where Hubert was bringing her up to date on the Augustus saga. He had just arrived back in his old rattletrap of a car from a long and hectic day in Fordham. He hardly ever used his car in \Kingscove as he could walk or bus just about anywhere, but he still stubbornly held on to it, and kept it in a rented garage a couple of streets away. It always amazed Abigail how easily it would start, given that it got so very few outings and that Hubert knew not the slightest thing about a car's innerds.

"Come and sit down and tell me all about your day," said Abigail, as she led him through into her sitting area. Felicity had rung Abigail the previous evening asking Hubert's help, and naturally he hadn't needed two invitings. Abigail had expected him to be more tired than he appeared, but she supposed he was running on excitement.

Strangely, he seemed more interested in the two cats, who apparently played a major part in the story.

"I cannot tell you how interesting they are. You know, I'm sure, what Mark Twain said is so true - *if we were crossed with cats we would greatly improve, and the cats would deteriorate.* These two are so intelligent, and so wondrously devious. I have to admit that I'm torn between the fascinating find in Felicity's attic, and the exploits of Freud and Jung - although a big part of me suspects that the cats and the find may be inextricably linked together."

"It does sound very interesting," murmured Abigail, her eyes glazing in preparation for a long evening of Hubertian pontifications. She felt a bit frail tonight as it was. One can be so wrong. As soon as he'd drunk his tea Hubert made his excuses and left. He just could not wait to settle down at the table in his garden summerhouse to peruse his borrowed treasures. He took a coat to combat the definite evening chill and climbed the stairs to the roof, consumed with anticipation.

His hands trembled with excitement as he began to sift through the bundle. There were several fading sepia photographs, some greetings cards, and a large bunch of what looked like letters, tied up with lavender ribbon, the edges of the yellowed paper gradually disintegrating into shreds of near-powder.

Which should he start on? The cards? The letters ? He knew he was almost certainly about to find out a lot more about Augustus.

Hubert was aware that letters and cards had been the only channels through which young Victorian lovers could convey their passions and emotions to each other in a world where strict convention normally forbade such openness. Once people became engaged it was permissible to communicate, on paper, heart to heart. So here on the table in his rooftop study he knew lay treasure trove indeed.

Hubert had decided he would take no notes at this first reading. He would peruse everything and then sleep on it all, and start in earnest the next day.

This could not have come at a better time. Yesterday he had accepted an invitation to be visiting Professor in Victorian Poetry at Joseph Banks University in Greenmount, Victoria, Australia. He hadn't told Abigail yet. He wasn't looking forward to the ten or twelve weeks away from her that it would entail and he had agonised over the decision for quite some time. Eventually he'd decided he couldn't let such an opportunity slip away. He hadn't asked her opinion. He'd known that she would just tell him in that non-committal rather hurtful way of hers that only he could decide. Perhaps he was hoping that absence might make the heart grow fonder.

One of the obligations of the Visiting Professorship was to give the James Salter Memorial Lecture. James Salter, Professor of English Literature at Joseph Banks for most of the 1970's and 80's, had been a renowned specialist in nineteenth century poetry. At an earlier stage he had been Hubert's tutor at Cambridge, and had had a big influence on his development. Hubert had been racking his brains hoping to hit on a fresh approach to make his lecture special. He read on eagerly, luxuriating in the thought that he might be going to find what he needed.

It seemed that the Stantons had come to \Kingscove for a late summer stay by the sea, and had taken one of the houses on Regent's Parade. Mrs Booth had met Mrs Stanton at the home of a mutual friend. Naturally the Stantons were invited to the next musical evening at Augustus House... and that had been that. Augustus and Emily had looked at each other and the bittersweet chemistry of love had transformed them. Putting two and two together while reading the letters, Hubert gleaned that Augustus and Emily were anxious to marry at once. Major Stanton, though not critical of Augustus in any major way, had decreed that they should wait a year, although he had reluctantly allowed an engagement.

Hubert found several half finished poems which he decided had been written by Emily. They were a mass of alterations - obviously eventually tossed aside in frustrated disgust. Poetry didn't seem to be her medium. She didn't have Augustus' talent for capturing eternal truths in two or three words but, although her poems were clumsily crafted they still had a profound effect on Hubert. He could feel her incipient anguish. She must already have sensed Death's messengers slowly invading her, strangling her creativity.

An uninvited tear fell upon the yellowed paper. Hubert was secretly soft hearted. He tried very hard to compensate, and consequently many people got quite the wrong impression of him.

Sadly, there seemed to be no poems from Augustus- just lots of letters from a young man languishing in love. Some of the letters spoke of his writing, of how he was struggling with new ideas and how his poetry had dried up. One letter seemed to be written whilst he was composing 'Fragments of the Sea'. Hubert was fairly certain that this had been Augustus' last poem, wrestled with for a long time and not completed till just before his death. He still hoped that one day he would find a copy of it.

His visiting cats always sensed his presence in the roof garden. One was on his lap now, the other sprawled across the table. Hubert began to sift through the photographs. There were several of Augustus, one with an older woman whom Hubert supposed was his mother. Hubert knew that Henry Booth had been very much into all things modern so it was likely that he had encouraged all the family to be photographed. Then he turned over one which showed Emily, easily recognisable because of her resemblance to the girl in the painting they'd found at the séance, with a rather pretty older woman and an army officer. Major Stanton had quite a serious severe face.

Yes, thought Hubert, I am sure you would be highly suspicious of love at first sight.

Suddenly the cats leapt up and were gone. Their acute hearing must have picked up a distant call of 'Dinner!' Hubert shivered. He was surprised to find how cold and dark it was getting, and realised he was becoming in need of his own dinner. He carefully gathered everything up and went downstairs. Tomorrow he would start work in earnest. He rang Abigail. "I've got some very nice looking sausages which I found in an old-fashioned butcher's in Fordham. Do you fancy bangers and mash?"

*

"So what did you make of the ghost in the attic?" Abigail sat at Hubert's kitchen table sipping sherry while she watched him cook. Watching other people cook was one of her favourite pastimes. "Imagination or reality?"

"Who knows," replied Hubert. "I thought about it a lot on the way home. If it was just that Felicity picked up a random selection of things without realising, which all turned out to be highly relevant, and then put them down without thinking on the table she'd cleared for the tea, then that certainly was a huge coincidence. But such things do happen – perhaps rarely, but they do.

Felicity told me that she's always been aware of something in that house . All very fascinating

He turned off the hob. "These are ready, Abigail. Would you like a glass of wine?"

Abigail decided she'd just carry on with her sherry. She had a nagging feeling that she might be sickening for something and wasn't even sure if she'd finish that.

First, Assam tea, and now sherry, he thought. What *is* happening to her?

The mash was even nicer than the bangers. He had mashed the potatoes with pesto and a little extra olive oil. She wasn't able to do them full justice and felt a bit guilty.

"I'm just taking my time, and savouring them," she assured him. "I've been meaning to tell you. I've decided what to do with my lottery windfall. First of all I'm going to lend it to Augustus House, so that James can make an immediate start on the roof. I shall get everyone to sign that they'll pay me back by late summer, and then in the autumn I'm going to Australia."

Hubert half choked on his mouthful of food. "Australia? Any special reason?"

"I'm going to look for my brother, John. I expect he will still be living there. My mother may still be alive too, but I especially want to find my brother. You seem to be somewhat amused, Hubert?"

"Well, yes," he admitted, "we've just been talking about big coincidences, and now here's another. You're off to Australia in the autumn, and so am I!"

*

Abigail's head was aching dreadfully, but every time she closed her eyes a huge computer screen demanded her attention. The computer was using a strange operating system and some essential part of it was malfunctioning. Emails rushed in non-stop and she just could not see straight enough to answer them. Every time she tried to use the mouse the whole screen jumped, and the emails would turn upside down then self- delete in a long rushing line across the screen. She was getting nowhere, no matter how hard she tried. She seemed to be working in an office and her boss was becoming extremely annoyed because she wasn't making any progress. Although she couldn't see him she knew it was God, but somehow, at the same time, it was Hubert..

Mrs Milburn seemed to be the tea lady. She didn't look one bit like Mrs Milburn, but Abigail knew that it was definitely she.. God wanted Assam tea, but Mrs Milburn had none left on her trolley. God was getting exceedingly grumpy about it - not behaving in the way one might expect the Deity to behave at all. He demanded that Mrs Milburn go out to the corner shop to buy some. She was having great difficulty in convincing him that she couldn't, because they were deep under the North Sea. The apparently long discussed project for a tunnel between Newcastle and Norway had finally come to fruition and today was the inaugural journey. That must be why God was on board. Abigail was the train driver who had to shoulder the responsibility of this first historic journey, whilst trying vainly to answer God's emails at the same time.

There was a loud insistent ringing. At first she thought

it was a recording of church bells but it turned out to be the signal for lunch. Andrew came in to her driver's cabin cum office, which seemed to have elastically expanding walls. He was wearing his purser's uniform and he began to serve lunch to God - spaghetti bolognaise topped with a sprinkling of coconut and grated paracetamol, along with a nettle and swede salad in a cocoa dressing, followed by spinach and banana trifle.

God complained loudly, "Just because this muck is your favourite food, Eliot, it doesn't mean I have to eat it."

At this point Abigail realised that not only was God Hubert, but her irascible Grandfather as well - a strange Trinity indeed - God, God the Hubert And God the Grandfather. God the Three in One aboard the North Sea Star hurled his main course out of the train window. There was a resounding splash, which shouldn't have happened. An alarmed Abigail could see water steadily rising up towards the open part of the train window. The wonderful new North Sea tunnel was leaking, its tiled walls with mosaic pictures of Geordie and Nordic gods - Alan Shearer, Woden, Cardinal Hume, Greig, Sting, Thor, Bobby Robson, Abba, Gazza... slowly disappearing under a dark watery blanket.

God began intoning a strange prayer:

"Rout out the dross,

Consign it to the heap..."

as his pudding followed his spaghetti out of the window.

A terror stricken Mrs Milburn began to shout, "Let my Freddie drive. Let my Freddie drive!" as she pushed forward a weedy man standing next to her.

Abigail asserted herself, "Freddie cannot drive. Freddie

is dead."

"What has that got to do with it?" screamed Mrs Milburn.

"This is a daytime train," insisted Abigail, "dead drivers only drive at night."

She summoned superhuman strength to heave the Milburns back into the passenger coaches, slam the door on them and pull the huge lever marked Uncoupling.

She could feel the lessening of the train's load as the passenger coaches hurtled backwards at bullet speed. Maybe they'd resurface near the Tyne Bridge whence they had come: maybe they'd be lost forever on the North Sea bed. Abigail found she didn't care. There was a thunderous noise from above. The tunnel was cracking and breaking. The driver's cabin was sucked into the vortex of swirling water and splintering concrete. It shot up and up into the turbulent brilliance of a North Sea morning. The light hurt her eyes, and she was drenched in sweat. Hubert was mopping her brow with iced water.

"I think that's the worst of the fever past, Hubert," Andrew told him. "Poor Abigail," he continued, "you *have* had a rough old time." Andrew was trying to appear sympathetic and reassuring, but only succeeded in looking fearfully worried.

*

For days Abigail was almost too frightened to sleep lest she re-experienced her dream. When she was well enough to recount it to the others even Hubert had been reduced to laughter - he did not often find himself equated with God. Abigail tried to find it funny, but it had been awful at the time.

"It was the fever, Abigail," Andrew tried to reassure her, "you don't normally have nightmares. It'll never happen again." And after two or three nights of dreamless sleep she did begin to relax.

Of course, unbeknown to Andrew, Abigail *did* normally have nightmares. Hubert, in his bedroom above, frequently heard her. That was how he had realised she was wrestling in the throes of illness. He had been so worried that he had called out a doctor. Once the doctor had assured herself that Abigail was not developing meningitis or pneumonia she had issued the usual instructions- most likely a bad flu, put a cold compress on her forehead, try to get her to drink, ring me again if she worsens - and left. Hubert and Andrew had spent a distraught night while Abigail hallucinated her way under the North Sea.

Once she was convinced she could sleep without her nightmare returning she began to enjoy her convalescence. She was thoroughly spoilt by all and sundry and found she could get quite accustomed to breakfast in bed. She decided to relax and just enjoy the loving practical help that all of Augustus House offered.

She had a naturally robust constitution and it was wonderful to feel herself improving every day. Each morning Hubert would bring in a newspaper and her mail. On one occasion there was a letter with a Tyne and Wear postmark, the address written in a faltering, spidery hand which she did not at first recognise. It was from Mrs Evans.

Hollybanks Rest Home,

April 17th.

Dear Lorna,

I wasn't sure if I should write to tell you this. Mrs Milburn has died. She never really seemed to recover from Freddie's death. It upset her much more than she let on. I think everything that happened probably upset her deep down. I knew her all her life. She always had a nasty streak. She must have been born like that. Perhaps we should just try to think that she couldn't help it.

Remember what I keep telling you and try not to let her spoil the rest of your life. She has gone now.

I don't want any of that money. I've always been a saver and I have a bit put by. If I have too much saved they will just take it away to pay for my care. You have it. I'm quite lucky on the lottery. I often win small amounts.

I hope you will come to see me soon. Bring that nice man you told me about. Harold, was it?

Happy Easter, Love,

Doreen Evans xxxx

Abigail felt a little strange, as the emotions she felt weren't what she would have expected. The anger, the resentment were no longer uppermost. She felt relief, and almost a lack of interest - a sort of mental shrugging of the shoulders.

"Should I feel guilty that I am so relieved by Mrs Milburn's death?" she asked Hubert later that morning.

"Did you actively wish her dead?"

"No, of course not!" There was a touch of indignation in her reply, "I just feel…" she searched for the word,

"...uninvolved."

It was as if her own personal albatross had floated away into the North Sea at the end of a very long tunnel.

Well, Hubert consoled her, relief was not the same as pleasure, nor was lack of involvement.

He thought her reaction might be similar to that of Macbeth when he heard that his wife had died. He was up to his ears in the mess he felt she'd landed him in and he was far too busy concentrating on his own salvation to spend time thinking about her - *"She should have died hereafter."*

That made some sense, she thought. Of course, she would much rather none of it had ever happened, but she was at last beginning to feel proud of the way she had put her life back together. She certainly hadn't been a failure. If none of it had happened she would most probably have left school as early as possible. The shop had never provided her family with much of a living. They'd eaten well but were always strapped for actual cash. All spare resources would have been channelled into John - he had been quite bright, just badly lacking in skills of social engagement. She would certainly never have gone to University if she had been at home, but she had been given the chance to do her A Levels while she was detained, and that had made it relatively easier to progress to getting a degree after she was released. If she'd not been accused she would most likely have worked in the shop - perhaps taken it over from her parents. She would have had to cope with financial crisis as the supermarkets gradually forced corner shops out of business. She would never have ended up in Kingscove, never have met Hubert... steady on! she thought.

"Hubert," she found herself saying, "I've had an idea.

When we go to Australia, shall we go a week or so before you're due to take up post? Have some time to sightsee together?"

He did his best to look relatively indifferent.

"That's not a bad idea," he told her.

Chapter 23

Cedric was deep into another of his regular agony sessions, but with one very useful modification - Ann, who had taken a day off, was there, chairing. At least there would be no risk this time of his rushing, panic stricken into the sea. He'd been thrown into consternation earlier in the afternoon when he'd got the call from his friend in high places, asking if he would be interested in having his name put forward as a possible candidate to be the next Dean of Norchester.

"It's only a first stage, old chap," his friend had explained, "it more or less goes like this - if you're interested then your name would join a list which the Prime Minister's Appointments Secretary will be discussing with the Bishop. Then they make a shortlist which goes to the Prime Minister, who recommends someone to Her Majesty. You're not deeply committing yourself - just decide whether you'd like your name to go forward for discussion. Let me know by Monday, OK? Must go. Sorry." And he rang off.

Monday!!! And it was Friday already. So here they were, deep in gin and thought.

"But could I really do it?" He was pacing up and down.

"Will you grow up," she demanded, "of course you can do it. That's not your dilemma at all. Do you *want* to do it?"

Cedric didn't really know what he wanted, although he knew what he didn't want. He'd had enough of the university, enough of dry as dust theology. The entire course needed a drastic overhaul, but as there were strong suspicions that the Professor of Theology had been at school with Abraham the chances of any modernisation were more than remote.

If only Cedric had felt a little more secure in his own faith he would have had no hesitation about going ahead, but he thought it would be dishonest to aim at an important post in such a stronghold of Christian faith as a cathedral given his present personal doubts and reservations. He started trying to explain this to Ann, but the gin on an empty stomach was beginning to have too much effect.

"Do sit down, Cedric," she begged, "all this prowling about is making me feel giddy. Isn't there anyone in the ministry you could speak to about this? Someone you could trust? It must be much more common than you think. Surely you're not the first clergyman to feel this way."

He'd actually had a long heart to heart with an old colleague he'd run into at a conference a few months back. This man had suggested he might be suffering from burnout.

When he recounted this to Ann, to his surprise, she nodded emphatically.

"You said you got really worn out by your parish work," she reminded him, "and that's why you took the university job."

"But that's five years ago," Cedric bit his lip. "I should surely be over it by now."

Physically perhaps, Ann agreed, but she wasn't sure, she told him, if the university job had done all that much to replenish his spiritual side.

"I've been meaning to tell you," she went on, "do you remember the Bishop about 20 years ago who caused a furore when the media twisted his words round to make him sound a total heretic? He'd been trying to get people to look at the resurrection in a different way."

Cedric nodded.

"Well," she went on, "I found one of his books in my bookcase the other day. You know how you buy books that look interesting but then you never get round to reading them? I took it with me on the train that day I had to go to Plymouth. It was so interesting. I think you and he might agree on lots of things." She fished a sheet of paper out of her handbag, "This is his declaration of faith -

I believe that there is something at the centre of things, caring about, and striving for holiness, for spirituality. I believe in the blazing beauty of justice, peace and love.-

Do you believe that?"

"Of course I do," Cedric replied, almost indignantly.

"Well, start from there. You've got to stop this self torturing business. You did your job too well. I reckon you very narrowly escaped a complete nervous breakdown. Your own good sense took you to the university for a breather. The fact that you're now taking this so seriously tells me that you're ready to dip your toe back in the water, re-enter the fray. So stop the agony bit - I sometimes think it turns you on, you know - and just get on with it."

She threw his jacket at him. "Come on," she nagged, "curry time. We need to soak up all this gin. Sleep on it. You can decide tomorrow. And for goodness sake, try to realise it's exciting. People think you're good. They want to promote you."

Even when Ann was a little girl she'd been almost too skilled at telling people how to run their lives. She would stand in the rectory kitchen looking up at her big brother, and laying down the law about what he should do - and more often than not he would do it - because even then she was usually right.

*

As one might imagine, Ann was a very early riser, and she had a protesting Cedric bundled on board the 7.34 London train next morning. Over their curry they'd sorted out a strategy. He'd go up to Norchester for the day on Saturday, have a good look around, come back to London and stay the night in Ann's loft. Then, on Sunday, he'd decide. Ann couldn't go with him to Norchester as she'd a clutch of appointments booked with people who never had a spare minute Monday to Friday.

It was a rather pleasant April morning, but even so Cedric was surprised to find so many people travelling from London on his train to Norchester. After a while it dawned - Norchester Wanderers were playing at home. He brightened up. Norchester's nickname, he remembered, was The Canons. That must surely signal that the city bore a measure of affection for its cathedral. Perhaps the Dean might…

Cedric had not even told Ann yet about his footballing past. As a boy he had had a trial for the local team in the Hertfordshire town where he'd grown up. When his father, a local doctor, had discovered, he was furious with Cedric, and horrified. He was too late to stop the trial, but he assured his son that if the team made him an offer there was absolutely no chance that he would allow him to take it up. Dr Wright was determined that only a professional post, preferably as a doctor, would be suitable for his only son.

Long dead, he might have been amazed to discover how much footballers earned nowadays, and how highly they were revered by a sizeable section of the population - veritable modern Medicine Men. Cedric's trial, to his great disappointment, was unsuccessful, but at least a massive rift in the Wright household was averted.

Dr Wright was no longer around to curb his son's passion for the beautiful game. I could get re-involved, thought Cedric, with ridiculous excitement - not as a team member - Crockchester Wanderers would be about his level these days - but he wondered if they had a chaplain...

He'd kept his football up at Oxford, and then at Theological College, even though his friends teased him about the incongruity of a footballing cleric. He'd pointed out that there'd been a famous Test cricketer Bishop and no one had found that funny - pure snobbery, he'd declared - cricket for the nobs, soccer for the plebs.

Sadly, there'd come a time when he'd had at last to admit to himself that he'd never set the pitch on fire. He still couldn't bear to hang up his boots, so he'd qualified as a referee. This made his friends laugh even louder, so he told them that if it was good enough for Shostakovitch... They laughed louder still.

He hadn't reffed a game for years now, and his boots and kit were hidden away in the little room he rented at the Self Storage Centre on the hill going up to the racecourse, but seeing the Norchester fans in their black and white shirts, keen and ready to go, did set him yearning.

A lot of people seem to harbour intriguing secrets, and the residents of Augustus House were no exception. There was Hubert, mother's little psychic helper, Tracie, purveyor of painful delights, Cedric, in a league of his own, and Abigail, with her darker, more distressing burden.

The express train was out of London now. When the trolley came round he thankfully grabbed a sandwich and a bottle of orange juice. He marvelled always at Ann's energy which sometimes seemed linked with a total disinterest in food. Spending a lot of time with her was quite an effective diet. She certainly wasn't anorexic - last evening in Kashmiri Nights she'd eaten very well indeed - but if she was doing something which required her whole attention she was able to go for hours and not give food a thought. That, and intelligence, he decided proudly, were the secret of her success.

He so wanted her to be as proud of him as he was of her, and would have been amazed if he'd known that she already held him in pretty high esteem. He saw himself as a dithering cleric, with a shaky faith and substantial human weaknesses, who had made a success of very little he'd undertaken. She saw him as a learned theological scholar, and a successful inner city parish priest. She had met many of his friends by now and knew all about how skilfully and selflessly he had undertaken everything he had tackled, wearing himself out in the process. She loved the way he could fit in effortlessly with people of every type, and his gift for preaching impressed her greatly. As for what he saw as his substantial human weaknesses - well - they were the things which had first attracted her to him, and she found some of them quite delicious.

By the time he'd eaten his sandwich they were in the Norchester suburbs and he made his way along with the fans to the carriage door. He couldn't wait to look this city over.

He'd read up all he could find about it on the internet the previous night. One thing had stuck in his mind - apparently no directions would be needed to find the cathedral. Built on raised ground, it stood high above the relatively small city, and it was blessed with one of the highest and most beautiful spires in the land.

Sure enough there it was, standing like a proud parent guarding its children. He hurried down the road from the station feasting his eyes upon it in admiration. It was hard to concentrate on the more mundane things like uneven paving stones and traffic lights. The only entrance to the Cathedral close seemed to be through a mediaeval arch with a huge wooden door, wide open at present. Cedric assumed it would have been locked tight shut at dusk in the Cathedral's early days - he'd read about murderous feuds and riots between monks and townspeople then. He wondered if it was still locked at night - say at midnight. He smiled to himself, imagining Ann, driving up to stay after some late night city function and battering indignantly on the ancient oak door. What a reputation the new Dean would gain in the twinkling of an eye. No, he was afraid the only solution should he become Dean would be for him to make an honest woman of her.

He'd already decided that was what he wanted anyway - more than anything else, wherever he was working, wherever he was living - but would that be what *she* wanted? He would never dare ask her because if she refused then he knew that things between them could never be quite the same again.

The cathedral was dedicated to St. Botolph and people had worshipped on the site since the area's first acquaintance with Christianity in the seventh century. He stood quite still in the nave, soaking up the atmosphere. It was impossible, he felt, to ignore the spirituality and timelessness of the place. One became part of the hundreds of years of joys, of tragedies, of wisdom.

Cedric knew that even some of his non-believing friends experienced similar feelings.

One had told him that there seemed to be a pair of invisible arms in a cathedral which wound themselves around him and gathered him up into a world of wisdom and tranquillity. Admittedly that had been one Christmas Eve, not quite roasting chestnuts by an open fire, but sipping an extremely affable cognac after a splendid meal with close friends. He'd asked Cedric if this was perhaps what Christians were getting at when they talked about holiness.

Cedric had quoted Philip Larkin at him :

A serious house, on serious earth… which… was proper to grow wise in…

Norchester Cathedral, Cedric felt, was somewhere in which he might grow wiser and, hopefully, holier.

All these worthy thoughts were making him feel hungry again so he retreated to the Crypt cafe for a quick bite of lunch before doing a proper investigation of the Cathedral Close. He was keen to find the Dean's house and take a photo of it to show Ann. It was undeniably a splendid Close, although some of the larger houses, including an extremely handsome one which looked as if it might once have been the Bishop's Palace were now being rented out as offices - sad in one sense, but the money generated had obviously been used to keep these buildings in pristine condition. They fairly sparkled. Between two of them stood a solid brick building in that plain eighteenth century style which is so unfailingly elegant. On the white porticoed front door was a discreet old brass nameplate - The Deanery. This house was neat and beautiful in a workmanlike way . He liked it and he took a couple of photos to show to Ann.

Cedric walked right round the close, discovering in the process that it was possible to gain vehicle access through another lovely entrance, an arch, but without a door to lock Ann out. Right by it was a path leading towards another entrance to the cathedral, through the cloisters.

Previous Deans must have been very important for the life of this cathedral, judging from the tablets and plaques dedicated to them on the walls. If he ever held this post might he, he wondered, perhaps aspire to being loved like:-

The Reverend John Michael Sanderson D.D.

The greatly loved and much missed Dean of this Cathedral from 1925 - 1935.

And in memory also of his devoted wife Mary, died 25.11.1939.

Give thanks for their commitment to the welfare of all, both in the Cathedral, and throughout the Diocese.

Stand up, and bless the Lord.

*

He decided he ought to make a lightning whistle stop tour of the surrounding area, but it turned out to be much like the area round the cathedral in almost any cathedral city - genteel, with ancient cottages, dainty tearooms and upmarket gift shops. The quiet atmosphere was blasted every now and then by roars of distant jubilant noise. The Canons were definitely having a good game.

Time to turn back, he thought. He really didn't want to miss Evensong, which, he always felt, was the yardstick by which the life of a cathedral should be judged and measured.

For the second time that day he made for the Crypt Cafe, footsore from his tramping around and wearied by his unaccustomed early start. The service was at 4pm. Just time for a cup of tea. The actual cafe occupied one corner of the vast space. The remaining area seemed to be used as a huge recreation room, where people could eat their sandwiches, write their postcards, rest their feet. The usual suspects sat about on a collection of old pews and trestle tables - gaggles of energetic old ladies on afternoon coach tours from the far flung outposts of this reputedly largest English diocese, knots of high pitched children, their leaders looking on the far, far side of worn out, and tireless parties of Japanese showing off to each other their souvenir purchases from the shop before stowing them away in their neat little backpacks.

Everything echoed. Chairs scraping across the stone flags echoed; the constant clattering of cups and saucers echoed; talking, laughing, excited childish screaming, mobile ringtones - they all echoed. Most of all the crescendoes of the Norchester choir and the mighty organ echoed from the last minute practice in the cathedral above his head.

Cedric knew it was a ridiculous contradiction in terms, yet he could only describe the atmosphere as one of noisy calm - a place to be noisy and a place to be still - a place for all people, with the organ and choir soaring again and again, their glorious sound drowning the cacophony below.

Time to get organised, Cedric decided, getting up and clearing his crockery and tray to the shelved trolley in the corner.

"Jolly good cheesecake," he told the waitress who was cleaning tables ready to close.

"Thank you, sir. The Bishop's wife makes it," she responded, "I'll tell her."

Cedric grinned to himself. He hated to think what Ann's baking skills might be like!

Upstairs the normal quiet of the Cathedral prevailed. Cedric's heart trembled with anticipation as he was shown to a seat in the choir stalls. How could Evensong, celebrated day in, day out for hundreds of years, manage to maintain this magical atmosphere of tranquillity and optimism.

He gave himself up into the service ...*O Lord, open thou our lips...*

*

The hoped for snooze on the train back to London proved out of the question. He was just too full of his day out. Thought after thought raced through his mind. Should he ask for his name to go forward? Was he up to it?

Should he wait? He just didn't know.

The train was full of euphoric Wanderers supporters. This was their first season in the Premiership and they were doing so well. Cedric had a table seat next to three of them, and gradually he was drawn into their conversation. By the time the train pulled in to St. Pancras he knew all there was to know about each brilliant save, the two stupendous goals, and all the rest.

That evening Ann found that it was much easier than she'd feared to persuade him to let his name go forward.

It can't last, she thought. He's bound to agonise about it all night.

And he, too, had expected to lie tossing and turning, but when Ann came in about fifteen minutes later he was already asleep.

Chapter 24

"What do you mean, I can't build an amusement arcade there? On my *own* land?" someone was demanding indignantly.

Abigail looked up in curiosity from her task of organising the dishes of food on her worktop. It wasn't a voice she immediately recognised.

"I'm beginning to think you're making these rules up as you go along," it continued.

"I certainly am not, Stephen," came Hubert's patiently pompous reply to the protester, "if you look on Page Five in the instruction book you will find it clearly stated that you cannot do that. You *cannot* establish a commercial venture like a traditional seaside amusement arcade in a residential area . There are far too many people round this table cheating. If there are rules they should be obeyed."

Abigail smiled gleefully. Her Kingscove SeaSaw Party was hotting up beautifully. She loved it when players started to get irate.

Ever since she'd played SeaSaw at home when quite a small girl she had delighted in how it seemed to bring out the worst (or was it the best?) in everyone. Her mother, who never really wanted to play, had always contrived to be knocked out early, and would then retire to sulk. She had that puritanical streak which seems to force people not to enjoy themselves.

On the other hand, Abigail, her father, and her brother John would play on for the rest of the evening. They would lie and cheat, and eventually end the game in one glorious squabble. They'd loved the squabbling. It was a central part of the game as far as they were concerned.

SeaSaw was the brainchild of Abigail's father. John, his troubled son, tried so hard to be happy, but most of his efforts ended in tantrums. There was one thing though that unfailingly made him happy – that was the sea.

When their Uncle Ernie's wife, Auntie Cath, had won the top prize in a national baking competition she had shared that prize with them – a week by the sea in Brighton, just a few miles down the coast from Kingscove. It was the best holiday of their lives. Even the British weather had obliged. John had never been so happy. When they got home his father conjured up the idea of SeaSaw and John helped him make all the props which were needed to play the game..

Every time they got it out to play John seemed to relive that wonderful holiday.

Abigail, too, had loved that week. It was one of the reasons why she had ended up so near to Brighton, settling for Kingscove because the Brighton places were more than she could afford.

Years later, here was the same game having a similar effect on Stephen - mild- natured, equable, verging on the saintly Stephen. Abigail surveyed the scene through her kitchen hatch. There had always been something, she thought, about Stephen, but tonight there was a rakish adrenalin- fired glint in his eye which made him very fetching. She had a strong suspicion that it was directed at Andrew. She was right.

Actually, Stephen had set his sights on Andrew when they were at school. They had always been friends, but Andrew had been the one who had stood out, with his long legs, good looks and sporting ability. Stephen's attractions had taken longer to manifest themselves.

One of the masters, worried about a tendency for larger, oafish boys to bully this small quiet child, had persuaded him to take up boxing. It turned out that he needn't have bothered. Stephen had begun to discover his musical talent, and his confidence and attraction had grown accordingly.

Andrew didn't notice.

Nowadays the women in Stephen's choirs swarmed around him. He could have had his pick. What a shame I'm gay, he thought mischievously. Nevertheless, his patient enthusiasm and charm wrapped them round his little finger. He sometimes coaxed them into turning out performances which were technically quite beyond their capabilities.

Andrew still didn't notice.

Hubert, Abigail supposed, wasn't behaving much differently from normal. Dear predictable Hubert. When she'd first announced that she wanted to hold this party he'd been aghast.

"What are you thinking of?" he'd asked her, "don't you remember the doctor telling you to take it very easy?"

That had been several weeks ago, she'd insisted. Surely Hubert didn't expect her to behave like an invalid for ever? And it was only a few friends and neighbours, for goodness sake. He'd reluctantly given in, but then she'd confessed that it was going to be a SeaSaw Party.

"You know I hate playing games. I'm not coming," he told her flatly. "Anyway, none of them will want to sit round a table all evening playing board games."

She'd smiled sweetly at him. She didn't want him to play, she'd explained. She wanted him to be the Game Master. The Game Master didn't need to play. The

/Game Master was in charge.

"You see, Hubert," she'd flattered him, "someone needs to make sure that no one cheats."

Poor Hubert, she'd thought, having a good idea what she was letting him in for.

He'd never played before and had no notion about the rules, but, being Hubert, he naturally applied himself so well to learning them that when the day dawned he was well versed enough to have become World Champion - if that sort of competition should ever be held for SeaSaw Game Masters.

His prediction about lack of interest had proved wrong so he'd taken over the organisation of the food as well, thinking that that would be one less thing to tire her out. He'd spent much grumpy time that morning transporting food down the outside steps from his flat to hers .

She'd told him that they'd not had an in-house party for ages, and that she was throwing it to celebrate her recovery and to thank everyone who had helped her.

Those were her excuses, but he suspected something ulterior. There usually was with her. She was busy now laying out his excellent food. She'd pacified him by agreeing not to play, so that if she really did get as tired as he feared she could have the odd ten minutes with her feet up just surveying the melee.

Ann and Cedric had arranged to bring Cedric's weekend guest Robert, a Board Game devotee apparently, and the three of them were all installed at the table.

Robert seemed to be in his mid forties, much like Cedric. They'd been at Oxford together, and then Robert had gone into teaching, eventually becoming headmaster of a boys' day prep school somewhere in West London – a pleasant, thoughtful looking man, whose dark hair was just beginning to recede. He was now doing his best to pour oil on Stephen's troubled waters.

"I'm afraid Hubert's right," he told Stephen. "From what I've had time to read there are very strict rules about what you can build in residential areas."

In fact, no one had had much time to read the rules. Abigail had dug out the only copy of SeaSaw in the world from a dusty pile of stuff in her cellar a couple of nights previously and had then printed off a summary of the rules for each of the players.

*

Felicity didn't seem very involved in the game. Even though she was at the table, taking her turns, making her moves, but somehow she seemed apart, elsewhere. Abigail knew why this was. Felicity had confided in her. She'd not yet managed to sort out the situation with Andrew, and she really missed his friendship. He would speak when they met, but she felt the words were uttered under sufferance, and surrounded by dislike. They had grown so close over the previous few months, and now everything was quite destroyed by misunderstanding, anger and jealousy.

Felicity had treated herself recently to a new desk and placed it by her sitting room window, looking out to sea. She and Dominic had sold the London house so she had, at last, a little bit of spare money to spend on her flat. She often saw Andrew's comings and goings while she was working at her desk high above Regent's Parade.

She was probably the first to notice how much Stephen was beginning to figure in his life. She really approved of that - she still felt gratitude to the kind man who'd taken her under his wing on that miserable morning at St. Hilda's.

She'd poured all this out to Abigail and, unbeknown to Felicity, the idea of the SeaSaw party had grown from there. Abigail hoped that an evening doing something pleasantly trivial, with lots of other people around, perhaps even ending up laughing at the same things, might turn the relationship around a little.

So Hubert had been right about Abigail's ulterior motives. Abigail thought it might work, though.

At least they were around the same table and they hadn't fallen out yet. Tracie, whose scars were at last beginning to quieten, was next to Felicity, coaxing the odd smile and feeding her doses of a rather nice rosé cava. Hopefully it would only be a matter of time before Felicity relaxed a bit and started to enjoy herself.

Abigail had laid out the buffet in the kitchen. Her idea had been that there would be enough people playing for there to be ample time between turns to go to the kitchen and load their plates. She hadn't reckoned with the paranoia which develops when a game of SeaSaw is in progress. Scarcely anyone would leave the table at all. Either they thought someone would steal their money, or their virtual businesses, or that someone would steal their turn or move their counter to an unfavourable position.

Even staying at the table didn't seem to stop things like that happening. Andrew turned away for just a few seconds to sneeze. When he turned back he was no longer resting on his own property but had somehow been fined £500 for being drunk in charge of a yacht,

"Who did that?" he demanded, outraged.

Everyone shrugged their shoulders, feigning innocence.

"Someone must have seen," he tried again.

"Perhaps it was Augustus," suggested Tracie.

What a mistake that turned out to be! From then on Augustus played a delinquent part in the proceedings. Any discrepancy on the board was attributed to him. Poor Augustus. What would he have made of it all?

It was as well that Abigail had decided not to play because she had to spend the rest of the evening waiting on all these stubborn people who refused to abandon the table to replenish their plates for themselves. At least Hubert was enjoying himself, keeping under control these grown ups who were conducting themselves like children and thoroughly enjoying it. Actually, it was more that Hubert *thought* he was keeping them under control. Almost everyone seemed to be developing new and surreptitious ways of behaving badly. Then the text messages started to fly, secretly manufactured under the table, zipping around between phones on silent.

Nearly everyone was enjoying gently playing Hubert up because of his usual high handed approach. It was a while before he noticed the text messages, but when he did he pounced in desperation upon Andrew, who had just replied rather too openly to a text from Stephen.

"Andrew," Hubert snapped, "it's cheating to collaborate with another player."

"I wasn't collaborating with anyone. It wasn't about the game at all." retorted Andrew, indignantly.

Hubert wasn't prepared to let it drop; everyone had worked him up into too much of a state. He declared that he would put nothing past Andrew because he knew he was capable of anything to get his own way. He would never know how grateful he ought to be to both Stephen and Felicity. He was very close indeed to discovering what a hot temper Andrew concealed behind that dazzling smile.

Stephen had kicked Andrew under the table, and frowned in warning. Felicity, just about the only player sufficiently uninvolved to leave the table to go for her own food, had been passing behind Andrew on her way back to her seat. Completely forgetting that they were no longer supposed to be friends, she'd automatically slammed her hand down over his in restraint, in a desperate attempt to stop him making as big a fool of himself as Hubert was threatening to do.

Felicity had noticed before how sharp Hubert could be with Andrew. She suspected jealousy, but had told herself at first that Hubert was much too sensible to behave like that. Jealousy, however, can break loose and wriggle around uncomfortably in the most sensible people, as Abigail had discovered in Malta.

Andrew had only just managed to retain his cool. He had, in fact, been telling the truth. Although most of the text messages spinning round the room were with mischievous intent, Andrew's was in justified response to one from Stephen. The Kingscove weather seemed to have returned to windy and wet mode. It was raging outside, and Stephen had texted to ask if he could stay the night. It seemed a very normal request and Andrew had replied agreeing, with an accompanying acknowledging nod and grin.

Stephen was certainly on top form. Everything was going well for him tonight. It was his turn and the resulting move took him round to win £1,000 in his own Amusement Arcade, which he had finally managed to build on the Promenade. Andrew wasn't having anything like the same luck. Within fifteen minutes he'd landed on yet another of Stephen's developments in which he got involved in a brawl, ended up in the police station, and was fined £200. In real life poor Andrew was pretty law-abiding. He certainly made up for it round that table.

"Winner takes all!" whooped Stephen, as he raked in Andrew's remaining assets, and looked hard at him with that glint in his eye which Abigail had noticed earlier. Andrew flushed crimson, but couldn't think of a good reply. He stomped into the kitchen to have a moan to Abigail, and ask her if she'd excuse him for half an hour while he went upstairs to get sorted for his overnight guest.

It certainly was wet, he thought, as he ran up the two sets of outside steps to the main front door. No wonder Stephen had asked to stay. This weather looked as if it was in for the night.

Andrew knew it was possible for SeaSaw to provide unexpected reverses, but at the moment it looked very likely that Stephen would end up as winner. You would never get a cab on a wild Saturday night, so a very wet walk, full into the wind, back to West Kingscove would go a long way to dispelling any euphoria that the win might produce. He'd just get things sorted and then go back down to enjoy watching them all tormenting themselves and each other.

He was pleased that Stephen had stopped him making a complete ass of himself. It was only a game after all. Perhaps, he decided reluctantly, he should be grateful to Felicity as well. He knew he was feeling ever more guilty about how he had behaved towards her.

As Stephen had pointed out so often, it was really Paul who deserved that sort of treatment. Once Paul had left Kingscove various friends had volunteered more and more about his previous escapades and his long list of immoderately seductive affairs. Deep down, Andrew had reluctantly accepted that Felicity and he were both victims. She was a lovely young woman, but Felicity as temptress? No! The trouble was that he'd dug himself into a deep bad tempered hole and he couldn't find any way of clambering out.

He'd watched her buying up and developing a Channel Ferry business this evening. He hoped it wasn't some Freudian sign that she was still thinking of leaving. It didn't seem to be a good time for selling. He'd not had many nibbles on his own place and was seriously thinking of taking it off the market. Keeping it in pristine-show flat condition just in case a viewer suddenly materialised was getting too much of a strain, even for his meticulous nature.

He was busy prising the vacuum cleaner out of his neatly packed hall cupboard when a cock suddenly began to crow. It was his message alert tone. It would be a much more suitable tone for Paul, he thought. He's much more the strutting stud than I'll ever be.

The message was from Felicity. She'd been bankrupted. Abigail had told her he was upstairs cleaning and suggested he might like a hand. Could she help? Mellowed by alcohol, he agreed.

"I'll vacuum and dust," she'd suggested when she arrived.

At least that would ensure no awkward silence. His cleaner always sounded like a plane taking off.

Conversation just wasn't possible, so he left her to it.

He found a clean sheet and put it on the bed; then he started to search through the airing cupboard for his spare duvet cover. Dammit, he thought, I must get that new bed. I suppose I'll have to give him mine. Paul's desertion of him like that had made a king size dent in his confidence. It hadn't dawned on him yet that Stephen, his oldest friend, was secretly courting him, biding his time.

The deafening noise suddenly stopped.

"I'll put the kettle on," he called to Felicity, "and then we'd better go down and see how they're all doing."

"I was very annoyed," she told him over their cup of tea. "I was only just beginning to enjoy the game when I landed at the lifeboat station on the Pier after one of my ferry boats sprung a leak and that was the end of my marine empire."

"So Stephen was your downfall as well?"

Yes, she'd continued. She really didn't know what had got into him tonight, she declared. He'd got a huge restaurant on the Pier now as well. It really was looking as if he was going to win. She might be thinking too far ahead, she conceded - there were still four other people left in - one of them might have a stroke of luck and tip the balance, but she thought not.

"He seems really cocky tonight," Andrew grumbled, "I can't think what's got into him. There'll be no holding him if he does win."

He was just taking the mugs to the kitchen to rinse them when his door buzzer broke into a frantic dance of sound. They looked at each other, puzzled.

"It can only be Stephen," Andrew decided, "perhaps he's

won already. He must be getting drenched out there judging from the way he rang the buzzer. I'll let him in."

He picked up the door phone pressing the entry button at the same time.

"Come on up," he called.

"Certainly will," came the chirpy reply.

Andrew could hear the front door already closing, and someone bounding through the common hall.

He turned, ashen-faced to look at Felicity.

"It isn't Stephen," he told her, "it's Paul."

Chapter 25

Felicity didn't even have time to return Andrew's horrified gaze before she could hear Paul's feet starting up the last flight of stairs. Seconds later he was throwing himself into the flat with all his old exuberance. Once again, down on Andrew's floor went the dripping jacket, off came the sodden shoes. Felicity couldn't believe it. Paul had been away for several weeks and had caused so much heartache and chaos, but here he was, behaving as if he'd just popped out for a paper and got caught in a downpour. The arrogance of the man - she did so hope that Andrew wasn't going to go all weak at the knees and let him get away with this.

She needn't have worried.

"I only buzzed you in because I thought you were someone else," Andrew told him coldly, "There wasn't any need to take your coat off. You can't stay. It's not convenient."

Paul looked taken aback. He wasn't used to being greeted like this but, being Paul, he couldn't just give up.

"Come on," he wheedled, "I thought we were friends. We had some really good times, didn't we? I just need putting up for tonight. It's bucketing down out there."

He was completely ignoring Felicity, as if she was just an ornament on the bookcase.

He must be a bit desperate to beg like this, she thought. She wondered who was lurking in wait for him just down the road - perhaps a burly opera singer, backed up with a few helping hands from the Men's Chorus?

"Come on, Andy," he was almost pleading, "just tonight. I'll be gone before you're awake."

"Yes," came a voice from the doorway, "we already know how good you are at that. Perhaps Andrew prefers his men to be still around the next morning, not halfway to Morocco." Stephen was leaning against Andrew's front door, steely eyed - still fired by his SeaSaw prowess.

"If you're worried about the rain," he went on, "I'll treat you to a cab to wherever you want to go in Kingscove. Surely there must be somebody still desperate for you to shag them." He threw two ten pound notes down on to the soggy jacket.

Paul was red with anger. He kicked away the money and picked up his things.

"Oh, it's the virtuous choirmaster. Didn't think you knew such rude words. Choirmaster!" he sneered, "what sort of a job is that?"

"*I* like it," Stephen told him, "that's all that matters. I really like it – and it means I don't have to get all my kicks out of sex, like some folk."

Paul made towards the door. "The three of you deserve each other," was his parting shot, as he passed Stephen.

"Well at least we don't deserve you," countered Stephen, "now push off."

Felicity couldn't believe this was Stephen. He had some nerve to take on Paul, who must have been a good eight inches taller than him. She found herself wishing he was straight - she'd take him home and keep him.

Lucky old Andrew!

Paul stared furiously down at Stephen. For a minute Felicity thought he might hit him. Then he blazed off down the stairs. As he turned the corner at the next landing he knocked into a slight figure coming up and nearly sent her flying. Fortunately Tracie managed to grab the handrail, so she was spared another trip to the County Hospital. Damn, she thought, why didn't I come five minutes sooner. I must have missed a wonderful scene up here.

“Stephen,” she called, “you're needed downstairs. Hubert says we're restarting in five minutes.”

Stephen, Andrew and Felicity came bounding down the stairs, giggling like naughty children.

“What *has* been going on up there?” she asked them.

“You're far too young to hear about it, Tracie,” Andrew told her, and they all started giggling again.

*

Things had been getting so out of hand round the SeaSaw table that Hubert had decided to impose a half hour interval - a sort of cooling-off period. He’d declared the dining alcove out of bounds, barricaded it with chairs to appease the paranoia of some of the players, and gone to have a cup of tea and a moan with Abigail in the kitchen. Tracie promised him that she’d round up all the stragglers when it was five minutes to restart and had then gone up to her place to take some stuff out of her washing machine, en route letting Stephen into the main house. They must have just missed Paul coming up the steps.

They were all back more or less on time - at least all those still in the game. Cedric and Ann were looking totally doom-laden, Cedric in particular. After a reasonable start to his game everything had gone completely wrong. His days as a marine entrepreneur were most definitely over.

He looked across the table at Ann. This wretched board game seemed to be mirroring his life. There she sat – with a cruise ship in the Marina, an oil tanker moored off shore, and a chain of upmarket fish and chip shops throughout the city. Whatever she touched seemed to turn to gold. And here he sat - skint. He was resting at the moment in a beach hut which apparently belonged to Robert, and which was costing an exorbitant amount of money per night. It had very nearly bankrupted him.

It was his turn again now. He looked round the board. Ann's prime properties were coming up. His end was nigh. Ann couldn't bear to look. She knew how wretched he felt. They really should have made their excuses and stayed away. It was only a game, she knew, but it had developed in the worst possible way for Cedric.

He picked up the dice, shook them, and rolled them. A four and a five. Ann knew before he did. She watched resignedly as he plodded his playing token round the board and got a telegram saying his remaining asset had just become shipwrecked on the rocks.

He left the table, leaving Hubert to sort out his debts, and went upstairs for a gin and tonic.

Of course, his bad luck in the game was not really what was upsetting him. He had put himself forward as a Norchester candidate and all had at first gone swimmingly. He'd got on well with everyone he'd met there, and he'd begun to feel that the job was all but his. He was sure he would be able to do really good work there. Then it had all gone wrong. This morning his friend had rung to say that the appointment had been offered to another, someone with more experience. Cedric had been shattered.

He gave himself a mental shake. After all, he had a

decent job, and a decent place to live. And a perfect girlfriend. Why was he getting so upset?

Because decent was just average, he thought, and offering something average to Ann was not enough. He'd been on the brink of something wonderful, life changing. He'd even begun to feel his faith returning - a different sort of faith, it was true, but possibly a better, stronger, more realistic sort. And he'd bought a ring, so that he was all ready to propose to Ann as soon as the perfect moment turned up. Once or twice he'd almost done it. He had been so exhilarated, but exhilaration seemed to have wandered off now, arm in arm with his courage.

What had he to offer her? She could even cripple him at a Board Game.

What a wimp he could be, he thought in disgust. He must find the willpower to start again. He made an effort to straighten his shoulders. He'd come too near now to give up. His go between friend had assured him it was just a matter of time, that there was bound to be another vacancy. He wasn't going to be defeated. He was going to cut down on this drinking. No more drinking alone, he decided. He went into the kitchen and tipped away the remains of his gin.

He'd better text her. She knew how he felt. She'd be worried. Better find his phone - he hadn't taken it to the party. When he ran it to earth he found there was a message on it from his go between - "Cedric. Ring me. Urgent. You've had your phone off for ages. We need to speak."

He looked at his watch - 9.30 - not too late. Better get it over with. It couldn't make the evening any worse. He pressed the number.

"Would you still like to be Dean of Norchester?" he was asked, when the connection had been made.

Would he?! Was this a joke?

"Poor Jack Sawyer," went on his friend, without waiting for an answer, "his wife had a hospital appointment yesterday. Turns out that what they thought was something routine is really a rather nasty illness - treatable, but not easily. Jack has decided they can't cope through all the upheaval of moving and a new job while they've got this to deal with. He's withdrawn."

"Won't they wait for him? Seems a bit mean if they won't," Cedric was feeling guilty. He was desperately trying to say the right things, even though inside he was beginning to bounce with anticipation.

"He's asked them not to. He doesn't want to have it as an extra thing hanging over his family. He's decided to wait till she's better and then start again. So would you like it? They want to appoint now. They've been without a Dean for some time so they'd rather not go through the whole drawn-out selection process again. They haven't had time to announce Jack's appointment officially so they have decided they are able to offer it straight to you. As I told you the other day, they were very impressed with you. They're very anxious for you not to feel second best."

I'll say yes, shall I?"

"Yes," replied Cedric, in stunned delight, and they said their goodbyes.

He was shocked to find himself crying, but they were tears of happiness. We all dream of a second chance but not everyone is fortunate enough to get one. He hadn't texted Ann , but now he needed to see her. He wiped his eyes and raced downstairs. Ann was in the process of bankrupting Tracie, who, of course, sensible girl, just found it very funny. He sat down in one of the growing number of empty chairs at the table and began texting. One look at Cedric and Ann didn't know what to make of him. No one else would recognise the signs, but she knew he'd been crying. She also knew he was very happy. Extremely odd. Then the text came through... "I am the next Dean of Norchester after all."

"In that case, are you going to propose to me, or do I have to do it?" she replied.

"Get on with your game, woman, and wait and see," was his response.

Fortunately Hubert had given up on text censoring, defeated in previous rounds.

*

Tracie wasn't a bit bothered about being knocked out. She went off upstairs to look for Felicity.

She was keen to find out what had been going on up there. Felicity seemed in a very good mood, telling Tracie that she thought Paul's appearance had done nothing but good. It seemed to have made Andrew able to start forgiving her. When they'd all come giggling down the stairs it had been just like old times.

"Do you think Andrew knows how much Stephen fancies him?" Tracie asked her.

"Surely he must have started to get the message. He'd have to be an idiot not to." replied Felicity, "and I don't think it's just that Stephen fancies him. Stephen means to have him. I'd not realised how gorgeous Stephen is till tonight. Such a waste, Tracie. I'm definitely going to sell and leave Kingscove - it's just not worth staying- all these lovely men I know - none of them available - all gay. What about you? You've got decisions to make. Have you any plans yet? "

Lots, Tracie told her. She and Martin had had a long heart to heart and, by mutual agreement, had sadly decided that their marriage was over. Martin was living temporarily at his mother's while he planned a future.

"I'm ahead of him," Tracie leaned forward in her chair," I know what I'm going to do. What do you reckon to this? I'm going back to Whitedean to do a PhD."

Felicity was very surprised. She hadn't realized Tracie was that academic.

"That's wonderful, Tracie. What will you research?"

"Haven't quite agreed a title yet. Probably along the lines of Changing attitudes to the provision of exotic therapy services in the last ten years of the twentieth century." Tracie tried to keep a straight face.

"Stop it," demanded Felicity, "what is it really about?"

Tracie was quite surprised. "You really have changed, you know. We used to say that a few months in Kingscove would finish off your education, and we must have been right. Last year you would have believed that. No, it's really going to be something to do with the Health Service and alternative therapies."

"What about money?" Felicity asked, "can you find any?"

Apparently there wasn't much around, and Tracie told her she was going to carry on part-time with the West Kingscove business. She looked at Felicity's disbelieving face.

"I'm not pulling your leg this time." she assured her, "I

don't want to end up with massive student loans round my neck. The Porridge Pot pays handsomely. I know you don't approve, I know you worry that something awful will happen to me, but I actually enjoy it. My clients enjoy it as well, and it doesn't do anyone any harm.

I've been thinking I might broaden the setup - make it a bit more 'academic' - mortar boards, gowns, canes, do the Porridge Pot out like a don's study - that sort of thing. Keep Teddy, of course. I've grown to love him/her. I change the sex to suit the client." She looked at Felicity, whose expression was far from approving.

"Stop it, Felicity," she laughed, "you're looking just like a forbidding maiden aunt."

"Well I'm not taken with the idea, I grant you. I am really pleased about the PhD, though..." she tried, unsuccessfully, to look less disapproving and decided the best thing might be to change the subject.

"Do you think we ought to go back?" she suggested.

Tracie sent her on ahead. She wanted to put some more loose covers in to wash. She and Martin would have to sell their place, and she wanted it spic and span. She wondered if deep down she felt that washing the covers might wash away their withered relationship.

*

The main front door opened just as Felicity levelled with it and in rushed a large dripping wet yellow labrador, tugging Robert on a lead. The dog suddenly stood still and shook itself thoroughly, showering both Robert and Felicity. Then he jumped up and down around her, excitedly.

"I am so sorry," apologised Robert, "Basil is normally much better behaved than this. It must be the Kingscove air. He's taken a great shine to you. You must like dogs."

"I do," she agreed, fondling Basil's ears, "immensely. I assume you've been knocked out? I'd half expected you to win. You were going great guns when I went broke."

"Ann and that Stephen stitched me up between them and that was that. They're the only two left in now. Not my day. How do you fit in to all this?"

"I'm a friend of Ann's and I live upstairs. But not for long. My flat's for sale. I'm going to move back to London."

Robert didn't have time to reply. There was an almighty crash, and Basil began to bark loudly in agitated alarm.

Augustus' picture lay on the floor, the frame splintered. The creased and crumpled canvas had distorted Augustus' face into a look of horror.

Robert didn't realise the deeper significance, but Basil certainly seemed to. He stood staring at the mangled picture, and his barking changed into a continuous, high pitched, desolate howling.

Chapter 26

"Calm it, Basil, for heaven's sake," pleaded Robert. "I'm very sorry, Felicity, he doesn't normally go on like this. The picture falling down must really have frightened him. I'll take him back out. Perhaps the fresh air will quieten him down." He tried to pull the agitated dog towards the door, but to no avail. Basil would have nothing to do with it, digging his claws deep into the hall carpet. His howling continued, developing a definite pattern. First there would be a burst of particularly loud wailing. That would gradually subside, as if he was beginning to pull himself together. Then the wailing would build up again, each time to an even higher-keyed crescendo.

Felicity and Robert looked at each other in amused resignation.

"Why don't you take him up into Cedric's?" she suggested, "He's bound to stop eventually. And he must need a drink after his walk and making all that noise."

So Robert pulled him as firmly as he could up the stairs. Basil seemed to think this was a good idea. Perhaps he had become bored with the sound of his own voice. He began to trot up the stairs, more or less to heel, in a seemingly docile fashion, as if bad behaviour was totally beyond his capabilities. Robert finally relaxed. He fiddled in his jacket pocket for Cedric's key, but it had got tangled up in a tear in the pocket lining. He let go of Basil's lead so that he could use both hands to dislodge the key. What a mistake that was! With one bound, Basil escaped, accelerated, and thundered out of sight round the bend in the stairs, dragging his lead mockingly behind.

*

Basil's efforts at coloratura could be heard down in Abigail's place. At first people assumed it was outside - perhaps a combination of emergency service sirens rushing hell bent to the next Brighton catastrophe, but when the noise continued, Abigail in particular began to be a little concerned. She turned her charms on Andrew.

"If it wasn't so wet out there, and if I wasn't so tired that I can scarcely put one foot in front of the other, I'd go up and find out what that terrible noise is. Could you be a real pet, Andrew, and go for me?"

Andrew was only too glad to have something to do. He was getting a bit fed up with this SeeSaw game. Stephen and Ann were battling it out to the death. Surely they could finish it off. Surely they must realise that they each had someone itching to have them to themselves. He could see Cedric circling in much the same way as he was, but these two board game addicts just kept going.

He was right about Stephen, who was really intent on winning at all costs. He was so wrapped up in the game that he almost felt that everything he wanted depended upon it. Stephen knew that it was stupidly out of proportion, but he couldn't help it.

Ann didn't feel like that at all. She kept looking across at Cedric and she could tell that he was fired up with excitement. She was almost certain that he was going to propose as soon as the game was over. She was doing her best to lose, but Lady Luck would not have it. The game had yo-yoed between herself and Stephen. On one occasion she was certain he was about to strike the fatal blow and then she threw the only possible score that could see her safely through his territory. Should she just give in, she wondered. She convinced herself that she couldn't do that because it would somehow detract from Stephen's ultimate victory. She was deluding herself really, because, deep down, she felt just the same as Stephen. They both wanted to win. They both had the same need for perfection, which they normally satisfied in different ways - she through her successful business, Stephen through his music, particularly his choir.

*

Andrew arrived in the main front hall of Augustus House at the same time as Tracie, who was just coming down from seeing to her final load of washing.

"I'm beginning to think," she announced, "that perhaps I won't be so sorry to sell up here after all. One fall down the stairs in West Kingscove was bad enough, but the same thing's started up here as well. First that prick Paul nearly sends me flying, and now a ruddy great Hound of the Baskervilles practically tramples me underpaw. He's sitting outside your place now, Felicity, whimpering."

When they went up to investigate, there he was, still sitting on Felicity's doorstep. Nothing would budge him. In the end, with some considerable difficulty, and egged on by Tracie , Robert half carried the still whimpering Basil down into Cedric's flat.

Andrew and Felicity trudged back to the basement to report.

"It's nothing," Andrew told Abigail, "a picture fell off the wall in the hall and practically brained Robert's dog. Dog's now behaving like a diva. Have you still got your smelling salts, Abigail?"

"Which picture?" Hubert had jumped to his feet, "was it Augustus?"

"Yes, I think so."

Hubert became quite agitated. He wanted to know how it had happened.

"It just must have fallen down," Andrew told him. "Perhaps the cord broke, or the hook gave way." Andrew shrugged his shoulders. He didn't see it as a big deal, but Hubert got even more worked up. He turned to Felicity and wanted a blow by blow account, but when she tried to remember she found she wasn't thinking very straight.

I must have drunk an awful lot, she thought. She hadn't meant to, but it had turned into one of those parties where somebody wandering around with a bottle would keep topping up glasses before they were empty, so it had become much harder to keep count.

Better make an effort, she thought. She knew what Hubert could be like.

"I was talking to Robert in the hall," she told him. "He'd just brought Basil back from a walk. He asked me how I fitted into the setup here, and I told him I lived on the top floor. Then the picture fell down and Basil started howling."

"There must have been something else. Think, Felicity. Think!" Hubert insisted.

Abigail looked at him. He was quite red in the face. She suspected that here was one very inebriated person. He was so worked up that he had quite forgotten that he was supposed to be Banker. Abigail was stone cold sober - just as well that someone was, she thought. She could only drink at lunchtime these days. Just waving at a glass of wine on the other side of the room after about six in the evening was enough to give her an almighty hangover. There was even a theory that she suffered other people's hangovers. She wouldn't mind if they paid her to do it, she thought.

Felicity was getting a bit agitated as well, but suddenly her memory started to function again.

"Of course!" she beamed in relief, "I told Robert that I was going to put my flat on the market."

Without another word Hubert dashed out into the rain.

Oh dear! What is he up to now, thought Abigail, as she plodded after him. "Come on, Andrew," she wheedled, "hold the umbrella for me up these blessed stairs."

Everyone was so busy talking about dogs and pictures that the end of the SeaSaw game went completely unnoticed. Ann finally had had no option but to concede defeat. Stephen, who wasn't that au fait yet with Augustus House intrigues, couldn't understand why she looked so pleased, almost victorious. An exceptionally good loser, he decided.

As Hubert, the Banker, seemed to have disappeared, Stephen began to pack away the SeaSaw props. He started with the boats. When he turned back to collect the shop fronts and the pier Ann had disappeared as well. If he'd been really observant he would have noticed that Cedric was missing also. It wouldn't have interested him anyway. He was much keener on finding Andrew, so he joined the never ending procession of people on the stairs.

When Stephen arrived at Cedric's door it was wide open. Cedric's sitting room was surprisingly quiet. Basil was sitting on Robert's knee and Robert was scarcely visible behind this very large dog.

"He's not here by invitation," he explained sheepishly, to the assembled company. "If I make him get down he just howls till he's back up. He'll probably settle better if you don't show him so much sympathy. He always plays to the crowd - big time. He's a total baby. I bet he's not half as upset as he makes out."

But a lot of people there were getting too much pleasure out of petting this beautiful dog, sitting like a dejected child on a parent's knee, his mournful brown eyes managing to convey with one moist stare the unutterable sadnesses of the entire world. Tracie was on her knees, stroking Basil's ears, gently patting his head, and murmuring all kinds of ridiculous sentiments in his ear. Basil was feebly responding in like fashion. Even Andrew, who always professed that goldfish were the only pets worth the bother, was rubbing Basil's back and echoing Tracie's encouragements.

Hubert, as much, or even more, the worse for wear than any of them, decided to take a man to man approach. He drew up a chair, sat down, and stared into Basil's liquid eyes. Abigail retired to a corner and tried not to giggle.

"Look here, Basil old son, you've got to tell us what's wrong."

Abigail was not having much success with hiding her chortles and Hubert cast her a withering look.

Basil, however, pricked up his ears. Here was an invitation to some really gross misbehaviour. He'd been dreading coming with Robert for a weekend at Cedric's. He'd been before and knew just how very boring it would be. The two men sat and talked and drank nearly all the time. Then he'd get taken for a pitifully short walk before being left behind while they went out for a slap up meal, no doubt with lots more talking and drinking. The picture falling off the wall hadn't really scared him after the first minute or so, but his game of pretend had certainly relieved the boredom. Now it looked as if he might be able to spin it out a bit longer. He struggled out of Robert's grasp and jumped on to Cedric's table as a shortcut towards Hubert.

"Basil!" remonstrated Robert in horror- but Hubert raised his hand magisterially.

"No! No! " he insisted, "this animal is about to proclaim! I know it!"

Basil looked quizzically at him, with his head cocked on one side. Anyone still sober could see exactly how he was thinking - he could have some really mega fun here.

"Now Basil," commanded Hubert." Bark for yes, whimper for no. Were you upset when the picture fell down?"

"Woof!" This was great, thought Basil - encouragement to bark indoors.

"Was the man in the picture sad because Felicity said she was moving?"

Basil couldn't believe this. It was a picture, for goodness sake. He settled for no response.

"I think that must mean the answer would be too complicated," interpreted Hubert. "Did you know that the man in the picture wrote poetry?" he went on.

Basil hadn't a clue what poetry was. Robert has grossly ignored my education - and he calls himself a schoolmaster, he lamented to himself. A whimper seemed the right response.

"Has he hidden his poetry in Felicity's flat?"

Basil hadn't a clue, but he felt he'd better say something, or else this old chap would lose interest. He gave a hesitant choking sort of bark.

"If I lead you round the house might you be able to sniff the poetry out?"

Basil didn't really think that was a sensible option. He still didn't know what poetry was; what did it smell like, look like, was it dead, could you eat it? However, no self-respecting dog could possibly turn down an opportunity to have a really good nosey round this lovely big house, up and down these long rambling stairs, and in and out of all these tantalising flats with all their different smells.

Basil mightn't be too sure about poetry, but he knew a drunk when he saw one, and there were a few here, ripe for being made to look real fools. This old boy who was interrogating him looked very unsteady on his feet. He had one of those posh voices and obviously thought he sounded mightily confident, but Basil could detect that tell-tale slight slurring in his voice. He'd heard it all before - too much of the red stuff. Robert wasn't completely without sin there either. Basil quite liked the odd drop of beer, but wine! Even with a gourmet tin of dog food to camouflage it – yuk. Basil was a puritan at heart. He so abhorred drunkenness.

Once he'd made this man look as silly as possible, then he could concentrate on the idiot who kept stroking his damned ears. *She* was obviously as drunk as a Duchess. Perhaps he could have another go at tipping her down the stairs. He'd nearly managed last time. There wasn't much of her. It would just take a bit more of a shove.

Then his better nature took over. How can you even

contemplate things like this, he thought. Is this the nature of the noble Labrador? He sat down, whimpering with guilt. When Robert had first acquired him, Basil had heard him extolling his virtues to his friends. According to Robert, a Labrador was kindly, of a tractable nature, adaptable, with gentle ways, intelligent, eager to please.

Does he mean me? Basil remembered thinking with amazement. He chuntered now in self disgust. How could he tarnish this wonderful reputation? How could he live with himself if he did?

He'd often wished he'd been born a Jack Russell. Lucky little things - they were *expected* to snap at people's ankles, *expected* to show their owners up. It was an important requirement of their mission statement. Consequently they had loads of fun.

Poor me, he lamented. I'm stuck with things like 'eager to please'.

Suddenly his ears perked up. Eager to please! Of course! A legal loophole! These people wanted to rush round looking for the poetry. He must please them. That was a major part of a Labrador's job. Give the public what they want!

"Come on!" he barked at Hubert," What are we waiting for? Go! Go! Go!"

The ensuing search developed epic proportions. Basil, followed by Hubert, Robert, and half the population of Augustus House rampaged up and down the stairs. He made them all hang about while he sniffed everything and everywhere. It was a cross between a French farce, the credits scene in those old Benny Hill shows, and The Pied Piper of Hamelin. Eventually, however, Basil began to panic. He still hadn't found any poetry and he still didn't even know what it was. What he did know was that Robert would soon decide to blow the whistle on this caper. He really must retrieve something for them, and soon. His reputation hung on it. But where to look? There had to be something in that huge dark smelly room at the back of the old man's flat, he decided. They'd been round it twice already - third time lucky? I'll find them something there, he vowed. I've got to.

Off they went again, with Basil in the front and Hubert almost tobogganning down the stairs behind him.

The heavy sliding doors to the Domed Room were closed. Basil scratched frenetically at them, howling, till Hubert opened up. Once in, he tore round three times. Actually, he was tearing round in total confusion, but the onlookers got quite excited, feeling he must be on the scent of something big.

Finally he jumped on one of the old wooden box-like constructions built into the corners of the room. He leapt about and scratched at it in desperation. He must find something. Suddenly there was a grinding sound and something rose up out of the wooden surface at Jack in the Box speed. It was forceful enough to cause him to lose his balance, and he landed somewhat ignominiously on the floor.

That's it, he thought glumly, I've blown it.

How wrong can a dog be? Hubert rushed towards the "box" and delved his hand and half of himself into it. After a moment or so he rose out again, his hand waving triumphantly and clutching, not Excalibur, but a large battered leather-bound book.

"Augustus!" Hubert cried in drunken triumph, "I think we have them! I think your poems are safe. Rest sweetly, dear friend. I will cherish them."

Everyone cheered and clapped. They all patted Basil and he soaked up every bit of adulation.

Nevertheless he was a self- effacing animal at heart, or so he told himself.

"All glory, thanks and praise," he barked, "to the brave and blessed Saint Roch, the patron saint of dogs, and those who love them." That took a long time and made a lot of noise.

"This calls for a celebration," decreed Hubert, and he began to lead the procession towards the front door. He's going to bring them all back down to me, thought Abigail in horror. Before she could say anything he had thrown wide the front door in triumph. Everyone gasped. There on the step stood a very surprised, very wet Cedric and Ann, her hand still raised with a door key in it. The noisy gaggle fell very silent, staring, waiting for an explanation.

As Ann said later, it was like those awful moments when a lift door opens and someone you really don't want to meet is staring at you from about two feet away. You have absolutely no chance of escape.

Cedric decided the only thing was to bite the bullet. He beamed at them all.

"Ann has accepted my proposal, and we shall be married in the summer!!"

*

Hours later everyone, including Basil, crawled off to their bed. His was a makeshift one in a very large adapted cardboard box on Cedric's kitchen floor. Even though it was quite well padded with old cushions he might normally have regarded this as a bit of a let down - the equivalent of a Z Bed for the hero of the evening, but he was too tired, too smug, and altogether too happy with himself to care.

That bloke Hubert, he thought, was right about one thing - I do know my quotations - every dog has his day, and mine has been a splendid one.

Chapter 27

Hubert took a step back to admire what was written on the two sheets of paper he had pinned up on the notice board in the main hall.

*

The Patient Sea

I have spent my life waiting for todays,
But they dart past and do not notice me.
I have no future, and yesterdays are not enough.
The sea stalks me, eternally frothing, patiently planning.
"I have waited for you a long time," it murmurs.
"It matters not. I can wait longer, but I shall take you.
You cannot escape,
Nor do you wish to.
Come! Tread my grey corridors.
Refine your sorrows in my caverns of tears.
Come! Come and claim your tomorrows within the deep -
Tomorrows of sleep.

*

Fragments of the Sea

Seemingly Augustus' final poem. Unfinished at his death. The crossings out are Augustus'.

~~Birds sing for you, as they sang yesterday~~

~~They do not sing for me.~~

Their ~~birdsong~~ music cannot cross the arid line clamped round my soul. My lonely desert.

~~Flowers bloom for you, as they bloomed yesterday.~~

~~They do not bloom for me.~~

Their colours pale to grey within the cloud ~~sunk low around my eyes ?~~ My anguished desert.

I offer you my treasures - but you stare, puzzled.

I tried to gather all life's riches. I sowed. I tended.

Behold this dismal harvest -

Within my outstretched hands these splintered fragments of a frozen sea.

*

Even Hubert would have been at a loss for words to explain how he felt.

He had been too exhausted to sleep at all. He did one last check of what he'd posted on the board and

almost crawled back to his flat.

As usual, Abigail woke up with someone else's hangover. It had been light years past her usual bedtime before she'd finally got rid of them all. She expected they were all still sleeping, but she couldn't help waking at her normal time. Her flat looked as bad as she felt, and it took several coffees and cold face washes before she could even contemplate clearing it up.

Eventually, slowly, with every movement provoking a wince, she put a first load of dirties into her dishwasher, and then went back to bed till she heard the beep-beep of the completed cycle. Most of the first load turned out to belong to Hubert, so she staggered into some clothes, packed the crockery into carrier bags, and took it upstairs. At least the rain had stopped. Quite a stiff breeze slapped her in the face. It helped considerably.

Hubert had found some more energy from somewhere and was back standing in the shared hall, with a hammer in his hand, staring up at Augustus' portrait. He had repaired the frame and rehung it.

"It really is strange," he told her. "I cannot see how it came to fall down in the first place; nothing vital seems to have bent or snapped."

Certainly Augustus looked quite composed again. The twisted look his face had seemed to hold was gone. Serenity reigned.

Hubert began to hammer again. She really wished he wouldn't. It was going right through her head.

"I've put up one of the poems, and a few jottings of another one," he explained. "I did a lot of work on them this morning. I was too excited to sleep much."

He smiled at her somewhat sheepishly. "These are just rough copies. The originals are so full of alterations and crossings out that they're almost incomprehensible, but I felt people might like the chance to see why I got so very excited." Again he looked at her sheepishly.

Abigail stood scrutinising the two poems. They both focussed on Augustus' tragic obsession with the sea. One tried to express the feeling of anguished loss which had invaded his soul. She assumed that this had been a reaction to Emily's death: the other portrayed the sea pulling him relentlessly into its grasp. He had seemed to see it as his comfort and salvation. Poor Augustus had been substantially depressed.

"There are lots more," Hubert told her, "we know his Muse deserted him after Emily died, but then he seems to have had a massive final burst of creativity. They're still at the draft stage," he warned her. "Had he lived I am sure he would have spent a lot of time reworking and improving them - but even like this they are so important for me. They throw such light on the reasons for his death, and they show us the way in which his poetry seemed to be developing."

Abigail racked her brains, She'd better try to say something intelligent, she thought. How she wished she had a clear head.

Was this poem not a bit avant-garde in style, she ventured. Not specially Victorian? It seemed more like twentieth century work to her. For instance, she could only find two lines which rhymed. Most Victorian poetry she'd read was much more ordered, with careful rhyming.

"You're quite right," he agreed. "That's one of the reasons I'm so pleased we found them. I think the answer is that we need to revise how we view Augustus Booth. We've fixed him in the Victorian era because he died so early. We forget what might have been. Had he lived on into a normal old age we would have been thinking of him as a contemporary of Yeats and T S Eliot and perhaps D H Lawrence. Imagine if he'd lived till 1945, say - we'd have a different attitude to his poetic style, woudn't we?"

Fortunately she didn't need to reply. Hubert was really fired up, and was quite happy to do all the talking.

Suddenly he stiffened.

"I must get on, Abigail. I've a great deal to think about. I'd more or less completed writing all the lectures for my Australian tour, and they now need massive revision and addition." He dashed off, complete with the clean crocks and brandishing his hammer, up to his rooftop desk and his cats, she imagined. It was lovely to see him so excited.

As he'd taken the trouble to put the poems up for perusal she decided she'd better make the effort to read them again. She hadn't got far when Andrew and Stephen came clattering down the stairs. They sounded very chirpy.

"You're a couple of early birds," she greeted them.

"I've got to be at church - someone will have to play the comb and paper for the hymns if I don't turn up," Stephen reminded her.

Abigail couldn't help noticing that Stephen's new found confidence of the previous night seemed still there. Although Andrew kept on about how starving he was, Stephen insisted on reading the poems before they went out to find some breakfast on the way to church.

As he read them one could see his mood visibly dropping.

"Did he just walk into the sea?" he asked Abigail.

She nodded gravely.

"He must have felt so desperately alone. Where is there for people to turn when things get as black as this, if they have neither faith nor friends to cling to?"

Abigail caught the sidelong private glance he shot at Andrew, but pretended not to notice. She went down the steps with them and out on to the forecourt.

"Why don't you come for some breakfast with us? Best cure for that morning after feeling," suggested the ever-courteous Stephen, but Abigail smiled and shook her head. She watched them, deep in conversation as they turned left off the seafront towards Veronica's, the local greasy spoon.

Should she go for a walk herself? It was really rather a nice morning. She was just deliberating when the front door opened, and Robert emerged with Basil. Basil was up to his same tricks. He didn't want to go out. First he dug his claws deep into the thick coir doormat, and then just sat down, refusing to budge.

"Come on, Basil!" Robert was cajoling him, "you need to go out. You don't want to disgrace yourself - not after your triumph last night."

But Basil wouldn't go. He kept looking back up the stairs.

"Perhaps he wants longer in bed, just like the rest of us," Abigail suggested.

"No, it's not that. He wants to go upstairs to see Felicity. He's taken an almighty shine to her."

Basil's ears pricked up at the sound of her name. He gave a happy little yelp and tugged again at his lead, smiling at Robert, his head cocked on one side.

"Oh, go on then, if you must," Robert told him, dropping his lead. "Go and ask her if she wants to come for a walk with us."

Basil rushed off up the stairs. They could hear him barking at Felicity's door. Abigail made her excuses and carried on down the steps to her flat.

Hmmm, she pondered, Robert certainly hadn't taken much persuading.

Epilogue

The great day dawned gloriously, with blue skies and birdsong. Ann had laid out continental breakfast for her house guests in the Deanery's spacious dining room, with its French windows leading into the lovely walled garden. She'd only meant to keep the windows open long enough to air the room – it was very newly decorated and the smell of paint still lingered – but by eight o'clock the world had warmed up so well that she decided to leave them open longer. Somehow open doors seemed to bring the long awaited event of Cedric's Installation as Dean of Norchester much nearer.

"Her" house guests! She had not yet grown accustomed to being the mistress of the Deanery. She and Cedric had only been married for three weeks. When they had first become engaged they had thought how fitting it would be to be married in the cathedral at Norchester, but after a while Ann had had second thoughts about this - far too many people would become involved, she'd decided.

"Let's do it really quietly," she'd urged Cedric, "it's *our* day. We don't want it taken over. Apart from anything else, if we get married quickly now I can be with you when you move in. I want to support you. I know what you're like."

Cedric agreed. He wanted her there too, but they both knew it might not go down at all well in the Cathedral Close if the Dean Designate were to be found sleeping on site with his lover.

So a very quiet wedding it had been, in the church where Ann had been christened. Her father had given her away. She'd tried to persuade him to marry them, but he was not in specially good health.

"I'll just totter down the aisle with you, on *your* arm," he'd joked. He had been so thrilled when they went up to Suffolk to tell him. *His* daughter married to a *Dean*, and a nice one at that. He'd taken to Cedric immediately, although Ann had retorted to Cedric later that she felt he would have approved of her marrying a monkey if it had been wearing a clerical collar. Part of her still couldn't come to terms with the irony of her situation – she had spent most of her adult life distancing herself from the church, yet here she was, marrying an almost Dean.

Naturally, Robert had been Cedric's best man, and mindful of his duty to get the groom to the church on time, had booked a more than spacious en suite for him in the best local hotel.

Felicity had always maintained that under Ann's hard bitten exterior lurked a beautiful nature, and it had certainly shown itself that day. As for Felicity, she did sterling service as Matron of Honour, in a stunning hat that almost put the bride in the shade. When people saw the photos, several of them remarked on how radiantly pretty Felicity looked, and wondered how they'd never noticed before.

Cedric had given them all a bit of competition as well, resplendent in clerical formal dress gear, complete with gaiters and all. It was quite possible that the little church hadn't seen the like for at least a century.

The newly weds had spent a sublime week in Gozo – Abigail's suggestion – and then moved into the freshly redecorated Deanery. They'd asked for white throughout. Jolly good chap this new Dean must be, Major Brunson, the Cathedral Financial Controller, had told himself when the decorators' bill landed on his desk. No airy-fairy expensive tastes – just good down to earth white.

Cedric was nervous this morning. It was a funny kind of nervousness – quite different from how he'd felt before the wedding. He was raring to go, but terrified at the same time.

"That's good," Ann had reassured him when she'd brought him an early morning cup of tea. "It's adrenalin. Means you'll show up at your best."

He hoped so! In the meantime he decided to take his mind off it by being a good host at breakfast, even if he himself didn't feel much like eating. Stephen, for instance, and Andrew, would be down soon from their makeshift sleeping accommodation in the attic. Stephen, who had the responsibility for directing the combined St. Hilda's and University choirs in this afternoon's service, would surely be nervous, and Andrew would probably have butterflies as well. They had all been amazed when Andrew had joined the choir a while back. Unbeknown to the Augustus House residents, it was the result of a bit of an altercation behind closed doors. Andrew was getting more and more irritated because he saw so little of Stephen, whose entire waking hours sometimes seemed to be one long round of choir practices, orchestra rehearsals and playing the organ for weddings and Sunday services. On top of all that Stephen now had a new passion. He had been very moved when he'd read Augustus' poems that Sunday morning in the hallway and he'd spent the evening closeted with Hubert, the cats, and a bottle of sherry (The previous night's party had cleaned Hubert out of everything else.) discussing an idea for writing an opera based on Augustus' tragic life. He'd long been looking for the perfect subject, and now he thought he had found it.

"It's not just me," he'd pointed out smilingly to Andrew in the middle of their minor set-to. It was just about impossible to ruffle Stephen, which could be rather annoying in itself. "What about you? You spend half your life either up in the sky, or swanning about in Hong Kong, or the like. But this is how we both earn our livings. I don't think either of us would want to give up and be a kept man, so we're stuck with it. We managed before. When I was on the rigs we sometimes didn't see each other for months and we always managed to pick up just where we'd left off."

As soon as he'd said that he'd realised what a stupid remark it was. They both knew things had changed forever on what they referred to as SeaSaw Night. Time spent apart was no longer so easy to bear.

"We'll just have to make do with an almighty Shagfest whenever we do have time together, I suppose," grumbled Andrew.

"You are so vulgar. Is that all you fancy me for? You've been spending too much time with Paul again," Stephen had told him, tut-tutting in mock disgust.

A couple of weeks later Andrew joined the St. Hilda's choir.

"I twisted his arm. He was in the choir at school, you know, though we were both trebles then. I was desperate for an extra bass, and he's been hiding a great voice," Stephen had explained.

"I decided it was the only way I'd get to see him," Andrew had growled, though secretly he really enjoyed the new experience. Stephen had done a bit of preliminary coaching before getting him along to choir practice, so that he had some idea of how to hold his bass line while the others sang different parts. Andrew had been amazed at how much he enjoyed having Stephen's tenor running up and down the tune just behind his own voice, as if it was chasing after it. Singing was quite sexy, he decided, but he certainly had no intention of letting on – not yet, anyhow.

When the two of them arrived at breakfast Stephen was all smiles, seemingly not a bit nervous, but Andrew was very subdued. It was quite simple. Stephen had rehearsed his choirs again and again, and had been performing for years. He had no qualms at all about the afternoon's service, whereas Andrew was still going through the long process of gaining the confidence that comes from performing experience.

Cedric found himself wishing that Tracie was there. She was always able to lighten up an atmosphere – but she was in San Francisco, on a term long Webster Scholarship, looking at aspects of alternative therapies in California. Cedric could only imagine how she was eking out her grant. She'd sent Cedric a very funny, but somewhat risqué, good luck card. He wondered how many Deans Designate received saucy cards from slinky little dominatrices.

*

Cedric, Stephen, and Andrew had all left for the cathedral to attend yet more rehearsals before Felicity made an appearance.

"Basil is playing up," she told Ann, "he definitely knows something big is happening today, and I'm sure he senses that he's not going to be there. We've just taken him for a walk by the river and he's been *so* badly behaved. He jumped in, got wet through and then rolled about all through the mud chasing ducks. He only stopped when two swans decided to see him off. He's absolutely filthy so Robert's having to clean him up. He'll be a while. And he was! Basil was in deep disgrace. Robert marched him out to the very large kennel in the garden, where the previous Dean's St. Bernard had been housed when the Dean's dog-fearing mother–in-law came to visit.

"Stay!" Robert had commanded, and as Basil felt in need of a rest anyway after all his exertions he'd decided to obey just this once.

Later, before leaving for the day's events, Felicity had gone to say goodbye to him.

"Be a good boy, Basil. This is a big day for your Uncle Cedric. We won't be long, and you've got all this lovely garden to play in. You can't come with us. They only allow guide dogs in the cathedral.

Basil had snorted in disgust. Guide dogs! My wagging tail, he may have been thinking. I've known a few of those who'd have guided me up the wrong path if they'd had their way.

"It'll be really boring," Felicity had gone on, tickling his ears, "lots of singing."

This got him going. He could sing. He'd jolly well show her.

And even after Ann, her father, her older brother, Felicity and Robert had left the Deanery for the cathedral they could still hear him howling a song of rage. He was never one, though, to waste energy, so as soon as he was sure they were out of hearing he gave up, and started chasing butterflies round the garden. His plans were going really well. Robert just didn't realise how securely his fate had been sealed. Basil had decided that he could not manage without Felicity, and was using all his wiles to bring together the two people he loved most.

*

Hubert and Abigail had booked into The Royal Oak, just outside the archway which led into the Cathedral Close. He had refused point blank to stay at the Deanery.

"The poor chap is surely entitled to some peace. If Ann invites anyone else she and Cedric will end up sleeping in a tent in the garden. He has a hectic day ahead. We are not going to add to his stress," he'd insisted. Abigail hadn't wanted to miss out on the excitement, but he did have a point, and The Royal Oak had turned out to be very comfortable.

After breakfast they decided to have a proper look round the Cathedral and the large Close because they wouldn't have time to play the tourist later. Just as they stepped through the arched gateway the cathedral bells began to ring. The joyful peals were to pursue them all morning wherever they went in Norchester. Past and present bellringers had gathered to ring a peal of bells, which would last four hours. One did not have to be very observant to realise that this was going to be a great day. The tea urns and trestle tables were already in place on the lawns. People were bustling around placing notices in every conceivable place, mainly about who was to robe where. Just how essential these notices were would only become clear when the processions commenced, and serried ranks and ranks of robed clerics flocked down the aisle like proud and elegant swans.

There were people in red cassocks carrying mysterious cardboard boxes, a man doing a last minute job on some beautiful glass doors leading into the cloister garden, and another one feverishly washing down chairs in the cloister.

"Don't worry. These will dry pretty quickly," he was reassuring another man, "I had to clean them. The choirboys make such a mess of them."

Does he mean those little angels? wondered Abigail. Surely not!

There was a big notice up in the Canons' Cookshop – 'No hot food today.' Of course not! *Far* more important things happening today. The Lord will provide.

But there *was* coffee on tap, so Abigail insisted they take the weight off their feet for a few minutes.

"Do you think Augustus is here?" Hubert surprised her by asking.

She slowly licked the spoon she'd been scraping round the remains of her cappuccino while she considered his question.

"No," she decided, "I'm sure he hasn't come with us. I think he will be keeping an eye on James while he restores the The Tower Room. I'm surprised you didn't decide to do the same, Hubert."

Hubert had retorted that she underestimated him. He was perfectly able to delegate to competent people and James and that architect fellow Monypenny seemed more than competent. How could he possibly miss this exciting event?

"And Augustus may be saving his energies to supervise

you in Australia," she'd continued.

As she'd expected, Hubert's eyes lit up at the mention of Australia. He had burnt the midnight oil constantly in order to get all his lectures rewritten with a completely new slant on the life and work of Augustus Booth. There seemed to be a completely new slant on Hubert Jeffries as well – he'd even bought new clothes for the trip.

Neither of them was ever really sure about Augustus. Abigail sometimes wondered if his whole ghostly presence hadn't been conjured up from the collective consciousness of the Augustus House dwellers, but on other occasions he seemed very, very real. He must be quite glad to have shaken off the fuddy old-young Victorian poet image. Perhaps he was relieved at being finally released from his long limbo of imprisonment in Augustus House. Perhaps the finding of the poems had provided the key to unlock the door of his prison – now the poems had been found there must no longer be anything to keep him there. Or perhaps she was right and he was scheming to go with them to Australia to keep an ear on what Hubert was going to say about him there.

Abigail's father had been fond of a saying he'd picked up in the RAF in World War Two – ' Enjoy yourself. You're a long time dead.'

Perhaps that was it - Augustus just wanted to see Australia – just one last bit of earthly enjoyment before he called it a day and decided to die properly? Who knows?

They went back into the cathedral. There were flowers everywhere. A Dean is the head of a cathedral and this cathedral had been without one for a good while. At last it was preparing to greet its new Dean, and the resultant joyful buzz was infectious. In the very heart of the building there were last minute moppings, dustings, cleaning of door handles. A frightening blue box on wheels was dashing around like a manic robot. It must have had someone directing its cleaning operations, but it did seem to have a mind of its own. Throughout everything Abigail could still hear the bells pealing in jubilant anticipation of the joyful occasion.

A charming elderly usher had warned them that it would be wise to be in their seats by 2pm.

"That seems inordinately early for a 3pm start," Hubert had complained to Abigail, but later they were to discover why.

On their tour they had bumped into Cedric, looking somewhat harassed. He was trying to find Stephen, whose choirs were having an extra rehearsal somewhere with the cathedral choir. They only found out later why Cedric looked so worried. The Cathedral Organist had been struck down suddenly with a strange bug. His Assistant was happy to stand in, except for one item. Stephen, at Cedric's request, had composed a new organ piece to be played as the procession returned down the aisle at the end of the service. The Assistant Organist felt he didn't know it well enough to perform it. He'd suggested that Cedric ask Stephen.

*

Hubert and Abigail wandered out into the city. Neither had much room for lunch so they just bought sandwiches and nibbled at them by the river.

"If I were to leave Kingscove," she told him, "I think I

might settle in a cathedral city. They do seem to have everything- beautiful locations, lovely housing, great shops, great culture, fast trains to London – to say nothing of cathedrals and lots of bells."

She dragged him back, protesting, in time for two o'clock and found the block of seats allocated for Cedric's personal guests. She didn't recognise most of the people assembling there. Old associates, parishioners etc from the year dot seemed to have descended in a fleet of coaches from all outposts of the nation to see their much loved Cedric installed.. Most of the Whitedean Theology Department had turned out too, and Hubert pointed out to Abigail Abraham's schoolmate, the Professor of Theology, ensconced amongst the bigger wigs up front, next to Ann's father. She could imagine the conversation – Ann's father would be telling him "Oh, didn't you know? The new Dean is my son in law".

There wasn't anything like enough room to house everyone who wanted to be present in the main body of the cathedral so extensive staging had been erected high against the West Window and this was rapidly filling up as well. The people up there wouldn't realise how ethereal they looked, silhouetted against a blazing sun.

Shortly after two o'clock the first of several preliminary processions took place. The parish clergy of the diocese in their clerical vestments sallied down the aisle to take up their reserved seats. A few minutes later it was the turn of the clergy and representatives of other denominations of the Christian Church , and of other religions, then the municipal dignitaries from all the administrative areas of this far flung diocese. Finally, came the Lord Lieutenant of the County, accompanied by his lady wife, looking like a pair of sumptuously feathered peacocks, both vying for attention with their grand plumes.

Fifteen minutes before the great procession was to make its way through the cathedral the mood was quietened with music from the Assistant Organist. He was obviously well used to the renowned Norchester Organ and was coaxing wonderful sounds from it.

Hubert looked at Abigail fondly. She looked quite lovely, he thought, in a face-cradling lemon coloured feathered hat. He was so glad they were going to have that week together before they went their separate ways in Australia. He knew how much she was looking forward to searching for John, and he did hope she'd find him. That might take her one step nearer to letting go of her troubled past. She'd told him a little about how she planned to start looking round Adelaide because that was the area from which Mrs Evans had had christmas cards for the first few years. She was really determined to find him, and when Abigail was determined...

But at the moment all Abigail's interest was in the procession. She'd intended to follow the order very carefully, but when it entered the cathedral and surged down the aisle to the crashing sounds of "Guide me oh Thou great Jehovah, Pilgrim through this barren land." she was so bowled over that she'd lost the place within moments. So she just watched intently, trying to pick out her own known and cherished participants.

The first of those came immediately after the Cross and Tapers – the Choirs of the Church of St. Hilda, Brighton and The University of Whitedean at Brighton, Director, Stephen Armitage.

First she made out the tall figure of Andrew, doing his best to look invisible. Stephen brought up the rear, just ahead of the Choir of Norchester Cathedral. His face showed no nerves at all. He almost looked to be thinking "Bring it on!"

There followed a lot of people she didn't recognise before she made out Cedric, the Dean Designate, side by side with the Prime Minister's Secretary for Appointments. Now Cedric really did look nervous!

Bringing up the rear in a swirling flurry of sumptuous vestments and robes came the collected clerics of Norchester Cathedral with their Bishop.

Abigail did not think she had ever witnessed a better procession. Nowadays, when we can watch great occasions in close up on television we have perhaps become a little blasé, but television just cannot convey adequately the awe of such an occasion. One has to be a participant. She'd heard from Ann how much effort had gone into choosing the content of this service. Its aim had been to draw Cedric, together with all his experience within and without the church into his new post and life at Norchester. Cedric saw this as being one of the most significant days of his life, and had chosen things to be included in the service which had special significance for him. The Installation was to be woven into Evensong, ever Cedric's most appreciated service, and he had chosen the music from William Byrd's Great Service. It never ceased to amaze and inspire him how the great ecclesiastical composers of Byrd's era managed to write their sublime music in such troubled times.

He took the text for his sermon from Ephesians Chapter 3, verse 19 – "...to know the love of Christ that surpasses knowledge, that you may be filled with the fullness of God." And he vowed to them that he would strive to that end. They were all pilgrims through the wilderness, the barren land of the first hymn, he reminded them, and the theme was echoed in the final hymn , Bunyan's To be a pilgrim.

Then the vast procession retraced its steps back down the aisle to the thunderously triumphant strains of Stephen's new piece – a set of variations on Haydn's great anthem from The Creation – The heavens are telling the glory of God.

They all whirled out of the cathedral, each to their separate disrobing areas and then flooded out onto the lawns for that well-earned cup of tea and a pile of cake.

One or two, who'd felt it wasn't very good form to have this unknown Stephen Armitage fellow from Kingscove playing for the finale of such a great occasion – (what if he messed up? After all, the Norchester organ was not one for amateurs-) found themselves unable to come up with any criticism at all, except perhaps that the man ought to learn a lot more humility. It just didn't seem right that he should have the confidence and ability to step into the breach and perform that well. Stephen had only grinned when the remarks had started filtering through.

"Perhaps the best thing about playing your own brand new compositions," he'd confided to Cedric, "is that no one but you realises if you make mistakes."

*

At 6.30 Hubert phoned Abigail to ask if she was ready to go down to dinner. She wasn't a bit hungry, she told him. She'd been a bit too appreciative of afternoon tea.

He wouldn't take no for an answer.

"We must, Abigail. The Royal Oak, Norchester is renowned for its food. It has two Michelin stars. And we've already paid – it's part of our package. Let's have a walk first. I think it serves until 9."

They walked along by the river mulling over the best bits of the ceremony.

"A truly splendid day," announced Abigail, "it will take something very good to compete with it. Although I am sure you will be throwing a mega party when your Dome is finished?"

naturally, Abigail was joking – Hubert? A mega party?!!! Small dinner parties yes but… She could not believe Hubert's reply.

"As a matter of fact I am. And I may even keep on throwing parties."

He owed Augustus and his contemporaries such a lot, he told her - he'd almost built his career on

them. Perhaps it was payback time. He was going to establish the Augustus Booth Foundation which would assist young musicians and poets in any sort of difficulty. He would organise frequent soirees of musical or poetic content and use the proceeds for the funding.

He'd been talking to the Professor of Music at Whitedean and between them they'd already developed an idea for the Grand Opening.

By this time they were back at the hotel. He lashed out on a bottle of champagne, which naturally lifted her mood no end.

On their way into dinner they peeped through the door of a function room where a lively wedding reception disco was taking place. The convivial guests had obviously been celebrating for several hours already and Hubert and Abigail were dragged in to drink a toast to bride and groom. The DJ was just starting up more music.

Hubert smiled to himself, drew himself up to his full height, and walked over to where Abigail, yet more champagne in hand, was talking to the bride and groom.

"Abigail," he asked, with the gravest of straight faces, "would you care to dance?"

*

At just about the same time James was putting the last lick of paint on the Tower Room walls, at the end of a very long overtime session. The daylight had all but gone, so he had already switched on the new wall lights. Just in time he remembered that he'd been going to give the new radiators a final check. Everything would have to be right for Hubert, that old perfectionist. Finally he stood back and admired his work. He had every right to be pleased. The room looked very special, very imposing. It didn't take a lot of imagination to hear music, and singing, and laughter.

There should be a topping out ceremony, he decided. He made himself a cup of tea, and proposed a toast – *To the Tower Room at Augustus House – past, present, and future.*

He was sure he heard clapping - joyful, approving clapping.

He turned, startled. "Who's there? Hello?" But there was no one.

Just the new radiators, of course!

And James and Augustus both went home.

The house basked in a gentle breeze straight off the sea.

Author Biography

I seem to have been scribbling most of my life. Doreen, my best friend from our days in Primary School, tells me that when our teacher needed to finish some marking she would ask me to read my latest story to the class. I can only vaguely remember this, but if Doreen says it happened it happened!!

I certainly still love writing – prose and poetry – silly and serious. I like the way that one can create characters and (usually!) make them do exactly what one wants.

I try to bring things I love into my writing - for example cats and dogs - and can't resist giving a voice to them.

I have the craziest dreams and like to fit them into my scribbles.

Whenever I am away I am looking for locations about which I might write- places to be the setting for my next tale.

I hope you like this one.

Happy reading!

Susannah.